DUELING HEARTS

"Will you always be a smuggler?" Harmony asked.

The abrupt question stopped Daniel, made him uncomfortable. "Will you," he countered, "always be your father's helper?"

Eyelids lifted with surprise, then very quickly, a mischievous grin followed. She clutched her chest and fell against his shoulder. "A hit!"

He blinked in surprise, entranced by her awakened sense of fun, by how quickly she adapted to cheerful laughter after a lifetime of solemnity. "Perhaps," he said, "we should let these questions lie dormant for a while. To prevent conflict when we are pretending to be sweethearts."

She shrugged amiably, then without warning, struck again. "My father said you refuse to use your title."

"Satan's teeth, Harmony," he said, reeling from her outrageous probing, "are you out for blood today?"

"Another touchy subject, Daniel?" She grinned again. "I believe I have found a method for your long-overdue retribution. You tease and torment me—I quiz and prod and generally make your life miserable."

When she found him speechless, she added, "You'll never know another peaceful moment, *Lord* Rockburne."

LOOK FOR THESE REGENCY ROMANCES

The Seductive Smuggler

Donna Davidson

Zebra Books
Kensington Publishing Corp.
http://www.zebrabooks.com

ZEBRA BOOKS are published by

Kensington Publishing Corp.
850 Third Avenue
New York, NY 10022

First Printing: July, 1997
10 9 8 7 6 5 4 3 2 1

Printed in the United States of America

One

Daniel Rockburne clenched his jaws and swallowed the scream that rose upward—in a straight line from the bayonet piercing the flesh of his lower back. Jab-jab-jab it came, always in threes, for Sedgewick, the damned, stiff-rumped officer marching behind him had no imagination, neither in his monotonous stabbing the same agonized spot, nor in the repeated command that followed. "Keep moving, you filthy smuggler."

Daniel sent a sharp glance toward his father, James Rockburne, climbing the steep cliffside track beside him. Their eyes locked, his father's promising a murderous retribution for Daniel's tormentor and a warning for Daniel to remain valiant. It was all he needed—that glimpse of strength—to endure whatever came, for a Rockburne never showed weakness, not in centuries past when titles and honors graced their respected name, nor would it now when that same tarnished name evoked shudders of fear throughout the countryside.

A powerful gust of cold, gritty sand swept up from the beach and blasted them from the side. Daniel tucked his chin downward and leaned into it, sharing a smile with his father as Sedgewick and his soldiers sputtered and twisted against the onslaught, cursing as their slick-soled shoes skidded on shale and rocks.

What the devil? Daniel's fleeting amusement died a swift death as Sedgewick reached the top of the bluff—and instead

of turning toward the village and the Martello tower beyond—
he turned the wrong way.

Then all the pieces tumbled into place.

Before them lay the home of Sir Roan, *the magistrate infamous for harsh justice, and, should the mood strike him, swift
penalties without benefit of trial.* Daniel's heart took a violent
leap as they marched onto the gravel driveway. He glared at the
multi-paned rectangles of light and uttered a silent curse—*blast,
the house was still awake.*

Sedgewick snorted his satisfaction and grabbed Daniel's arm
to tug him forward. Ashamed of the shiver of relief to be away
from that prodding blade, Daniel halted, deliberately pulling his
arm free of Sedgewick's grasping fingers. Unable to mask the
panic that contorted his features, Sedgewick delivered a vicious
gun-butt to Daniel's ribs.

His honor satisfied, Daniel moved easily forward, feeling
much like a lazy black panther sauntering alongside an uneasy
keeper, the balance of power teetering precariously between
them.

It was strange, he thought, the personal animosity Sedgewick
had directed toward him from their first meeting many months
ago, almost as if they were opponents. In competition for what,
he couldn't imagine, for two more opposites surely didn't exist.
Sedgewick was handsome; Daniel was not. Sedgewick in his
mid-thirties, was fair, slim and compact and the epitome of manners, dress and social correctness; Daniel, at ten years and nine,
matched his father's towering height and dark coloring, wore
loose sailor's garb and could barely remember his mother's attempts to civilize him. Sedgewick—an eligible *parti*—enjoyed
the attention of a dozen flirting *ladies;* Daniel—the smuggler—
received only haughty aristocratic glances and skirts hastily
brushed aside.

"Move up here, smartly now," Sedgewick snarled, dragging
Daniel up the worn steps to the square Georgian mansion. Placing Daniel on the second step below him, he took a moment to

arrange them all—father beside son, with the four armed soldiers relegated to the step below.

It was a foolish maneuver, one a battle-seasoned soldier would never have made. While it created a handsome picture, the soldiers were now so close that the bayonet-topped muskets were necessarily pointed upward, rendering them useless in a sudden skirmish. His blood quickening, Daniel sent his father an inquiring look—*Escape?*

James shook his head, looking pointedly at the door before them; Roan, they both knew, was just as apt to turn them free as he was to condemn them forthwith, an option preferable to a battle with Sedgewick's armed men.

Sedgewick, oblivious to the silent interchange between father and son, hoisted his chin like an actor in a play, raised the knocker, and pounded loudly. Daniel smiled, for the officer had just made a serious error in judgement, putting himself in jeopardy as well as his prisoners. The thunderous noise at this hour and the foolhardy demand that the magistrate-cum-scholar *leave his books* to attend to a matter of law was something the merest child in the neighborhood knew enough to avoid.

Unwisely filled with his own sense of importance, Sedgewick knocked a second time and shuffled impatiently, giving Daniel an idea for their deliverance.

"I never marked you as a coward," he drawled. When Sedgewick turned to snarl at him, Daniel hurled another insult. "Kidnapping *unarmed* men . . . why that smacks of cowardice at its worst."

Sedgewick took the bait and spit out his rebuttal. "I'm an officer of the Crown arresting two smugglers." A brisk, arrogant reply, Daniel noted, but full of emotion, for all Sedgewick's attempts to appear unruffled.

James, alert to Daniel's game, joined in. "Ah, but you attacked us on our own beach, without a boat or contraband in sight."

"Everyone knows you and your son are smugglers!"

"And it was so galling when you tried to prove it," James

purred, "but were entirely . . . impotent." Sedgewick stiffened. *A hit.*

Daniel kept up the pace. "What will your commanding officer say when he finds you have neglected to deliver us to the Martello tower?"

"My commanding officer," Sedgewick said, his voice rising, "is bedridden with the ague, and could not be disturbed no matter how important the matter."

"Ahh, cowardice breeds treachery . . ." Daniel began, but Sedgewick in a fury now, turned to beat the door more loudly than before. Immediately, the door opened, casting a dim light across the tableau arranged on the steps.

The apparition before them would have—to anyone but the inhabitants of Shingle Spit—filled any visitor with amusement, for his white hair stood virtually on end and his querulous words only added to the impression of an aged retainer disturbed from his slumbers.

"Go away and leave me alone," the old man bellowed. He gave the door a hearty shove and turned to shuffle away.

Sedgewick managed to lodge his heavy boot in the aperture. "Look here," he said, insult in every word, "go fetch your master, else I shall inform him of your insolence and see that you're turned off."

The man stopped where he stood, squared his shoulders and turned slowly around. Daniel and his father exchanged knowing glances, but Sedgewick, oblivious to the tension crackling in the air, pushed the door fully open and began a heavy-handed tirade. "I've captured smugglers operating along the coast and have brought them to the magistrate. Run up and fetch him at once." Then he waited, toe tapping, for the servant to grovel and move at his bidding.

The older gentleman reached into the pocket of his jacket— worn green velvet, Daniel noted, permanently creased from repeated wearing, but clearly made from the best cloth available—and retrieved a pair of spectacles which he positioned carefully in place. Totally ignoring the impatient

Sedgewick, he took his time and carefully studied each participant upon his doorstep.

Daniel tensed, his every sense alert to the magistrate's reactions. Roan was everything that Daniel despised in the society his grandmother and cousin enjoyed—arrogantly believing that as a matter of birth, he was superior to the villagers, that he had the right to trod over those beneath him without a spark of humanity—and yet, having stated his hatred of smugglers in particular, guzzled down illegal French brandy and wore French silk as if they had not reached England's shores by way of free-traders.

Sir Roan recognized James and Daniel at once, yet surprisingly did not direct his ire at father and son. Instead, he turned to Sedgewick, furious with the interloper who had thrust this unwelcome predicament upon him. A chilly wind gusted into his face, and Roan, turning away, jerked his head sideways in an irascible motion for them to follow. "Come in," he snapped. "I'm freezing my balls off."

"These prisoners are not moving," Sedgewick blurted out, "and you'll do as I say, or else . . ."

Roan swung back around. "Who *is* this horse's ass?"

"Lieutenant Sedgewick," James answered, a careful respect laced through his words. "Newly assigned to the Martello tower."

Sir Roan's bushy eyebrows twitched upward and his startlingly blue eyes slewed sideways. No sleepy, absentminded retainer now, he froze Sedgewick where he stood. Still unable to quite believe the truth as it hit him, Sedgewick's response emerged as a weak question. *"You* are the magistrate?"

"Sir Temple Roan," Daniel interceded in way of introduction, hoping to warn Sedgewick away from his blatant rudeness. *"Baronet,"* he added for clarification, hoping that Sedgewick—who looked ready to explode at Daniel's usurping the conversation—would comprehend the respect due the titled gentleman, if not the danger in pushing him too far. For the moment, Sir Roan seemed fairly reasonable, and if they could just get this over quickly, he might be guided away from one of his infamous tantrums.

Slanting Sedgewick a meaningful look, Daniel explained. "I believe the lieutenant wants you to lock us up for the night so you can hear his complaint at a more reasonable hour tomorrow. If you want, we can doss down in the barn and not disturb you—"

Before Daniel could finish, Sedgewick's self-control shattered.

He stepped toward Daniel, fury and loathing in every word. "I'll decide what's to become of you, and if you don't want to find yourself skewered at the end of a bayonet," he said, stepping back to swing his musket toward Daniel's chest, "you'll shut your mouth." Sedgewick jabbed his bayonet forward, the tip grating painfully against Daniel's ribs. James lunged toward Sedgewick, but the soldiers seized him and beat him about the head, gasping and grunting as they brought him to his knees. Barely conscious, he swayed unsteadily, blood dripping down his face onto the chilled stone steps.

In the doorway above them, Sir Roan's face turned red, and he began to swear. Dear God, Daniel intoned silently, praying fiercely there was yet a chance to halt Roan's dangerous tantrum.

He prayed in vain—Sir Roan and reality had never dealt well with each other.

His eyes wild with rage, Sir Roan pointed to the beaten man and bellowed, "Get that bloody mess off my steps."

Daniel's heart sank as Sedgewick, using his intellect for the first time, stepped back from Daniel and queried the hysterical old man. "Shall I hang them, or shoot them or have them transported, Sir Roan?"

Clinging to the last word uttered, Sir Roan answered. "Transport them, for God's sake, and do it now. Or," he hissed as the rest of the conversation sank in, "hang them if you wish. Just don't shoot them and wake up the hounds."

"Certainly," Sedgewick began, but the patter of running feet turned his attention toward the foyer behind Sir Roan. "I'm sorry, Father," a feminine voice intruded, its gentleness almost jarring against the tense lunacy of the moment.

Harmony, Daniel thought, identifying the newcomer, while Sedgewick quickly brushed his fingers through his windswept hair and pasted on an engaging expression for Sir Roan's daughter. As Sedgewick's attention shifted to her, Daniel edged closer to his father's side. Bracing his legs to provide a resting place for his father's drooping head, he let himself hope that a miracle might have arrived in the guise of this remarkable daughter of Sir Roan.

And wished that he hadn't spent the last few years terrorizing her.

"I was in the library, Father, and didn't hear the door," she said, her gentle voice soothing and apologetic all at once. "Come away from the cold and finish inside." Her skirts swirled into the doorway ahead of her as her hands reached up to grasp the tasseled scarf that hung loosely around Roan's neck. Ignoring his mumbling curses, she swept the scarf once around his throat to ward off chill and patted it, *clucking* and *tsking* as she went.

A tall, coltish young lady no more than fourteen or fifteen, Daniel conjectured, yet she was a mothering caretaker for her father. She turned then, and began a skimming glance across the group on the steps—stopping like a marble statue when she saw the bloody carnage below her.

Daniel observed her carefully, noting her whispered petition. "Dear God in Heaven." Her cheeks paled like those of a porcelain doll too fragile, he decided, to be an aid to their plight— then, as he watched, she gathered her composure about her like a matron who had raised a rowdy brood of children and seen it all. Never taking her gaze from the injured James Rockburne, she said calmly, "I believe one of your guests needs a plaster, Father, shall I attend to it?"

That shook Sedgewick out of his surprised fascination with her, for clearly his anticipated glory in capturing a dangerous band of smugglers had not impressed the young lady. "He's a convicted criminal, Miss Roan," he said, a hurried resumption of authority in his proclamation, "and I'll be taking them both away with me now."

Harmony noticed Daniel then, and flinched, unable to hide that familiar flicker of fear he'd seen so many times. She shook it off, staring directly at him as if to say, "Take note, Daniel Rockburne, I'm not afraid of you."

She turned to Sedgewick, calmly calling his bluff. *"Convicted?* Surely not without a trial, sir, you must be mistaken." Before he could reply, she waved toward Daniel. "Bring your father into the hall, Master Rockburne, before we're all chilled into icework statues. And you, sir," she said coldly to Sedgewick, "come in and close the door behind you. Your men may remain outside."

His nostrils flaring, Sedgewick opened his mouth to object, but the girl forestalled him by patting her father's shoulder, saying, "You don't mind my taking care of this for you, do you Father?" Sir Roan shook his head, smiling at her as if his outburst had never happened.

Daniel quickly hefted his father into his arms and carried him the length of the hallway, striding past Meadows, the wrapper-clad housekeeper now rushing into the foyer. Careful not to aim for any furniture—for Daniel was not so far lost in manners to forget how females fuss over carpets and such—he gently laid his burden on the wooden floor at the warmer end of the room. Kneeling, Daniel stripped off his own coat and made a pillow for his father.

With a mutinous expression on his handsome face, Sedgewick stepped in and closed the door behind him, his eyes fastened upon Sir Roan and his daughter. His face grew uglier each moment as Harmony's soft monologue calmed and convinced her father.

James grasped Daniel's arm. "Now we're inside, there are a dozen ways out. If this goes sour, I want you to escape."

"Not without you."

"Escape," James bit out between clenched teeth, "the better

to rescue me. Gather the men to help." When Daniel remained silent, James hissed, *"Promise."*

Daniel hesitated, swiftly calculating the unlikely chance of safely moving the wounded man. Resigned, he nodded. Readjusting his kneeling stance for a hurried move upward, Daniel turned his attention to his fragile rescuer.

Head cocked to one side, Harmony was smiling up at Sir Roan as she gained his permission to carry on as she saw fit. Daniel wondered for a brief moment if he were in the throes of a particularly nasty nightmare, and he would wake and find everyone gone—female wizard included.

"Sir Roan," Sedgewick interjected, "I shall just take my prisoners now, and . . ."

James's hand tightened on his son's arm; obediently Daniel tensed, ready for flight.

Sir Roan's head jerked up at the sound of Sedgewick's voice, the wild look hovering about his eyes once more. Sedgewick hesitated briefly, but continued despite the clear warning sign. "You did say I might hang the prisoners forthwith, and I wish only to carry out your command."

For a second, it seemed to Daniel that Sir Roan might concede the point, but once again, Miss Roan cut him off. "Tell him, Father, that he has misunderstood you. We often have barrels of brandy floating in from the sea, and if he saw the Rockburnes with some of these, he must understand that it's only tradition to clear them from the beach to protect children who might find them. If he wishes to punish the prisoners for this error, I'm sure the father has received quite enough beatings from the soldiers, and a servant can administer a nice whipping to the son on the morrow."

Stunned at her daring brilliance, Daniel bit back a gasp of admiration. Did she, he wondered, comprehend how very clever that whipping was, to have assigned a punishment for an accused crime, one that satisfied the law and thus prevented Sedgewick from taking him away?

Daniel held his breath as Sir Roan, now calmed and back in

control, nodded. "Sedgewick, is it?" he spit out distastefully. Waving his hand at James's sad plight, he barked out a protest. "You have stepped outside the bounds of civility with this barbaric display." When Sedgewick would have objected, Sir Roan stepped closer to the officer. "Stick to guarding the tower, young man, and leave my beach alone. I do not want to see you on my property again."

Sedgewick's temper deepened. "My brother is an earl, Sir Roan. He shall hear of this." Sir Roan smiled then, and Daniel knew that Sedgewick had just sealed his fate.

Pulling a rumpled paper out of his pocket, Sir Roan waved it and murmured, "As someone who is translating literary works for the Prince of Wales, I do not tremble at the mention of your brother."

A muffled bit of amusement escaped James, and his fingers relaxed upon Daniel's arm.

Sedgewick paled at Sir Roan's *coup de grâce,* but returned the magistrate's amused regard with a silent rage too far gone for prudent apologies.

"Harmony," Sir Roan said, "please show Lieutenant Sedgewick out. I shall be retiring now." He shuffled away as if the entire event had never happened.

Daniel watched as Sir Roan's daughter neatly chivied Sedgewick out the door, but not before the irate lieutenant bestowed upon Daniel and Harmony a glare that promised retribution in full. She lifted her round little chin and glared back. Once the door closed upon Sedgewick, she turned to Daniel, her willingness to do battle with him clearly emblazoned upon her face, should he protest his own allotted punishment.

Ah, not so much rescuing angel as determined little termagant, Daniel thought, dipping his head in silent acknowledgment of her victory.

She fascinated him, this strange girl, nervous as a fawn ready to dart away, yet bright and brave. An enigma to solve another time and a favor to be returned, for he never left a debt—especially one of such magnitude—unpaid.

* * *

Harmony hated looking into Daniel Rockburne's penetrating eyes, hated the power he wielded in that capturing gaze that so easily held her transfixed. A strong emotion traveled that strange, frightening path between them, suspended for a brief, intense moment before he released it into words, the first sound she had ever heard from his lips. "You have my solemn promise, Miss Roan, that someday I shall return this favor."

Oh, *unfair* that this uncouth giant should speak with the lilt of a Welsh poet—in a deep voice that resonated like a ship's bell echoing across the water. *Unfair* too, the vow he made, for she wanted no such entanglement. She did not want to be this close to him again—ever. She closed her eyes briefly to break the spell, and her voice emerged a faint whisper. "Please, sir, nothing is required . . ."

She looked down at his father, relieved to concentrate instead on the unconscious man. "Meadows," she said firmly to the housekeeper, the better to lodge firmly in everyone's mind that she was truly in charge, "send for the doctor to care for Mr. Rockburne . . ." She glanced at the blood spreading across the front of Daniel's shirt, ". . . and for his son as well. And, Meadows," she added, marshaling her thoughts, "prepare two bedchambers and send soap and hot water to each. Bring footmen to transport Mr. Rockburne to his room."

"Call off your servants," Daniel drawled as Meadows rushed away. "I'll take my father home."

She wanted to strike him, this caustic, ungrateful oaf who probably had no idea of how dangerously close he had come to hanging. She raised her chin. "You do that, sir, and then when Sedgewick discovers how you have evaded your punishment . . ."

"I'll be back in the morning for my whipping."

"And," she continued as if he had never interrupted, "when your father dies because you are too stubborn to take advantage of proper care . . ." Her words trailed off, challenging, daring him to refute her. Then some fleeting expression on his features gave her pause . . . and a glimmer of understanding.

No man, least of all this dangerous male, liked being forced into the ignominious position of being rescued. To accept what amounted to charity from Sir Roan, who so loudly proclaimed his contempt for the *illiterate peasants and smugglers,* must be more painful than his wounds.

She tried a gentler reasoning. "You are injured as well, Daniel Rockburne," she said, waving her hand at his chest. "If the doctor deems it wise, I will provide a carriage to carry you and your father home tomorrow, but tonight . . . no matter that you're strong as an ox, you cannot carry him all the way to the castle, both of you bleeding every step of the way."

Clearly confused at her words, he glanced downward. Surprised remembrance flitted across his face as he stared at his blood-soaked shirt. He sent his father an assessing look, and grimaced at seeing his unconscious state. After a tense moment, he squared his shoulders in proud defeat. Through gritted teeth, he relented. "I thank you for your kindness."

A wave of relief flowed to her knotted stomach, and a tiny breath of hope rose. "Perhaps as the favor you offered, we may now be . . . pleasant when we meet?"

"Pleasant?" he asked as if the word were a stranger.

Oh, why had she even opened the subject? "Smile . . . nod . . . ?"

The look he gave her—strangely amused as if he knew something she did not—was nothing less than condescending. "You think I would offer so little for so great a kindness from you?"

A small kernel of anger sparked. How dare he withhold this small boon? Oh, no he must promise some majestic—and imposing—repayment of a favor, as if only some daring deed would suffice so great a man. Well, she would not be content with so paltry a gift, nor would she hold back her own true feelings.

"Until that great moment, then," she said, not caring how it might offend him, "if you must persevere in the clandestine idiocy that brought you to our doorstep, please refrain from using our beach to do so."

She might just as well have thrown a feather at the wind, for his steady response bore no hint of contrition. "We were captured on our own beach, Miss Roan, and entirely innocent of wrongdoing."

"Do not quibble about details, Daniel Rockburne!"

He dipped his head to acknowledge her words, but belying the gesture was an unmistakable lift of his twitching lips. No matter how serious she found the situation or how true her scolding words, his monumental ego remained unbruised and his brash confidence stayed firmly intact.

Worse, now he found her amusing.

Incensed, she studied him as he knelt beside his father, his long, muscled legs straining against weathered nankeen and his loose shirt doing nothing to conceal the spread of dark hair across his broad chest—*indecent,* she thought—like an oversized statue hastily draped with clothing as it came lustily to life.

And his face—so harsh and tanned, so lacking in finesse— bore traces of age-old experience, unforgiving disillusionment. A dark shadow covered his cheeks and uncompromising chin, a face framed by long, thick hair the color of ebony. His eyes, though—they were the worst, as if some stranger hid behind those sun-squinted slits, looking out at the world with the wisdom of an ancient seer. Green they were, dark as moss, but glowing, lit from within.

Rushing footsteps interrupted her reverie as Meadows came bustling along the hallway with two footmen in tow. They soon had James Rockburne hoisted gently into their strong arms and on the way up the stairs. When Daniel rose and turned to follow them, she gasped, horrified to see what the soldiers had made of his back—a sieve of bloody stabs above his waist. Sympathy overwhelmed her for a moment, but the closed, dark look she had seen on Daniel's face as he turned to trail behind his father only demonstrated how little he would welcome her pity.

She waited a moment for them to disappear, carefully devising a plan for this unexpected intrusion into her life. She would see to their healing as any compassionate person should, but only with the goal of speeding them from her life. She would order Daniel's punishment, but with a light touch, for he was, after all, a doubly wounded man. She would keep them isolated from her father and his guests. As for any necessary conversation, she would not cower from Daniel, but conduct herself as the intelligent, capable person that she was.

And should she and Daniel reach a future confrontation, she would simply whip up her justified anger as a barrier against her fear of him—for he had not accomplished their rescue—she had done it all. She would be the one to lie awake all night, her nerves jumping and her mind racing, replaying the horror of finding blood-soaked prisoners at her door. Then, too, the incident had unnerved her father, a spoiled, tantrum-throwing man who let his brilliant, delicately tuned mind teeter and fall wherever it willed, never mind the consequences.

As she strode up the stairs, she thought of words she might have added, choice items one of her favorite gothic heroines might have hurled at a villain. To prove her superiority over Daniel's uncultured ways, she muttered militant insults in German and then composed an elegant imprecation in Portuguese. After a pause, she threw in a few guttural Russian oaths to polish off the job.

"What?" her father called from beyond his bedchamber door. "What are you saying, Harmony? You know I don't understand those languages, and it's rude of you to forget that."

"I'm sorry, Father," she gasped, alarmed at how far she had slipped into a world peopled only by her and Daniel Rockburne. She was tired, she reasoned, and only needed a good night's sleep for her usual calm to reinstate itself. She needed a change as well, needed to get out of this house where she was trapped in a life of books and languages and her father's friends . . . her entire life dedicated to immortalizing Sir Temple Roan.

A few more weeks until summer, she thought with a sigh, then she could escape to Aunt Beatrice's house. She clung to the thought. It was her salvation, that annual holiday. What would she do without her aunt, for there in the gentle society of Bath, she was rejuvenated by the *illusory* pampered existence her aunt lovingly thrust upon her, able to return home refreshed and ready to accept her own life, able to tamp down the small rebellions that so often rose within her.

And there were rebellious moments, times when she wished her father had never discovered the capacity of her splendid brain—her ability to read entire works, remember every word and spew them back in the language of one's choice—for how had she been rewarded for such precocity? Twelve-hour days, six days a week, with visitors to perform for on demand. And responsibility for scenes like the one tonight.

Remorse immediately filled her at such ungrateful thoughts. Remorse and regret that she was not stronger, that she could not endure with good cheer, that she so needed the frivolous summers with Beatrice to keep from sinking into a weak, female decline.

Why, she wondered—a fruitless exercise she indulged in far too often—did she fight against her destiny, a destiny her father continually reminded her surely meant she was to accomplish something great? Why else would she have been so favored in her mental faculties? For a man, it would have been a distinguished honor to be so gifted, but for a woman . . .

She motioned to her father's valet, rushing toward Roan's chamber, obviously surprised to find his master retiring so early. "Give him a posset, John, and warm his sheets well. He's been disturbed, and needs a good night's sleep." Within the hour, Sir Roan's tantrum would turn into a painful headache. John, dutifully efficient with Sir Roan's comfort and valuable beyond words, nodded calmly, opened the door, attending his master with a stream of tranquil words.

She knelt beside her bed that night, fervently giving thanks for averting her father from his folly. "And God grant that . . . ," she finished with a rush of emotion, ". . . that I never have to rescue that Rockburne devil again."

Two

Daniel followed the small cavalcade into the dining room, with a contented smile playing at the corners of his mouth. Before him strode his father and a small contingent of craftsmen come to examine their collection of ancient furnishings with a view to repairing them. The dining hall they now entered, with its polished oak panels and rich, exotic carpets, signaled the end of the tour and the culmination of his father's dream—the final restoration of Rockburne castle—an undertaking of many troubled years.

Looking at his father's contentment now, one would never guess at the agony that had preceded it, nor the wounding memories that still had the power to torment James Rockburne.

At nineteen, James had inherited this ancient stronghold, a long-neglected fortified manor house, surrounded by long-dormant land, along with a name so disgraced by his father, Neville, that no decent person would exchange a civil word with him. Not that gambling, whoring and enthusiasm for vile societies were grounds for social banishment, but illegal schemes that resulted in the loss of fortunes belonging to the aristocracy drew considerably more unfavorable notice.

The scale-tipper had been Neville's despoiling a duke's beloved daughter, who then took her own life. The outraged duke petitioned the crown to strip away the Rockburne title. The *ton*, lemmings all, embraced the idea with a vengeance; suddenly, after months of cutting Neville, they found abundant excuses to address him, but only to call him *Mr. Rockburne* to show their united displeasure.

Gradually, though, a trickle of reason smote them. Could one, in a matter of moments, be stripped of one's title *socially,* if not legally? Panic grew. Arguments erupted. Solicitors, barraged with questions, assured them it was impossible, while the growing hysteria sent them scrambling to the law books for further verification.

Before the legal community could begin to seriously argue over such an unlikely matter, Neville Rockburne died mysteriously, choking on an opium pipe that seemed to be jammed deeply into his throat. His obituary, however, labeled the deceased—sans title—as *Mr.* Neville Rockburne.

Neville's son, James—Daniel's father—had spent his childhood running wild, wresting pleasure from life with cunning and an unyielding determination. Upon his father's death, James's focus immediately changed. Upon that day of emancipation, he vowed that he would someday take back all that his evil sire had lost.

James promptly rented out his land for sheep grazing, gaining immediate coin for his coffers. His devil-may-care attitude sobered, and he took the local smugglers in hand. A motley bunch with little ambition, they were the laughingstock of *gentlemen* all up and down the coast, more likely to sink than succeed. The only reason that the excise men had not captured them was pure lack of interest, for no glory could attach itself to such a puny endeavor.

Excise officers, if driven by any ambition at all, sought either the glory of capturing smugglers or the far more sensible reward of generous bribes. So prevalent was the practice of officers accepting gifts from the local free trading—subsequently retiring as wealthy men with lands of their own—that the Crown instituted a rotation system for the excisemen monitoring the coast. Far more feared were those excisemen who ruled their local smugglers by violent force, siphoning off the profits and terrorizing entire villages into poverty-stricken submission.

Dangers notwithstanding, smuggling was James's deliberate profession of choice, for it offered an ambitious man a quick fortune—and James was not only fiercely ambitious, but bright enough to know that wealth was the avenue upon which his ambitions would travel the swiftest.

James concentrated on his goal, whipping his gang into a frenzy of greed and pride. They paid their bribes and everyone prospered.

Then, at twenty-two, with an impressive pile of coins neatly tucked away, he surprised himself by falling in love—with Caroline Talbourg, a friend of Sir Roan's wife. He was afflicted by the Rockburne hex that always struck with sudden, irreversible power, leaving in its wake a hopelessly smitten Rockburne male.

She was older than he, unlovely and awkward, but she had the sweetest laugh . . . and the longest, most graceful legs in the kingdom. Neither liked the tumult caused by their romance, an alliance between a duke's daughter and a hastily retired smuggler, but she was of age and a formidable match for her father's objections. Their son, Daniel, came into the world nine months and six hours after the wedding, the nine-month propriety belonging to the strong-willed Caroline, and the six-hour swiftness belonging to the virile lustiness of her husband.

She played house in the castle, importing London servants to bring a womanly comfort to Rockburne and its master. She moved furniture and hung drapes and rearranged James's life to suit her own personal idea of his happiness. He grinned and agreed to everything.

With her immense dowry marching alongside his illicit fortune, they traveled, taking Daniel with them, along with a retinue of servants—and later a tutor for Daniel—to smooth their path. She showed him London and her version of civilization; he showed her hunting in the wilds of Scotland. She took him to vast libraries and museums; he took her fishing and taught her to sail. She loved and laughed and prayed for more children. He found himself praying as well—in thanks for their wonderful years of happiness.

Then her wish was fulfilled; she was once again with child.

It was an uneasy pregnancy, punctuated with unmentionable complications. Frightened beyond thinking, James let her parents convince them to move to London for "better access to learned doctors." The doctor came to her lying-in dressed for better things and full of himself. While he pranced and pontificated, Caroline and their baby daughter died. James went crazy, and it took several strong footmen to pry his fingers from the doctor's throat.

He escaped to the solitude of Castle Rockburne, taking Daniel, a confused and heartbroken boy of twelve summers. James's grief left him a shadow of himself, gaunt and lost in another world.

Daniel endured his father's folly for several months, then seeing no improvement, convinced him to sail away from England. He was old enough for such an adventure, Daniel argued, for at eight years a boy might serve as a squeaker in the navy. At his own age of twelve, midshipmen were considered men.

It was a request borne of desperation, and turned out to be a moment of brilliance. Thrown into a life completely devoid of memories of Caroline, and forced to safeguard his son from the very elements, James began his return from hell.

Daniel was his father's only link to sanity, and he knew it. He let his father teach him the dark side of life; no pupil was more apt, more diligent. He learned to sail, to navigate, to forecast the weather and the actions of violent men. He learned to fight, to see the treachery in every opponent, to attack at the first hint of danger.

James was fierce, but Daniel was ferocious. Where James hated, Daniel despised. Where James fought like a wild man, Daniel fought like a demon, giving no quarter—for in truth, that was his mission, to fight his father's fight before his own, to guard his back, to supply whatever his father needed to be safe and content.

On the occasion of his fifteenth birthday, Daniel sat watching his father pace the pine deck of their 56-foot cutter, restless and out of sorts. Amused by antics of their crewmen in avoiding his father, sometimes scrambling around the low teakwood cabins to stay out of James's unswerving path, the words, *you need a good fight* rolled down his tongue. And halted. The words were true in fact, but false in spirit. His father was addicted, not to fighting, but to escaping his own cruel thoughts. He was driven, but never satisfied. Despite all they had seen, all they had done, his father was unhappy, and it was Daniel's self-appointed job to remedy that.

It took Daniel hours of concentrated thought to come up with a solution. Finally, he swung the cutter about and began sailing toward England. At his father's questioning look, Daniel replied, "We've mourned long enough. We're going home."

James balked; Daniel bullied and reasoned and talked his way home. James sulked and prowled the castle, kicking furniture and yelling at Daniel's newly hired servants; Daniel yelled back and raised the servants' wages. James reached for the bottle; Daniel hurled it in the fireplace where it promptly exploded—setting fire to a wing chair.

James stared, dumfounded—then laughed for the first time in three years—it was a beginning.

As if a fog were lifting, James turned his energy back to restoring their holdings—a project sadly neglected in his absence. He reorganized the smugglers and ambitiously invited other gangs to join him. Reassuming his role as father, James relegated Daniel to watching the inn—fondly called "The Wreck," short for "The Wreck of the *Amsterdam*," a ship which ran ashore sixty years ago—which boasted the only coaching stop in the area. His task, James announced, was not only to monitor the coach traffic and the gossip of bragging soldiers from the tower, but ensuring that the excise officers gave honor to their bribes.

Daniel cheerfully sloughed off his mantle of command, but balked mightily at James's other edict, that of sending him to London to visit his Talbourg grandmother each year on her birthday. He managed to keep the detested visits brief, but upon the recent demise of the duke, his grandfather, his stay had been prolonged.

He rather admired the old lady's impenetrable facade, for she never shed a tear in company. Even better, he liked the manner in which she managed his cousin, the sly little bookworm, Robbie, who had always done his best to throw Daniel in a poor light. He called him a lawbreaker, and twisting the old story when they'd almost been hanged, said they'd been *caught smuggling*. Daniel explained that they'd been charged falsely by Sedgewick, but Robbie liked his version better.

Even when Daniel was a child visiting in London, the duchess had always given fair hearing to the squabbles between Daniel and her sister's grandchild, and when Daniel told his side of the story, she believed him.

The thing he couldn't abide was her determination to mold him to her London ways—clothes, manners, social events— never believing that he preferred his country ways and had no intention of changing.

Nevertheless, he was home now where he belonged, grateful to watch James press forward unhindered toward this day. James had fulfilled his vow to restore what Neville had destroyed, Daniel thought with fierce pride, and in doing so, had finally found peace.

James stood just inside the room, a proud tour guide saving the best for last, for they had spent the day exploring each room in the castle. Pleased with James's enthusiasm, Daniel strolled toward the marble-framed fireplace on the opposite side of the room. Trotting alongside him, his mastiff pup, Juno, surveyed the newcomers with glee. "Don't even think of it," Daniel murmured, pointing to the hearth. "Sit." Deprived of a friendly tussle with the strangers, Juno sent Daniel his finest canine pout and settled his considerable bulk upon the hearth rug.

Amused, Daniel turned his attention to the awestruck crafts-men James had retained to restore the castle's furniture, Joseph Fossey, Furniture Restorations Ltd, London, and his son, Paul, who acted as clerk. Behind them strolled the Head Finisher, Charles Bernard, a wide-shouldered, solemn-faced craftsman whose contributions to the conversation consisted of expressive grunts as he recognized the treasures sitting so complacently waiting for his healing touch.

Fossey's precise description launched the cataloging cere-mony. "Twenty Charles II walnut dining-room chairs." His son obediently noted the information in his bound book. Bernard ran gnarled fingers across the top of one ornate chair, dispens-ing an alarmed grunt for a missing knob, a satisfied one for the strength of the turned back-posts; then as his fingertips slid disinterestedly down the threadbare oval back cushion and stopped to stroke the shredded cane bottom, he emitted an un-derstandable grunt of disgust.

Daniel bit his lip, trying to banish the vision of Bernard sub-jecting a female bedmate to just such an inspection.

"One table," Fossey catalogued, "oak refectory, oversized." Bernard ran his own fingers across the scarred planked surface, then stepped back to examine the sturdy legs cross-braced in pairs to the center piece near the floor. He stooped down, frown-ing as his keen eye examined the long beam. Daniel's gaze followed as a series of grunts counted the foot-propping scars that decorated the long planking.

Fossey's critical gaze scurried back and forth between the walnut chairs and oak table, clearly questioning the disparate wood and styles insulting each other in this grand room.

Watching Fossey closely, Lord Rockburne cheerfully sup-plied an unsolicited explanation. A reminiscent smile appeared on his strong, weathered face. "M'bride stood for no nonsense when she came here, cured me of my ignorance and civilized the household. She tipped me out of the kitchen and into the dining room, then brought out the plate and polished the silver. Bless her bright soul, she gathered together all the sticks of furniture in this old ruin, dragged them out of attics and store-rooms and set them where you see them now."

He paused, skewering Fossey with a unwavering look. "She *liked* these pieces together."

Fossey gulped. "As do I, Rockburne. Splendid choice." His eyes raced toward another item, blinked at yet another incongruous style, but his voice held steady. "Seventeenth-century oak sideboards—two." He hesitated, then added, "Excellent balance of . . . size."

Bernard added his approval, cooing gentle grunts as his stain-darkened fingers caressed the wide, ornate carving along the top edge and down the legs.

"By George," Fossey whispered, staring at the mantel. "One Sung pottery bottle, A.D. 1200. And," he added in a strangled voice, "look at this priceless Chinese porcelain bowl . . ." After that, speech ended as he moved openmouthed along the length of the enormous fireplace.

Without warning, Juno leapt to his feet. The sheer size of the mastiff's body sent Fossey tumbling sideways. "Wha—" Fossey began, his fingers clutching at the mantel.

"Down!" Daniel roared.

Fossey obediently dropped to the floor.

Daniel shook his head and waved the man to his feet, while Juno cheerfully ignored his directive. Blast the pup, Daniel thought, sometimes he couldn't remember a command longer than it took him to think of some new atrocity to commit. Juno cocked his head at his master, then his attention swiveled back toward the other end of the room as if seeing something beyond the tall, glass-paned doors—his massive body quivering with anticipation.

Suddenly alert, Daniel exchanged an unspoken message with his father and snapped his fingers to release the dog. Juno, responding to his overpowering guarding instinct, bounded across the room to stand silent sentinel.

Daniel glanced once more toward his father, not surprised to see his parent already leaving the room.

"Excuse us," Daniel said, following the older man into the hall. He regretted leaving Juno behind, wishing the mastiff were older and less volatile; seasoned, he would have made a fine accomplice for their present purpose. A few moments later, father and son were armed, James with his Twigg sliding-safety musket, Daniel with a pair of Manton pistols. They moved silently through the back entrance, its well-oiled hinges permitting a quiet exit. They stood unmoving, listening to the sounds of the night while their eyes adjusted to the dark. Fog moved up the bluff, ghosting the seaward panorama, muffling the wailing sea breezes.

James shrugged and moved forward while Daniel guarded his back. Around the house they went, slowly examining every bush for unfamiliar silhouette or movement. They headed for the stables, shunning the direct route over the cobblestones, choosing instead the soft dirt path that skirted the paved area.

James opened the stable door a crack, and they entered the warm, hay-strewn shelter. The horses' hooves stomped a restless pattern as they caught their masters' familiar scent. Newgate, Daniel's bad-tempered stallion, snorted an arrogant greeting, too proud to join the others' whinnying, while the lazy stable mongrel rose to lick James's hand. Nothing untoward there, they glided back toward the door, Daniel once again following.

James slid silently out the door with Daniel close behind. The double-flash of a flintlock pistol flared briefly across the stable yard and a hot, searing pain sliced into Daniel's thigh. A second weapon barked, its deadly missile tearing into James's throat.

Daniel threw himself awkwardly across his father's falling body, his scream denying the truth, cursing God and praying to him all at once. As they landed on the ground, he rolled to face the enemy, straining to raise one gun-fisted hand to squeeze the trigger. He fired the gun toward the acrid smoke drifting toward him, exulting at the agonized scream rending the air, then tried to raise the other hand which—damn it—seemed to be pinned beneath his useless leg.

Time slowed then, etching each pulsing second indelibly into Daniel's brain. Another small flash of fire from the pan of an enemy's gun merged with the brighter flash from the barrel's tip; a bullet sliced across Daniel's ear, nudging his skull as it passed. The noise deafened him as an incredible pain roared through his head like the explosion of a cannon. He battled the whirlpooling darkness.

Stay alert . . . Father . . .

Strong fingers pulled his trapped hand free and tugged at the loaded pistol, but Daniel gripped it with all his might—he would take it to hell with him. "Easy, Master Rockburne. It's me, Bernard." Bernard tugged again and Daniel relented.

"My father?" He wasn't sure he'd even spoken aloud.

"Quiet," Bernard warned, just as the assailants' voices floated across the gun-smoked stable yard.

"Did we kill them both? If you leave one alive, we're dead men for sure." Daniel recognized the voice—*Lark,* fellow smuggler, friend. Traitor.

"We'd better have," another familiar voice—*Flemming*—whispered, "he wants ring-and-finger from each of them before he'll pay us."

"I don't trust him. What's a bloke like him wanting those two dead so bad?"

"Who cares?" Lark hissed. "Go get the fingers."

"Me? I'm already shot. Why not—?" Bernard's gun blasted, terminating Flemming's complaint.

Bernard grunted softly. "I'm going after the other one—d'ye want him dead or alive?"

"Not . . . dead . . . talk." Cold air moved into the space Bernard left behind, chilling the hot ache of Daniel's head. He let the spent pistol slide from his hand and reached out to find his father, immediately touching him. His fingers trailed across his face—his *still* face—slipping next to his neck to find a gaping hole where his pulse should have been.

"Nooo!" His agonized protest pierced the evil night as Daniel embraced the welcome slide into swirling darkness.

* * *

He awakened—immediately alert to danger—then slowly relaxed as he discerned that it was daytime and he was safe in bed, his head resting upon a pillow and the weight of clean linens tucked neatly across his bare chest. Hushed voices rendered a background for the painful ache of his left leg and the throb of his tender head. Sickroom smells assailed his nostrils—sharp lye soap, basilicum powder, and alcoholic tincture of opium.

He cursed his wakening and the full remembrance of his last conscious thoughts. He let his eyes drift partway open. An unsmiling Bernard stood at the foot of his bed, his massive arms folded across his chest. Bernard—grunting furniture restorer, powerful comrade in arms, and hopefully, captor of the enemy.

"Still here Bernard?" he rasped, furious that his words had no more strength than a mewling barn kitten.

"Yes, sir."

"What happened last night? What time is it?"

"What *day* more like, sir, but save your strength for better things while I give you the news, bad and good."

"Thank you," Daniel mouthed, directing a steady gaze toward the man. Bernard nodded, his solemn expression acknowledging the full meaning behind the words.

Bernard grasped the footboard and scowled. "You've slept four days, and the doctor thinks you'll live. We buried your father on the second day. The vicar blessed him and the entire countryside stood watch."

The news wasn't unexpected, but it slammed into him like a swinging boom. It hurt too much to weep, but he thought he might die from the pain of it.

Bernard cleared his throat. "Got a prisoner trussed up waiting for you. You've a fine dungeon, but he doesn't seem to be enjoying it. Best you get well enough to end his misery, one way or the other."

A surge of passionate hatred filled him. "I'll do that."

Bernard nodded at Daniel's grim promise, one that issued forth with solid strength surprising to them both.

"Where are Fossey and his son?" Daniel asked, "What about your employment?"

Bernard dropped his hand from the footboard and squared his shoulders. "D'ye want me gone?"

"Don't be an ass, Bernard. You saved my life and buried my father for me—and you're still here guarding my interests. I just don't want to cause you any grief over it."

Bernard folded his arms and stared at Daniel. A disbelieving grunt followed. Finally, he relented. "Fossey's gone back to London. I'll tell him what my plans are when I'm ready."

"And how does a furniture restorer learn to shoot, to go hunting men in the dark?"

Bernard smiled. "I crawled up from the gutter, Rockburne. Had my turn behind His Majesty's rifles—scouted after that. Took a ball in my arm and they sent me home."

Daniel studied the older man as he spoke, a growing respect compelling a careful consideration of his words. "Tell me how I may serve *you*. I won't insult you with a token reward for assistance rendered, for if I gave you all I had, it wouldn't be enough. Name what you want, and it's yours."

"A fool's promise, Rockburne."

"My word is good, Bernard."

A silence followed while Bernard deliberated. "I've a son who's mad for the army," he began.

"Done," Daniel replied. "And your wife?"

"She's been gone these ten years, but I've a mother who's lost her employment."

"Would she like the seashore?"

"Here?"

"She can sit on a cushion in her own snug cottage and have a lifetime of servants waiting upon her if you wish."

"She'd like the cottage, but she'd rather be bossing your servants, if you had any up to her standards."

Daniel smiled and began negotiations. "She'll need her family nearby. A mother needs her son . . ."

Suddenly, the thought of his father smote him, wrenching his heart. He had to close his eyes to breathe as the pain filled him, flowed through his bloodstream and filled every corner of his body. He couldn't believe they'd never have a chance to talk again, or that James would never be here to see his castle finished. They had gone through hell together, been father to each other in turn, and come out the other side with years ahead of them, all the bad behind and the good ahead.

Pictures flashed in his mind. The two of them upon the ocean, following the winds and currents as it suited their pleasure, filling their hours with talk of anything that would diminish their mutual grief. Hours spent listening to James recounting his life.

If only he'd had a chance to say good-bye, to tell him . . .

Daniel could barely breathe. He didn't think he could stand it, not one solitary, lonely, meaningless minute of a future without his father . . .

"Your father talked about your mother the other night."

Daniel had to run Bernard's remark through his brain twice before he could make any sense of it. He swallowed the ache in his throat and forced himself to respond. "Yes, he did."

"D'ye suppose they're happy to be together now?"

Daniel couldn't answer as the idea took root. He let the thought grow, fill his imagination. His father together with his love, and his mother with hers. What a picture to carry with him when he began to feel the loss.

Bernard took a deep breath. "I'm staying here 'til you're on your feet, Rockburne."

Daniel nodded. "I suppose we're not up to your standards either."

Bernard snorted. "You've only a handful of servants; my mother will take care of that. Unless," he said, "you wish otherwise."

"I'm too weak to argue. Do whatever you want."

Bernard gave him an enigmatic smile. "Are ye hungry now?"

Daniel considered the question. The image of food was unappealing, and the thought of garnering enough energy to chew and swallow seemed impossible. The prisoner downstairs awaited, though, and revenge was a fine barrier against the yawning abyss of grief that loitered, anticipating any moment of weakness.

"I'll eat."

Questioning the prisoner lacked the enjoyment that envisioning the deed had promised, but it had a satisfaction of its own. Two weeks in the dungeon had weakened the assailant's bravado, and Bernard's tales of Daniel's cruel intent had done the rest. The smuggler resisted long enough to make it worth Daniel's painful trip down the stone steps, for he was soon babbling out everything he knew.

"We never knew who hired us. He was no stranger to free trading, but well-dressed for all that, who'd only meet us in the dark. Offered us command of the crew and a king's ransom in gold," the prisoner whined, "and gave us half up front, so you can see why we couldn't say no."

"We sailed together, Lark," Daniel answered evenly. "We were mates."

Lark hung his head, shaking his head at his own stupidity. "I know that, Dan'l. It was a cruel choice to make."

"Well, I'll give you another choice then, Lark, seeing how you like to make them so much."

Lark lifted fearful eyes, pleading, pitiful eyes, but Daniel's voice held firm. "The hangman—or my own swift justice."

Three

Bath, February 1813

Harmony walked steadily down the carpeted stairs, each step taking its toll of her waning strength. Following another difficult night at her aunt's bedside, she longed to rest her pounding head upon her own pillow. Instead, she must now deal with the trouble waiting below in her aunt's foyer.

John, Sir Roan's valet, waited politely for her descent. Beside him, with his soiled boots planted carelessly upon her aunt's spotless floor, stood Boris, her father's surly coachman.

Boris, cruel to his underlings and to the horses in his charge, was never called to answer for his acts, for when her father's fury engulfed him, Boris bolstered his employer's darker self, offering approval and justification for his judgements. No matter how petty the crime or how undeserved the punishment—a bewildered coachman whipped for scraping their passing carriage, a horse put down for biting Sir Roan, a hungry boy-thief she had barely been able to save from hanging—Boris provided an unquestioning means to accomplish it.

As executioner for *Sir Roan, the magistrate,* Boris implemented the sentencing with such dispatch that very often no record was made of the incident, especially if the convicted person were a stranger. There were laws against such actions, but she knew that all over England—and indeed, the world— that Lady Justice could not prevent what she could not see.

The villagers hated Sir Roan, but as Harmony began circumventing injustices, they gave her a cautious respect. Sometimes she longed to be magically whisked away from home, to forever leave the tumult behind.

Yet, she and her father were so closely intertwined that his work was hers, his goals what she had striven for all her life. If she left without fulfilling his purpose, she would not be able to endure the misery of failure, of disappointing him, of leaving him without the fame and fortune that awaited him in London this season. And, she loved him as he loved her, despite his unreasonable demands.

As for Boris, she admitted that he frightened her. Harmony's conspicuous influence with her father was the single barrier that kept Boris on the submissive side of the invisible fence between them.

John, however dedicated by duty, was no man's creature. Having raised himself to the position of valet from a house of squalor and poverty, his fervent goal consisted of never again being subjected to such a life. Discovering very quickly that Harmony not only single-handedly battled her father's mercurial temperament, but issued the servants' wages as well, he'd promptly negotiated an outrageous salary for himself. In exchange, he saw to Sir Roan's wardrobe—a distinguished ensemble for his at-home Sundays and old, comfortable garments for weekdays—and dedicated the rest of his time to helping Harmony keep Sir Roan calm.

What had brought these two men to her aunt's door in person? To mask her unease, she adopted a serene mask. "What is amiss?"

Boris stepped forward. "You're to come home—"

"He's sent us without a note this time," John said, waving Boris silent. "His orders are to carry you home by force if necessary."

Harmony gasped. "My aunt is dying. I cannot come now."

The coachman stepped forward, barely leashed aggression in

his stance. "He sez to take you as you are, never mind your trappings, Miss Roan."

The mental image struck with a wave of nausea. *Boris's brutal hands on her* . . . She swallowed hard and prayed for a calm voice. "Very well, let me just say good-bye to the housekeeper."

Boris's mouth dropped open in surprise as she turned and walked away. Hoping her shaking knees would make it back to the kitchen, she prayed that the servants had not finished their breakfast. The door, already opened a crack, swung inward as she neared.

"Shall we come?" This from the enormous butler, Biggins, husband to her aunt's dresser, Sorrel, and a man clearly hoping for a fight. How she would like to remain here, she thought fervently, secure with the alertness and protection her aunt's servants afforded her.

"Would you?" At his nod to the gathered male servants, she led the way back to the front hall.

"Wot's this?" The coachman's scowl deepened as the liveried servants arranged themselves around her.

She ignored him and addressed John. "I will not leave my aunt to die alone, no matter what the consequences. I am sorry to give you this burden, but I have no time for anything else. If he dismisses you, then you come to me here and I will make it right." She smiled at the relief in his eyes. "In the meantime, go home and tell him that when things are finished, I will return and catch him up. Until then, I am no good to him whatsoever."

She turned to the coachman. "And Boris?" She waited for his temper to ease into a muttered "yes miss" before speaking. "Do not ever challenge me again." He gave her a stony, calculating look and left without a word.

"Take care," was the valet's enigmatic farewell before he followed the coachman out the door.

Harmony paused to gather her composure before turning to thank her aunt's grinning servants. That done, she trudged back up the stairs and opened her aunt's door for a quick peek to assure herself that Beatrice still rested quietly. Surprised to see the invalid's alert blue eyes staring back, she hurried forward. "You're awake, darling? Can I get you something—a drink?" Without waiting for a reply, she lifted her aunt's head and shoulders, reaching for the water-filled glass that stood sentinel on the nearby table.

Poor Beatrice, her lips cracked and dry and her hair brittle and dull, seldom remained awake long enough to consume the liquid her body craved. She drank the glass dry, giving rise to hope, foolish though Harmony knew it to be.

"Thank you," Beatrice said, then sighed as she settled back into her nest of pillows. "You look fagged, Harmony. You must rest more, else you'll lose your looks, then I shall steal all your beaus."

Harmony chuckled softly. Dear Beatrice was her oasis, her lifeline to cheerful humor and undemanding enjoyment of life. Tales of her travels with her late husband filled Harmony's imagination. Beatrice *adored* her, and she in turn soaked up that uncritical love. "Well, move over then Auntie, for I shan't have that."

Beatrice smiled and sighed again. "May we talk?"

Harmony hesitated. Her first impulse demanded she caution rest, but she sensed that Beatrice needed this conversation. "Could I stop a chatterbox like you?"

"Will you listen and not humor me? Will you promise to take my words very, very seriously?" At Harmony's nod, Beatrice's voice caught and tears filled her eyes.

"I'm so *sorry*," Beatrice said fiercely. *"Sorry* not to be able to do as we planned. I meant to travel with you, to see the world once more through your young eyes. And then," she added firmly, "I would have brought you back see you married . . . and now to leave you so unprotected . . ." She shook her head and blinked her tears away. "That said, let me tell you what I have done to shield you. It's," she added with a lighter, teasing air, "somewhat bizarre, even for me."

She drew Harmony's hand into her own. "I've told you before that you are my heir, so if I should do something so thoughtless as to trot off to heaven in the near future, you won't be surprised to hear that I have left you my worldly goods." Ignoring Harmony's anguish, she took a deep breath, and with a confiding tone, lowered her voice. "I have left you a generous inheritance that will, of course, be under your father's guardianship." Harmony nodded, touched by her aunt's kindness.

"That, however," Beatrice said with a grin, "is a decoy." She smiled apologetically at Harmony's start of surprise, then embellished the story.

"The balance is a rather impressive legacy. The principal is over ninety thousand, an amount I have never needed to spend, so it's growing like a mushroom." She ignored Harmony's awestruck expression, her voice quickening as she went. "I have safeguarded it for you to a certain extent. It has been yours for many years, placed in a hidden trust until you reach your majority with instructions to Soames, my solicitor and your trustee, to follow no one's instructions save yours. Do not . . . ," she said with a pointed command, ". . . do not ever let your father know, else you'll never see a penny of it, or ever be free of his demands."

"Oh, surely not, he wouldn't . . ."

"Listen to me. Your father will interfere with any bid for freedom, Harmony, for you are far too valuable for him to lose."

She paused, then rushed forward. "I know it's unheard of, but when you reach your majority, you must break away and set up your own household. Find some impoverished matron with impeccable standards, one who loves to travel, to live with you. When you look for a husband, find one who wants you more than your money or your talents. Better yet, keep your inheritance a secret from everyone.

"Biggins and Sorrel will remain here with the house. I've settled an extra amount on them, to be granted upon your emancipation. They will keep this place in readiness for your visits, for the house will be yours along with everything else."

She closed her eyes, a troubled expression upon her face. "Give yourself time to *think* about the best way to arrange your life. It needn't be done immediately. I only want you to be as happy and fulfilled as I have been. I had my dear husband and then I had you. No one has ever known greater joy."

"Oh, Beatrice," Harmony managed, her throat clogged with emotion.

"Give me your word you will do what I have asked."

"Very well . . . I do promise."

Beatrice smiled, drifted into a restful sleep, and died before the cock crowed on the morrow.

Days passed before Harmony could face life again. Oh, she performed the necessary formalities, arranging her aunt's affairs, receiving visits from her aunt's legion of friends, but there seemed no purpose in doing anything else. Once those details were finished, however, she went to bed and stayed there twice around the clock, waking only to go numbly through her ablutions, eat a light meal pressed upon her by Sorrel, then find escape once again under the soft, scented covers of her bed.

Then her mind began to intrude . . . the memory of what Beatrice's life consisted of . . . humor, affection, shared interests and never enough time to say everything they wanted to before Harmony once more returned home. It was the *possibility* of such contentment that roused her from her bed.

Weakly, she rose and dressed, Beatrice's words still enticing her with things possible, strewing a path before her of cheerful, colorful visions. A faint euphoria smote her, lifting her thoughts like the wings of a butterfly, then floated them effortlessly through a fragrant garden of images—traveling to countries that females were only allowed to *hear* about, writing descriptions of home and village, describing fragrances of garden and kitchen, sharing the songs of children—vibrant images seen from a woman's interested eyes. Fulfilling her own destiny, magnifying her own gift. Although she hated to admit it, sometime in the *very* far future she might like *kisses* like the heroines of the beloved romances to which Beatrice had introduced her.

Energy filled her. She must complete her father's work first, of course, must take his present projects to London for publishing, then explain to him that she wished a life of her own. Her aunt believed he would never let her go, but she knew him better. Surely, he would want her to see the world as he had, would be proud of such ambition. She suddenly wanted to rush home, to whirlwind through the tasks awaiting her, every action bringing her closer to her new, exciting life.

Biggins and his wife, Sorrel, protested when Harmony made her intention known. "I don't like you going back to face Boris by yourself," Biggins said, his chest swelling like a large, protective frog. "Who's going to keep him in his place?"

Before Harmony could form an answer, Sorrel clutched her hands together at her slim waist. "And, when are you coming back?" Tears filled her dark eyes. She looked to Biggins for help, and Harmony wanted to weep at their lost expressions.

"I'll write." It was a perfectly worthless answer, she could see that at once.

"I'll write *often*," she amended, "to tell you how I'm faring. Beatrice has explained the situation, so you see that I must wait until I reach my majority so you can join me in my own household."

"We'll drive you home, Miss Roan." Biggins's announcement eased Sorrel's worried expression, and a smile creased her delicate face. "I'll order the kitchen to pack a basket."

"Not today," Biggins told his wife. "The coach must be cleaned and the horses groomed."

Harmony managed to hide her amusement at the blatant lie, nodding just as if his slur on the immaculate stables could possibly be true. "May I leave tomorrow morning?" Harmony held back a smile while her two self-appointed guardians exchanged glances, seeing nothing wrong with the little miss asking their permission. They nodded their approval. So, it was settled.

A quiet peace accompanied Harmony home, a time for anticipation, for reflection upon her recent rebellion against her father—for he hadn't contacted her since—and for envisioning scenarios for her future. Almost two months before her twenty-first birthday, plenty of time to begin edging out of her father's life and into her own.

Biggins rode outside with the coachman, and Sorrel rode inside, sleeping soundly on the bench opposite Harmony. As they neared her father's land, she suddenly felt compelled to postpone the end of her journey. She called out of the window. "Biggins, please stop here. I'd like to walk along the bluff."

Biggins nodded and nudged the coachman. The coach slowed to a stop, and when Biggins opened the door, Harmony stepped out and strolled to the edge of the cliff. Overhead clouds recast the vast ocean into moving patches of green and blue, while farther away, the water glittered with dancing waves of brilliants upon a sea of turquoise.

As Harmony's gaze followed the curving coastline, her pulse quickened at the sight of Rockburne castle—so powerful, so imposing on the horizon—Zeus, even the sight of the Rockburne stronghold could make her heart pound.

She had hoped to erase the memory of Daniel Rockburne from her memory, to forget that compelling gaze, that stirring voice. Yet, as if no interval ever ensued, his image came back to her time and time again . . . that night as he knelt on her floor, undiminished by Sedgewick's power, untouched by her disapproval, loath to be in debt to anyone. She could still see those powerful muscles poised for action, for she'd known what that whispered interchange with his father meant. Daniel Rockburne could have modeled for statues she'd seen in books, could have been a warrior in some exotic tale.

She had prayed that night that she'd never have to rescue that Rockburne devil again and her fervent prayer had been granted— precisely as she had requested.

Perhaps she should have asked for more.

Oh, Daniel Rockburne had indeed stayed out of her life and off her beach, but still he managed to haunt her. As if she were an unwilling lodestone, bits and pieces of his infamy found their way to her, and then refused to be dislodged. Over and over she tried to purge her mind of him, yet back the thoughts would come—like a tune one dislikes, yet hums without thinking.

Sedgewick, furious so the story went, found himself transferred out, but not before he'd been thoroughly thrashed by someone in Shingle Spit—*Rockburne Revenge,* she heard. *Disgraced,* some said through no fault of his own, but rather the machinations of someone who had access to the formidable arm of justice—*Roan Retaliation,* she suspected, but had no wish to hear more.

Subsequently, French brandy arrived regularly upon her kitchen doorstep, something her father enjoyed very much. Sometimes when she spotted the proffered gift, she was tempted to send it back with a request for calico or silk to repay the females of Roan House for their care of the wounded Rockburnes.

His Grace, The Duke of Talbourg—Daniel Rockburne's maternal grandfather—died, and an impressive coach bore Rockburne away to comfort his widowed grandmother for the ensuing weeks, just as it had done every year on the duchess's birthday. Scowling, he went. Scowling even more fiercely, he returned and refused to discuss it with anyone.

As if jarred to realization of his splendid London connections and his father's not-quite-forgotten title, wealthy cits, looking to import a title into the family, began courting Rockburne's good favor, a phenomenon that had been amusing Shingle Spit ever since his return. Strangers, mostly sturdy matrons and their eager daughters, turned up to fatten the coffers of the local innkeeper. Rockburne leered at the flirting damsels and was rude to their mothers, all to no avail, for the endless stream of females were a hilarious fact of Shingle Spit.

Every personal tidbit about Daniel Rockburne managed to assail her ears as well. His father died recently, shot in a cowardly attack at the castle. Harmony had wept over the tragedy, remembering the devotion between father and son. When she pictured the anguish that must be tormenting Rockburne, all alone with no one to share his grief, it seemed almost unbearable to contemplate.

The villains had wounded Rockburne in the left leg and sent a bullet searing a path above his right ear that left him unconscious for days. Other attempts had been made to kill Rockburne since then, and word of an enormous reward spread like wildfire—offered by Rockburne for discovery of the villain who ordered the attacks.

The assassins, she heard, were fellow smugglers, trading their loyalty for coin and their lives for betraying a Rockburne. Daniel had his revenge, so the story went, for one body washed up around the spit a few days later and two weeks later another one joined the grim list.

After his father's death, Rockburne installed a steward, Bernard by name, who brought his mother from London to serve as housekeeper to the castle. Bernard had saved Daniel's life the night his father died, and captured one of the assassins.

The local gentry gossiped and speculated about Rockburne. Lawless he was, for he was a smuggling Rockburne, and you knew what that meant—evil deeds and wealth beyond measure. Then conversely, they whined as they sipped illegal French brandy, why did not Rockburne, with a title and all that apparent affluence, take his rightful place in society?

Rumors flourished and grew, fed by the excitement of hearing any news about the castle and its unsociable master.

Shivering as a cold gust blew up the hill, Harmony wondered why she still felt so certain that she would indeed—despite her fervent wishes otherwise—find Daniel Rockburne disturbing her life once more,

Four

Shingle Spit, March 1813

Harmony finished the last piece of Thomas Moore's *Irish Melodies* with an enraptured sigh. "Mr. Lewis, I cannot thank you enough for bringing me this delightful music. However did you acquire such a treasure?"

Before the fair, pink-cheeked, Tony Lewis could conquer his blushing shyness, his older brother, Mark, Lord Haughton, supplied the answer. "Our sister lives near the chap who put the words to music." His short fingers dipped into an enameled snuffbox with the same focused attention as a plump matron might pluck a chocolate from its flowered box. "Tolerable little tunes if you like the Irish," Haughton drawled before sniffing elegantly.

"John Stevenson by name," Tony interjected quickly as his brother sneezed twice. "He'd be delighted to hear how perfectly you played it, especially for the first time." He whipped out his own snuff tin and balanced it on his sleeve.

"A simple matter for our Harmony, drawled the third gentleman in the parlor. Robert, Lord Beckman, with the arrogance of one who, having the honor of sponsoring the father-genius, assumed a subtle credit for the she-cub as well. *Marked his territory,* Harmony mused with an earthy humor that surprised her.

"She memorizes it the first time through," Beckman added, "and after that, plays by memory."

"Oh, I say." Lewis's exclamation mingled with the sound of his snuff tin clinking upon the floor tiles. As he stooped to retrieve it, Harmony wondered if his outcry denoted horror at his clumsiness or admiration of her abilities.

"A simple parlor trick." Offering her hand to him, she dipped a curtsy, extending her smile to the other two. "You'll excuse me?"

"But, surely," Haughton protested, bowing over her hand as well, "you shan't go back to work like the veriest slavey, Miss Roan?"

"She has always done so," returned Beckman, leaning over to kiss her cheek. "Even as a child she has been driven to work long hours—the cost of greatness, you see." He draped his arm over her shoulder and walked her to the door.

An amusing man, Harmony thought, this wealthy patron of her father's. He was a thin man no taller than she, who nevertheless assumed an air of command among the others. In private, he was relaxed and comfortable, but when guests were present, he needed this *cachet,* a bit of authority and prestige from his position in their lives.

He could be pompous occasionally, showing how knowledgeable he was and how his intellect had won him a place in Roan's select group, but that was not unusual with scholars, since admiration was their measure of worth. The only fault she found in him was his disparaging the reputation of his cousin, Daniel Rockburne, the *local smuggler.* When Beckman named Rockburne a smuggler, she argued that he'd never been convicted of such a crime, nor would he, if her father had any say, for once he'd let him go, Roan wasn't about to call attention to that fact by convicting him later.

Harmony gave Beckman a faint smile and escaped into the cool hall where a few deep breaths prepared her for the ordeal ahead of her.

Once in the library with her father, Harmony glanced across to the immense desk where her father was completely immersed in the final philosophical paper he wished to add to the publishing basket.

It was a strange time, she thought, a phase for many changes. An ending and a beginning. The winding down of their work, topped by a week of final endorsement. This evening's visitors had been invited to review Roan's work prior to sending it to the publisher. Following the flurry of critiques, she would be busy making changes. And then . . . they were finally off to London.

Before that, another task awaited, one she had been avoiding far too long. She sighed. She'd been home from Bath for some time, her thoughts wandering to and fro, arguing with herself over how to take the first step in determining her own future. Why did she still hesitate?

Although *fear* was the first culprit that came to mind, she quickly discarded it. Had fear ever held her frozen, she would have long since atrophied like an old lady in a rolling wicker chair. No, she battled that particular dragon every day of her life, refusing to bow to its power.

During her childhood, fear struck with each meeting of a stranger, because she knew full well that since tales of her oddity invariably preceded her, the gauntlet of their reactions to meeting her would prick like a dozen tiny knife wounds. Her fear of Daniel Rockburne had been a separate matter, for he had not viewed her from the distance of adult to child. Instead, his gaze had easily detected the fragility of her calm facade and in return lazily let her know he might inflict terror at his leisure.

As an adult, she found that *fear* had taken on a more realistic flavor. Strangers became a mere source of nervousness, and Rockburne a childhood aberration. Indeed, she thought, when had fear ever stopped her from so simple a task as the one before her—a question asked, an answer given—especially when the information sought was so vital to her future?

A simple matter of disproving her aunt's accusation.

So, do it and get it over with.

She cleared her throat. "Father, I wish to discuss something."

He waved his pen at her—a signal to wait until he finished a thought—then, after a furious spate of writing, he looked at her as if just remembering that she had spoken. "What did you say?"

"I wish to discuss my inheritance from Aunt Beatrice." He

remained so still that she wondered if he had even listened to her.

He tapped the end of the pen on the table. "Why?"

"I need to know the amount if I am to put my plans into motion."

He looked surprised. "What do you mean, *your* plans?"

She laughed. "Father, you are completely hopeless. We have discussed it many times—my plans to travel and to write as you do."

"Childhood dreams, Harmony. Women do not *travel*."

"Not many, it's true, but you have always said I may as soon as your work is done. So, next month, perhaps after my birthday, I thought I might begin with a small trip to see if I like it."

"You are serious then?"

He paused, then frowning, he shook his head. "I cannot remember how much it was Harmony, but I shall look through my papers and tell you before we leave." Tapping his pen once more, he stared off into space. She waited a few moments, then gave up. Once Sir Roan drifted off, she might as well disappear and remind him another time.

"I'm going for my walk now."

"Hmm . . ."

Harmony smiled fondly. How foolish she had been to give credence to Beatrice's worry. There had always been a rivalry between the two adults over Harmony's visits to Bath. She had always thought her father rather selfish for his reluctance in letting her go. She never realized until now that it must have been fueled by jealousy over her time and affection. The thought pleased her, turned the burning worry into a curl of warm pleasure. Imagine being so well loved . . .

What about her real inheritance? She had promised her aunt to keep it secret, to keep it from her father. But when her travels depleted her aunt's smaller bequest, as they might, she would want access to the interest from the larger amount. Would her father keep a close eye on her expenditures and then discover her secret? She hated the thought of hurting him. Oh, why had her aunt made it so difficult for her?

Another dilemma to contemplate.

Which is why she found herself walking along the beach, ankle deep in water, shoes in hand, an hour later. And how she found herself wandering far past the boundaries of her father's land.

One moment she was lost in thought as her toes curled into the wet sand, absently wondering if the water had warmed up, or if her feet were merely frozen. It was a riddle with a far easier solution than the puzzle that had brought her out here tonight.

The next moment the lapping waves before her held a weathered boat—a wooden craft that blocked her way, with muffled oars and dark-clothed men with casks in their arms who leapt onto the sand with silent grunts and surprised oaths. Torches were lighted and held aloft, the better to see her, the harder to see them. Where was she? Who were they, leaping from the boats and circling her?

Smugglers.

"What have we here?" one said, reaching for her, sliding his fingers around her waist. Others joined him, touching her, tugging at her clothes. Fingers tangled into her hair, dropping pins to the sand. Howls and whistles punctuated their rough actions. "I saw her first," another barked, hauling her close and sinking his wet lips against her neck.

"No," she whimpered, dropping her shoes as she pushed at his face, twisting to get free.

An enormous shadow blocked the torchlight and a giant grabbed her, neatly culling her from the crowd. With an effortless grip, he raised her up in the air—and she found herself staring into the face of the devil himself—Daniel Rockburne, salt-matted hair, tangled and wind-blown, with a face blackened like Lucifer himself. And in the middle of that darkness, mirroring the flickering flames of the circling torches, were his green eyes, glittering with anger.

Keeping his grip on her arms, he dropped her onto the sand. "Satan's teeth, girl, what are you doing here?" His melodious, fallen-angel voice trumpeted straight from the bowels of hell while his minions' torches flickered around him.

Her teeth began chattering, and she couldn't make them stop.

They'd probably chip and blacken, she thought irrelevantly, picturing the villagers of Shingle Spit pointing out the ugly hag who'd gone crazy after one night at the mercy of the smugglers. If she lived . . .

"Ho, who's there, Dan'l?" Another huge smuggler raised his torch for a better look. She ducked her head to avoid the identifying light, but it was too late. She was recognized, and as her surname—*Roan*—passed through the crew, they fell silent. Looking quickly around for whatever escort she might have brought with her, they produced weapons with one hand and with the other, plunged their torches into the sand.

And disappeared.

The new inquisitor stayed behind. "Come here, girl," he snarled, reaching for her—but Rockburne moved first, twisting to pull her tight against his chest. Wool roughed her cheek as he claimed her, and a powerful warmth radiated from his broad frame.

"Off the beach," Rockburne snapped at the other man, then he grabbed her hand and took off in a loping run away from the water, dragging her behind him as they headed for the bluff. His bruising fingers pulled her along, sending her tender feet racing through sand, then across rough shingle and shale. She mourned the loss of her shoes with every painful step.

They flew up the track without more than a token effort from her. Rockburne's hands were everywhere, around her waist, under her arms, grazing her breasts and even under her buttocks when they shot up the last overhang. It happened so fast, she couldn't keep up with the indignities he heaped upon her person. Then they were running once more, her feet barely touching the grass or the dirt in the lane.

Into a low rock hut they went, a windowless box that shut out the thin sliver of moon and left them in total darkness. She was too frightened to speak, and tried not to breathe too loudly while Rockburne lighted a lantern that sat upon a stack of crates in the corner.

The door flung open. "Whyd'ya bring her here, Dan'l?" The slower-moving smuggler slammed the door closed behind him.

The bearded speaker, a black-faced goblin, reeked of brandy and fish, and his arms hung out sideways over the gross bulk of his body. His gaze passed over her as if she didn't matter at all; his challenging attention was directed entirely—and accusingly—at Rockburne.

"She's a foolish girl walking on the beach, Saul," Rockburne barked. "Leave her alone."

"She's seen us with the goods, you fool. She could testify and bring down everyone. You know what we have to do. Make it look like an accident."

Harmony tried to object, but when she opened her mouth, no sound escaped. Rockburne stared at her for a brief second, then gave her an intent look. "You were supposed to come *tomorrow night,* Harmony. I told you, but as usual, your mind was off dreaming of something else."

"You planned a meeting with Roan's daughter?" the foul-smelling smuggler growled. "What are you up to, Dan'l? I just joined my men with yours—I didn't know you had mush for brains."

Rockburne heaved a great sigh, then pulled her roughly to his side. "It's none of your business, Saul, but she's my girl. She just got her nights mixed up, and I'm not throwing her to the fishes for that."

She stiffened, a disclaimer exploding within her, even as her brain held her back, cautioning silence. Rockburne dug his warning fingers into her side, while Saul snorted, "Hah! Old Roan's get is *your* girl? Tell me another, Dan'l."

"You calling me a liar, Saul?"

"Just wanting the truth, is all." He turned to pin his attention on Harmony, leaning down, close enough for her to see bits of sand on his charcoal beard. "And I'm thinking I'll get it from Roan's get 'afore I'll get it from you."

Harmony swiftly glanced at Rockburne. Oh, he was a cool one, the swaggering devil, but telltale beads of moisture covered his forehead, telling her that her answer had better be good or they were both in trouble. Unfortunately, she was incapable of uttering a single word, much less a coherent lie that would assuage Rockburne's tense expression.

Then briefly, he flashed her one of his old terrifying scowls. Their thoughts met in midair, and she knew the answer. She'd have to put on an act . . . *just as she did every time she spoke to strangers, just as she had this very night with her father. In fact, had she not been performing before the villagers for years?*

"Well?" Saul breathed into her ear. "This your man, Miss Roan?"

She forced a shaky smile. "Since you do not believe your own associate, Mr. Saul, what can I say to convince you?" When he frowned, she elaborated. "Why do you not ask me questions, and I shall tell you whatever you wish to know?"

Saul shot an angry look at Rockburne as if to say, can't you make her do better than this, but Rockburne, smiling now, shrugged his shoulders as if to reply that since Saul started it, he could just as well finish it.

Saul turned to her, snarling his rough demand. "Tell me something about your lover that no once else knows."

"Well," she replied, frantically searching through every novel she had read, "He's very sweet . . ."

Saul doubled over and bellowed with laughter. Harmony thought that might be a good sign, so she continued in that vein, looking toward Rockburne for some inspiration. "His kisses are divine . . ." What was it that her heroines always said? ". . . divine . . . thrilling."

Rockburne's eyebrows shot up.

"His poetry is . . ."

She hesitated as Rockburne glowered a warning at her. ". . . quite horrible, really. I've begged him not to quote any more of his own, but to stick to plain speaking."

That sent Saul off in another paroxysm, slapping his knee and blubbering into his beard. She relaxed, feeling quite clever about the whole thing. Saul finally quieted, then surprised her by saying in a deadly voice that made her heart pound and her mouth dry up, "Tell me something I can *check on,* missy."

She stepped back and looked away. It was a sign of weakness, but she couldn't think with his face near hers, breathing all the air. "This is most unseemly, but I can see that you would not have an opportunity to hear his poetry . . ." She retrieved her handkerchief from her pocket and fanned her face, pacing away from them to search her memory, ". . . nor, of course, to experience his kisses."

A gurgling sound escaped Rockburne's throat.

She wondered if she should stop and see what was wrong with him, but her mind was far too busy racing through her mental inventory of his history. Ah, there it was, tucked away like a recipe in an old cookery book, a nice little chronology of Rockburne's mishaps.

She began again. "So . . . something very personal you might be able to *check on* would be . . . a few very *private* scars that have marred his poor, dear person over the years."

She turned and paced back toward Rockburne, who was now red-faced and clearly horrified. "You may have seen his leg wound. It almost broke my heart to see him suffer so. And then there is . . ." She turned away to pace the opposite way, for fear his tortured expression might send her off into a paroxysm of her own, ". . . the injury above his right ear. I have told him to cease this foolish scrapping with others. One of these days he might scar his dear face."

Having gone the seven steps that encompassed half of the hut, she was forced to turn and face the two men. They were both staring openmouthed at her. Was she doing this wrong?

"Perhaps a man might not mind a scar ruining his handsome face," she assured them in her most convincing tone, "but I can promise you that a lady does not wish to be seen on the arm of a beau who will frighten her friends."

Saul looked at Rockburne like he'd grown two heads. Rockburne's teeth clamped ferociously upon his lower lip. She supposed that the two injuries she'd described might not completely suffice since they were not entirely private, but she did have two more scars to tally.

"And then, of course, there are the small stab wounds on his back and a larger one on his lower chest. Right about here." She tapped Rockburne's ribs. "On the left side."

Rockburne grabbed her fingers, squeezed a painful warning, then released them. "Now dearest, you need not say any more."

"Whoa!" Saul grabbed Rockburne's arm and pulled Rockburne around to face him, clearly not wanting any interference with her fascinating performance. The two black-faced gargoyles eyed each other, jaws thrust forward in a silent battle of wills.

Finally, Saul backed down and burst into laughter. "Old Roan's girl, eh? Wait 'till I tell the men."

"You'll say nothing, Saul."

"The hell you say!"

"You want Sir Roan on a rampage against our men, yours and mine? He'll make the toy soldiers from London look like schoolboys if he hears a word of it, Saul, and you know it. Hell," he said, throwing an arm over her shoulder, "when Harmony and I meet on the street, we don't even pass the time of day for fear her father will hear of it."

Saul turned to Harmony and looked her over as if she were a horse for sale, his eyes narrowing while he looked for some worthwhile feature. He examined her hair, once a tight bun, now fallen into her face. Her figure which must seem paltry compared to the voluptuous women who worked at the smuggler's ale house, drew his manly scorn. Finally he shook his head in disgust.

"Must be your blue blood, m'boy, makes you like 'em puny as this one." He scratched his crotch. "I wouldn't tell anyone about her either."

Shaking his head once more, he turned and left the hut.

Rockburne waited a long, silent moment, then stepped outside the hut, leaving her alone. She didn't move, but her mind raced. She was alive, she thought exultantly. She'd babbled and postured and Saul had believed her—and had left. He'd believed her, and she was still alive. She'd never felt more alive.

Rockburne stepped inside, leaving the door open behind him. Neither of them moved. Then they spoke at once.

"He's gone."

"I am sorry. I didn't realize how far I had come along the

beach . . . and I want to thank you for defending me." At his scowling silence, she began to babble. "It's been a long time since we've seen each other . . . that is, I've wondered . . ." Then she remembered the last story she'd heard. "I'm sorry about your father."

He nodded, his lips tightening so fiercely that she feared he would never speak again. She followed his piercing gaze as it swung down to her bare feet, then seemed to curve around her as it rose, stopping here and there to examine various parts of her. Beneath the loose cloak she wore a serviceable brown poplin she had never minded until this moment, stiffly starched and buttoned to her chin, its dignity lost where bare feet peeked out beneath its sand-etched hem.

He gave a curious examination to her right hand, with its ink-stained fingers; her left hand rated no such pause-and-examine, just a quick to-the-point check of her unadorned wedding-ring finger. Her person above the neck drew a frown, but no wonder, with her hair stuck to her face like a rowdy crofter's child. Then down and up he went once more, this time following what he could see of her feminine curves. She flushed, grateful for the screen of unruly hair.

Then he spoke. "We find ourselves in the midst of another crisis, Miss Roan." *That voice, she'd forgotten its power.* It rippled—like the wind in a hay field, like water over a rocky waterfall—low and invasive, like the shivery pleasure of a roaring fire on a cold winter's night. Chills raced down her spine and a heated flush made the return trip.

She wanted to leave.

"And this time all my fault," she replied, stepping toward the door. "Perhaps . . ." she hesitated as a wonderful thought flitted through her mind. "Perhaps now we're even?"

He looked away, shaking his head as he did so. *Zeus, what would it take to escape from him?* While he stared into space, she quickly took a brisk inventory of her own, determined to replace the frightening specter of his fiendish appearance at the beach with one more civilized to take away with her.

He had not grown that much taller, she calculated, perhaps it was the heavy wool coat that gave such an illusion—or perhaps his shoulders. Heavens, he was broad. Hard to tell about his torso, though, swathed in a wool sailor's coat that hung below his hips. She hesitated at examining his thighs and calves, so tightly delineated by damp nankeen trousers clinging to muscles that had carried her up the bluff without a trace of exertion. No, she would not look, for a glance was enough to make her realize it was not seemly for a lady to examine a gentleman anywhere, especially not parts that seemed so *personal*.

They would be, unfortunately, difficult to forget.

"You compare your rescue of me and my father with this little bit tonight?" he mused aloud, snapping her attention back up to his solemn face. "More like comparing a mountain to a grain of sand."

Her heart dipped even as she attempted to gain back the advantage, to erase any speck of debt on his part. "Shall we call it even, though, lest we spend the rest of our lives hopping from calamity to calamity trying to equalize the debt?"

He smiled. Well, as close to a smile as she might ever get from Daniel Rockburne. It was a nice way to end the evening. Safe. Noncommittal.

Willing to take his smile for an affirmative reply, she nodded. "I truly must be going now." She picked up her skirts and made her way carefully across the dirt floor.

"You cannot be serious."

She stopped, a new sense of unease racing through her. "I'm late and my father will be unhappy . . ."

"He'll be far more unhappy when you turn up dead."

"Dead?" Was *he* threatening her now? Dear God, what did he want? She turned to face him, her heart pounding in fear at what she might find there. His expression told her nothing, but his words were almost comforting.

"You're the one with the brain, Harmony, use it. Do you think our assurances will be enough to satisfy Saul?"

"Oh, Saul," she said, relaxing. "What more will he want?"

"He will be watching us to see if our story is true."

"But you told him we never speak when we meet in the village."

"And how often do you see Saul strolling along in front of the shops?" At her look of comprehension, he continued. "He will, however, be looking for our meeting tomorrow night on the beach."

"Oh, heavens."

"And of course the men will all hear about it."

"But you warned Saul not to tell them."

"Believe me, he won't be able to resist. All I accomplished was to convince him to warn the men to secrecy."

"But my father . . . heavens, he must never hear. He's never forgiven your father for the trouble he caused."

He leaned back against the wall and folded his arms across his chest. "The trouble with Sedgewick?"

"Not that—I mean when he married Caroline. My father didn't want my mother to speak to Caroline again, but she wouldn't agree, and that made him angry. Then too, your cousin is always telling tales on you, which doesn't help my father's attitude."

"Robbie? Good grief, what's he saying now?"

"Robbie?" She grinned at the nickname. "Do you call Lord Beckman *Robbie?"* At his amused grin, she answered his question. "He keeps calling you a smuggler, but I—"

"You what . . . call me worse?"

She raised her chin. "Of course not. You've never been convicted of the crime, or even accused, except for that awful Sedgewick, and he hadn't even *caught* you at it. Not only that, but what kind of person vilifies a member of his own family behind his back? I would like to see him tell you that face to face . . ." Realizing finally what she was saying, she blushed furiously.

Giving her sputtering words an amused attention, he shrugged. "It's too bad you have to put up with him, but you can't choose your father's friends. As for the villagers telling your father about us, don't worry. Their lives depend on keeping him ignorant."

She looked down. "You're right, of course."

Then she made the mistake of looking up at him. He hadn't moved an inch, but continued to stare at her with that unwavering regard. The hut seemed airless. "Well, then," she said, suddenly in a fever to be gone, "tomorrow night it is." She took a step toward the door, the skin on the back of her neck tingling.

"I am afraid that won't be all."

She looked at the door longingly; a few more steps and she would have made it. She ached to be outside, to be running down on the beach away from him. Then, like a net surrounding her slowly, he sealed her doom. "Every time something goes wrong Saul looks for someone to blame." His voice grew harsher. "From now on, you and I will be suspect."

"No," she whispered. How could this happen? How could *he* let it happen? "Then, quit the gang and move away. You cannot be enamored of their company, surely." Her voice shook.

"If I did, you would still be in danger." He strolled over to stand before her. "Or if we seemed to separate, getting rid of you would be Saul's first priority. At any hint of trouble between us, he would expect you to immediately turn against me and the men."

"You're trying to frighten me." Solemnly, he shook his head. She studied his face. He was deadly serious. "You mean from now on . . ."

"I don't like it any better than you do," he said, his voice rising in exasperation. "You should have known better than to wander off your own land. You've lived here all your life and know enough to stay off our stretch of beach at night."

Gulping back tears, she dipped her head in agreement. He was right. She knew better, and had mindlessly brought about her own ruin. One thoughtless moment. One unlucky melding of times and places and people. And she couldn't take it back.

Or do anything but go forward. "Tell me what to do."

He nodded, his temper held in check. "We have to make plans. If we are to fool Saul, I need to know more about you."

She was horrified. This was worse than anything she could have imagined, sharing her private life with Daniel Rockburne.

"Such as what?" She wasn't going to do it.

"Oh, not your scars, he said, surprising her with his light tone as he clearly enjoyed a little revenge, "or if your kisses are . . . divine."

She could feel the heat rushing into her face. This was surely a nightmare, a quagmire envisioned in her dreams. She couldn't be snared like this, at the amused mercy of this man, who even now outlined the parameters of her confinement.

"First, I must know if you already have a sweetheart, for that would be disastrous. What were you doing out on the beach to-night? Meeting someone?"

"No! Of course not!" Seeing his disbelief, she made another attempt to explain. "I have a . . . problem I was thinking about, and I couldn't come up with a solution. I just lost track of where I was."

She studied his scowling face to see if his opinion had changed, but she couldn't tell with only his greenish eyes showing in the middle of all that blackened skin. He evidently had a similar problem seeing her expression, for he pulled back the hair that straggled across her forehead and stuck to her heated cheeks.

Briefly, he studied her features. "No man, then."

The wretch said it without a shred of doubt. *Wonderful, all I have to do to convince someone that I have no beau is to let them catch a glimpse of my face.* She wanted to hit him, but still she had a little more sense than that.

Trapped. She was trapped.

He would know if she was lying. As in all their previous silent encounters, he always knew what she was thinking. Like the chanting snake charmer in the traveling fair. Like the gypsy who told your future. Like the vicar who promised you the fires of hell if you gave false witness.

She blurted it out, the entire truth, exultantly knowing it would shock him. "My aunt left me money she didn't want my father to know about. I was wondering how to spend the interest from ninety thousand without anyone finding out about it."

Five

"Why the hell," Daniel roared, "would you tell me—someone you hardly know—that you have access to that kind of money? Use your brain, girl. There are a dozen ways I could take it away from you."

She cringed, shrinking from his harsh words. "How could you possibly do that?"

"I could hold you prisoner and demand ransom, I could threaten to hurt someone you care about, I could woo you and gain your confidence . . ."

"Nonsense," she whispered valiantly, her wide eyes watching to see which of these actions he might attempt.

That sobered him entirely.

He could not do this.

He could not frighten her into being sensible when she had no idea of life in the real world. Not to her. This was Harmony Roan, the girl who had outsmarted Sedgewick those many years ago and saved his father's life—and his. No matter that she hadn't a drop of common sense or a speck of self-protection, he had no business treating her, or even thinking of her, in any way other than with respect.

The time had finally come for repayment of that priceless gift.

He took her elbow and guided her to one of the upended barrels that served as chairs in the hut, then seated himself beside her on a matching keg.

"Nonsense, you say?" He adopted a gentle, reasoning tone.

"What do you know about people other than in your own little world? Every day heiresses are sweet-talked out of their money. Of course," he included for her education, "marriage might be part of the bargain, but the result is the same."

She nodded, a faint line of worry between her brows. "I shall concede that point, but what has that to do with . . . Saul?"

Exasperated, he gritted his teeth, "First promise me you will never tell anyone about that money again." Lord, this girl was stubborn. Protecting her from herself could take a heavy toll on a man's time.

She considered his words for a moment. It was a charming little trick, Daniel thought, the way she chewed things over in her mind. Her head tipped to one side and her eyes crinkled almost closed. Then, when she finished, she issued a soft little sigh.

What a curious little mouse she was, so serious, so intense. In all the days he'd watched her, he'd never seen her smile.

She stiffened her back and gave him one of her *looks*. "Very well, I do promise, Mr. Rockburne. I will never discuss this with anyone." Then she rose from her perch, clearly ready for flight.

He gripped her shoulder with a heavy hand and lowered her back onto the keg. Alarmed, she looked up at him. Then, startled, he forgot what they were talking about, for there among the wreckage of her dirty face and tangled hair, was the most kissable mouth he had ever seen. Full and soft and inviting, made even more so by the pink little tongue licking a path across its upper lip. *Say something, you fool.*

"First, you must call me Daniel—"

He could feel her shocked resistance to such familiarity. "I shall do so when we are around Saul," she said, tucking her bare feet out of sight, "but when we're here alone, it seems more comfortable to use the correct address, don't you agree?" It was a tidy speech, delivered in a prim, dismissing tone. With each word, however, her hands betrayed her, twisting her lace-trimmed handkerchief into a tortured string of linen.

Seeing the disgusted look he made no attempt to hide, she

began to squirm as if seeking a comfortable perch on the rough surface. "But then, you are right," she admitted finally, looking at her bare toes. "I must practice doing so in case we meet again."

When she looked up again, he half expected to see her barriers up, valiantly ready for his next assault.

Instead, she seemed to have lost her eagerness to fight, looking at him instead with a questioning, almost whimsical expression. *Had she discerned his lustful attraction?* He was tempted—more than tempted—to discover the emotion behind that enticing look, but tonight was not the time to delve into some new facet of her complicated personality.

He had plans to make, and a brisk, seaside walk to Rockburne castle would make a fine place to begin. First, though, he had to see her safely home.

"We're both tired, Harmony. There's no need for us to leap all our hurdles tonight. Meet me on the beach tomorrow night. I'll wait for you where I found you tonight. And remember that we are supposed to be sweethearts."

"What do we have to do . . . ?"

"It's very simple," he lied, trying to imagine how a smuggler and a *lady* would conduct a seaside rendezvous. A smuggler's brand of courting—a quick tumble on a soft patch of sand—was out of the question, of course, but a lady's proper stroll along the water's edge without touching at all would never convince Saul. "We'll meet and talk and appear to be a most affectionate couple."

Then he reached for her.

Despite her most emphatic protests, he heaved her up into his arms and carried her down to the beach to search for her shoes. Oh, it was sensible to spare her tender feet the rough going, but that was no excuse for forgetting the proprieties.

She didn't know the precise rules for keeping a proper distance in a situation like this, so she tried to hold herself stiffly erect, thinking that if a twelve-inch gap served for the disgraceful waltz, then half that distance would suffice for a giant carrying a foot-tender damsel across a windy bluff. He, of course, only chuckled in that stirring, cave-echo rumble and tossed her closer, commanding her to relax.

When she finally gave in and rested against him, she had another worry on her hands.

She liked it—she liked it far too much. She liked the way he smelled, all salt air and healthy man. She liked the way he held her as if she wasn't a burden, as if he was having fun and didn't want anything from her other than a laugh and a mutual enjoyment of the dark sea breezes.

From whence had sprung this frivolous defect—this newly discovered penchant for things rough and uncouth and the sneaking suspicion that she was looking forward to being Daniel's girl, if only in pretense?

Why, even the most fragile heroine in her beloved novels hadn't turned to mush over one lusty look—and somehow she *knew* what that fierce darkening of Daniel's eyes had meant a few minutes ago—nor did the most enthralling romantic hero have the power to instantly weaken the heroine's moral fiber and make her long for earthy pleasures by simply heaving her into his arms like a sack of coal.

Almost as dismaying was the breakdown of her reasoning power.

She'd always researched a situation thoroughly, analyzed the facts before taking action. Tonight, however, she'd agreed to entangle her life with a smuggler's without considering all the ramifications. Oh, she knew enough to agree with Daniel that the farce must go on, and she had seen enough of Saul to know that the danger was real. But how unlike her to jump willy-nilly into a plan that now seemed in retrospect to be far too simple.

Even the surprise that Daniel, her nemesis, was not completely the evil ogre who had haunted her childhood gave her little comfort, for the edges of their lives that had met in the middle tonight were all that they had in common—the need to alter their daily activities to keep them both alive.

She had no hope of understanding him, a criminal who swam with sharks like Saul. Nor could he ever comprehend her, an uninteresting scholar whose life was totally immersed in the written word.

Daniel maneuvered his way down the cliff in an easy, rhythmic steadiness that amazed her. At the bottom he strode out to the water's edge and deposited her onto her feet.

Thank you," she began, frowning when, without a word, he sat down and began removing a boot. Poor man, she thought, he must have gathered a rock.

She sent a glance down the beach, impatient now to hurry home. What on earth would her father be thinking? "I'll be going now . . ." *he tossed his boot aside and began removing the other one* . . . "What are you doing?" she whispered. Was he going to disrobe? Had he discovered this weakness she had for him and was going to ravish her? A slow terror began . . .

"We've got to find your damned shoes and I'll find them quicker with bare feet. Start moving around, just skim across the sand so you don't bury them."

"Oh." She exhaled the word, trying to dispel the image so frightening in her imagination. It wouldn't vanish completely, but instead fused with her old fear of Daniel, renewing her uneasiness at being alone on the beach with him.

As she scuffed off through the sand, he called, "Over here, you're going in the wrong direction." She turned back just as he bent over with a grunt of satisfaction. "Here's one little run-away shoe, let's find the other before it gets away."

Bits of the beach rasped inside her shoes as she marched up the cliff path toward her home. She gritted her teeth and kept an even stride, for Daniel watched from midway up the track. Should she falter—or stop to empty loose debris out of her shoes, he'd be leaping up behind her and carrying her home as he had threatened. He'd laughed when she yelped at the idea and shook his head at her timidity.

She had yearned to join in that laugh; instead she doggedly trudged forward, telling herself that she belonged up in her own world, that she didn't mind that the library windows were never opened, that the sea breezes were unwelcome at night and that sunshine was a daytime enemy to the household furnishings.

That was not all she wanted, of course, a dull life at her father's elbow. No, now more than ever, she wanted an exciting life of travel like her aunt's. Perhaps, she thought as she quietly opened the kitchen door and tiptoed inside, her husband—in the far future—might like to *laugh*.

Daniel picked up a rock and threw it far out into the foaming waves. Damn, blast it all to hell! It was difficult enough to feign submission to Saul, but to give the fat walrus Harmony's safety to hold over his head—but what else could he have done tonight?

Thank goodness, though, for Harmony's clear thinking. She'd played Saul like a fiddle. And, he recalled with an involuntary grin, how she had gone on about his own *divine* kisses . . . where did she get that stuff? She was a natural comedian, did she but know it, with a sense of the absurd that made their story too outrageous to possibly be a falsehood.

Satan's teeth, what a surprise she turned out to be, that termagant of long ago who now so fascinated him with her mercurial personality.

Her looks had not changed greatly. Her tall, slim figure had rounded out nicely, what he had seen of it. The golden child had matured, and the childish fragility had deepened to more earthy tones—golden hair now streaked with an earth-toned wheat, ivory skin now flushed with rosy good health, thin wavering voice now low and husky. Even so, she was far from his ideal woman.

Not even close.

But, he thought with a stir of unease, that tug on his loins, that purely animal lust she had inspired, whence had it come? He liked his women earthy and matter-of-fact—discreet widows who welcomed a bit of fun with a man clever enough to see to their needs.

Yet, here he was, by his own vow and hers, betrothed to Harmony Roan.

He threw another rock, wishing, as it landed exactly where he wanted, that his own life would be so predictable.

"What on earth are you doing, Harmony? Loose that drapery and get back to work. It's almost time for tea and I want Pierre's work finished today."

"Very well, Father," She cast one last glance toward the cheerful clouds floating out over the ocean. "I cannot believe that with all we must accomplish in the next few weeks, you are taking time for that French parasite's book. He wants credit as the author, yet I'm to write it with no remuneration. He's discovered the craze for walking tours and wishes to profit from it. He lives in Alfriston, let him write it himself."

"He and his fellow scholars in France admire my work, Harmony, and when this war is over, I'll be an honored guest at their club. A woman cannot understand a man's pride, I know, but honors are the true payment of the literary world."

"Very well," she said, an idea forming in her mind. What if she just made up any gibberish that would send dear Pierre and his friends on a nonsensical tour? Her father never bothered to read the small commissions she executed for him. A twinge of guilt sobered her for a second, but the naughtiness of it was too delicious to resist. And sometime she would enjoy describing it to Daniel. Grinning, she dipped her pen into the ink and began to write.

Hours later, she was still smiling. Interspersed throughout her wicked piece of work had been moments when she had let herself drift off, envisioning a dozen scenarios in which she and Daniel were confounding Saul. Her sole interest lay in keeping Daniel and herself alive, and, she assured herself, if that prospect filled her with an unaccustomed euphoria, it was certainly understandable.

Daniel placed his lantern on an outcropping of rocks and walked away from its light. Looking up, he chuckled, for there upon the ridge bobbed the dark outlines of several unkempt heads. Their murmurs and sniggers wafted down the bluff, as did the clinking of bottles and flasks getting a hearty workout.

Harmony would have a fit if she knew.

He had gotten used to his men following him around ever since the villain's third attempt on him a few weeks ago. It was easier, they calculated, to snap up Rockburne's reward by waiting for the villain to come after Daniel than it was to go out hunting a villain whom no one except Saul could identify. He benefited by their surveillance, especially tonight when it would afford Harmony's safety as well.

He paced back toward the light and continued on beyond, the first step in his little drama for the benefit of Saul and his fellow voyeurs. The rogues uphill would have never *spied* like naughty boys on one of their own, for a quick joining after a drunken game of slap and tickle would have been too commonplace to bother with. This courtship, however, was akin to a royal parade—so far removed from their own lives that it demanded an audience—and no one could resist discovering what comprised a courtship between a smuggler and a lady.

The wind blew in forceful gusts, making her journey down the path an awkward business, clutching the lantern on the leeward side and her other hand shielding her watery eyes from the fierce wind. Her heart flipped about like a newly caught fish, and for the first time this day, her brain seemed to be working clearly.

That work she had done for Pierre, she must never send. First thing tomorrow morning she would correct all those ridiculous directions. But, she thought with a twinge of regret, what fun to have sent Pierre and his friends along a serpentine route to view the great marine spectacle awaiting them below, the nightly beaching of Old Saul, the great hairy whale.

What had possessed her to view this meeting with such frivolity? What on earth did sweethearts do during a clandestine meeting? What if Saul did not believe her and Daniel—and he killed them both? What if Daniel had decided to leave Shingle Spit to save his own skin?

She stopped halfway down the path, shivering despite her warm woolen cape. *She could go back.* She could confine herself to the house. The smugglers would not storm her house to kill her. Why had she not thought of that sooner?

Quickly, she turned and retraced her steps, breathless with the pace she set, frantic to cocoon herself in her own safe home. She paused at the top and caught her breath. She gazed at her lighted windows glowing through the trees. *Go home now and end this foolishness.*

She took a step in that direction, her heart pounding so loudly now that she could hardly breathe. But then she froze where she stood. Why, she asked herself, did she hesitate? No one in her right mind would embark on such a crazy life, consorting with a smuggler . . .

A smuggler who could have tossed her to the fishes last night. A smuggler who had no reason for saving her life, but still had put himself in just as much, and perhaps more, danger as she. A smuggler who now had to watch his every step and trust that she would do the same . . .

What was she doing, indeed? Her heart slowing to a comfortable, steady beat, she turned back toward the cliffside path.

He watched her approach, her slim frame wavering with each gust of brisk ocean air. He stood, waving his lantern to show her the way. The sounds emanating from above escalated briefly, then fell silent.

"Good evening, Daniel." She marched forward steadily until he could see her face.

"Come closer."

"Closer?" The word squeaked out.

"This meeting is for Saul's benefit, Harmony." He replaced his lantern to the rock beside him. "He'll need to see us embrace. If we stand here like statues, we might as well forget it."

"Embrace?"

Satan's teeth, if she was going to parrot every word he said, he'd ring her neck. "Put your lantern here on the rock beside mine."

She obeyed, then moved closer, peering around him like a timid child hiding in her mother's skirts. "Where's Saul?"

He hesitated. She wouldn't like it. He had intended to keep it from her; but, what the hell, she was already a wreck and maybe the truth would make her more cooperative. "They're up on the bluff."

"They?"

Exasperated, he pulled her hands forward and propped them up onto his shoulders. "Look at me." Her head jerked up and she looked into his eyes. "Now, there are at least half a dozen dangerous men up there . . . no, don't turn your head . . . and they are expecting something special from us. They've been waiting for some time, drinking to keep themselves warm and now they're in a festive mood. If you don't want them turning mean, you'd better make this good."

"Oh," she sighed. Taking a deep breath, she closed her eyes and puckered up her lips. He hadn't intended to really kiss her, for at that distance, the men couldn't see details, but it was either kiss her quickly or give in to the laughter rising inside him. He lowered his head and touched his lips to hers.

It was his last coherent thought.

Six

It wasn't the kiss that ensnared him—for she was an innocent and offered him a child's mouth, puckered for a quick, smacking salute. Nor was it her startled gasp that wrested the breath from his mouth, then returned her own, hot and sweet.

Even when her lips parted and he paused to discover if they trembled in dismay—and an uplifted curve gave him leave to continue—even when he answered that demure invitation with a second kiss, moving his mouth the way his worldly widows liked, still he was his own man, pulling quickly away at the first blazing jolt of lust. No, even then, he almost made it to safety.

Until a soft moan escaped her, and he made the mistake of looking into her face. *How could he have missed it?* Even with his ingrained image of her—the determined, sober-faced child baring her teeth to show her courage—even now with the wind-whipped clouds casting shadows upon imperfect features, *she was exquisite.*

More than that, she quivered with sensual promise—calling to him with innocent enticement—one his vow of protection forbade him answer.

The quicksand of lust tugged. Sensuous pleasure drew him, left him shaking with need. He had only to loosen his hold on an iron willpower that his companions found far too serious. . . . *But he would not . . .* neither, he reasoned, could he be so unchivalrous as to let her first step into womanhood be met by rejection.

He gathered her to him, careful that his arms did not crush her slender frame. Slowly, not to frighten her, he comforted her, nuzzling her neck, inhaling the clean, sweet essence of her. Gently, he let the barest touch of teeth and tongue discover the flavor of her skin, the intricate secrets of her ear, the edge of her upraised chin.

Even as he bartered with his conscience, suspecting that he wavered too close to the edge of her world, a world he had vowed never to enter—that he tempted himself with more than just her embrace—still, he could not resist its somehow-familiar welcome. Even as he hovered at the warmth of her parted lips, he promised himself only one taste. *Just one* . . .

Daniel tightened one hand at her waist and wove his fingers into her thick hair. Slowly, deliberately, his mouth took what it wanted—and imparted what she so innocently sought.

She surprised him by leaning into him, her fingers lifting from his shoulders to entangle themselves into his hair, naively pulling his head down to end the gentleness between them. Satan's teeth, but she lured him. The taste of her mouth made him drunk with pleasure, wild—

"Woo-hee! Go get her, Dan'l!" Bottles crashed and broke up on the bluff in celebration of the moment. Jolted out of his trance, Daniel quickly pulled her tight against his wool coat, covering her ears to muffle the sounds until the howling men hushed each other into silence.

This was insanity.

Appalled at his near loss of control, he held her a few inches away from him, almost unable to face her, to see the deep shock that must surely await him—and saw instead—a look of wonder. Her lips, swollen now with pleasure, gifted him for the first time in their strange association, a blazing smile. She glowed, meeting his gaze with the delight of sweet discovery. Tipping her head to one side, she issued a sigh. "So, that was a kiss . . ."

And in that moment, his world shifted. *After all these years, one smile had done it—just as all Rockburne men before him— he was well and truly snared.*

Satan's teeth, what kind of family curse was this, to link him with a woman who was totally impossible? Of all the women in Shingle Spit—in the world—she was to be *the one?*

Aye, he was to show up on her doorstep with flowers, asking permission to pay his addresses? Roan would have him hanging on the nearest tree before the sun had set.

And should he make it safely past that barrier, what was he to say to her, "Come cast your lot with the local smuggler. Give up your fancy visitors—or bring them to the castle where they may browse through the dusty books your husband hasn't read in years? And for heaven's sake, don't think of taking me to London, for I cannot abide the place?"

And when they went walking out, he could slip her a little hint for safety's sake, "Don't walk too close to me, my dear, there's a man who wants me dead, and I'm not too sure about his aim—he's tried twice since my father died and hasn't hit me yet."

Ah, but he wanted her, and the scent of prey to a Rockburne was a heady challenge.

All in good time, my lad, a Rockburne doesn't act on emotion, he plots and plans and uses the cunning that runs hot through Rockburne blood. For now, he would simply enjoy her surprising reaction to their embrace, the flush of awareness as she snatched her hands away from where they had snarled into his windblown hair, falling now to rest on his arms that still surrounded her.

He watched her head tip and her eyes crinkle as she reflected on what had just happened, clearly searching for some way to hide her loss of control, some way to obscure the truth of what had sparked between them. What stratagem had she decided to hide behind? Composing his face into bland acceptance, he waited for her words.

Finally, she sighed. "Oh, Daniel, they had it all wrong."

"Who?" he managed, hiding the smile that threatened.

"The authors of ladies' novels. They've got it all wrong."

She was going to *chatter* about this earth-shaking moment? "How exactly do they err?"

"Kissing, Daniel, *kissing.* The heroine spends all her time avoiding a gentleman's advances, simpering and hiding behind her fan. When some brave soul finally kisses her, she slaps his face, then secretly tells her friends that it was thrilling, divine."

So that's where she got that nonsense . . .

"Or," she continued, "if some wicked count steals a kiss, she shrinks away like he'd poisoned her. Oh, I can see why she mightn't want *him* to see she'd *liked* it when he's such a villain, but to not even admit it to herself . . ."

"You *like* kissing," he said to encourage that line of thinking.

"Of course! It's better than fresh strawberries or dipping one's toes in the ocean on a hot day. I think it must be better than flying if we could only figure out how to do that." She sighed. "It's too bad I must wait so long to be courted, for I would never be so foolish about kissing."

"Courted?" His eyes narrowed. "I thought we'd established that you cannot—"

"Not here in Shingle Spit, Daniel, but years and years from now—if I decide to marry. First," she said in the cajoling manner she used with her father, "I must go to London to get my father settled, and then I shall—"

"London?" he said in a strangled voice. "When are you going to London?"

"A week or two," she answered, studying the harsh lines of his face. "To get my father's work published. This is what we've worked for all these years—"

"You cannot go now, Harmony, too much is at stake."

She stilled, far too alert for his comfort. "You're not telling me everything, are you Daniel?" She snatched her lantern off the rocks. Gone was the nervous, chattering girl, and in her place was an intelligent, perceptive woman. "Would it be better if I knew all the story?"

He looked out to sea. With every step, one more silken strand of web lashed the two of them together . . . the enormous debt he owed her, the lies spun to pacify Saul, Daniel's idiotic sense of humor tempting him to kiss her tonight and then, blast it, demon lust entangling him long enough to allow a jolt of Rockburne lightning to strike.

He retrieved his lantern. "Yes, you should know the whole."

They strolled along, side by side, a golden streak of moonglow on the water keeping pace with them. "If you leave, Saul will act immediately—coming after me first, then you—and I'd rather not kill him, because Saul can identify the man who hired my father's assassins. He tried to hire Saul to do the job, but he declined the offer—and now he's helping me."

She nodded. "So Saul is a friend, then? He refused an assassin's offer out of friendship for you and your father? But, Daniel, he wouldn't kill *you* if he thinks we were lying last night. He'd just go after me."

"We're not *friends,* he only joined his gang with mine last year. But we are mates, which demands a certain loyalty. Even so, if he killed you, he knows that I'd come after him."

"Even if he found out that we were lying? Why would he think you would retaliate if we weren't really . . . lovers?"

"I swore that you were mine. If he decides that you are not, that doesn't change the fact that as of that moment, you were under my protection."

She stopped. "You're serious."

"In my world, Harmony, a man's word is law. When I claimed you—and you gave your word—you became my betrothed. Had we been in Scotland, we'd be married. It's not a whim that will blow away."

"Until . . . ?"

Satan's teeth, for a brainy woman, she needed a lot of words to understand a simple situation. "Until we marry—or Saul is dead. Even then, we have to agree between us to end it."

"And you *knew* this when you saved me last night." Her voice trembled. "Daniel . . ." Her voice broke. He could see her pulling herself back into that efficient person who took over when emotion threatened. "So Saul is the important party in this dilemma. But why does he *now* endanger himself by agreeing to help you? . . . Ah," she said, supplying her own answer, "because he's terrified of your superior strength and intelligence." Daniel doubted that, but it had a certain pleasant ring to it.

"But," she continued, "now I've shaken his trust in you, made us both seem a threat to him . . ." Absently, she paced slowly in front of him while, God help him, there he stood bemused, helplessly sinking deeper into the pit of illogical enchantment.

She stopped, turning to study his face as if the answers awaited there. "If he learns I'm going to London, he will think you have lost my . . . loyalty to you. He'll try to kill you, and you will have to kill him, and then you will lose that valuable witness.

"However, there is no way to keep him from hearing about my plans, so we must make him think I do not want to go, that I will come back to be with you as soon as I may. How can we do this?"

She paused then, allowing Daniel ample opportunity to interject a comment if he wished. But, why should he be so foolish, he mused with an inward grin, when he had her exactly where he wanted her—in charge of their safety, bless her imperious, organizing mind—leading him where he wanted to go.

"You must explain it to Saul, talk about how we hate to be parted, . . . ask his advice." She smiled at him, a bright-eyed kitten displaying her catch for his admiration.

Daniel choked. *"Ask his advice?"*

"As long as Saul doesn't lose faith in us, we should be safe."

"Excellent," he managed with a serious arrangement of features. And, as he mulled over how *entranced* Saul was over their romance, he realized that the damned idea might work. Daniel rewarded her with a friendly arm thrown over her shoulder—for Saul's benefit of course—and strolled slowly toward the path to her home.

Keeping it from Roan was another matter. Secrets couldn't be contained; the more shocking the secrets, the faster they flew. It was a race then, to find his father's murderer, to shield Harmony from Saul—and from his own base desire.

"You know," she said, as they reached the cliffside path, "I used to be frightened of you."

He smiled and waved her up the track. Then with a somber voice strengthened by resolve, he offered his fervent reply to the howling wind.

"You should have clung to that thought, my dear, for it's too late now."

Seven

"D'ye not want the carriage, Miss Roan?"

Harmony stared at the puddled drive, a challenge she would have enjoyed as a child, but which now played havoc with her plans for walking to the village. She could take the carriage, but Boris always drove her then retired to The Wreck while she did her errands. He liked to park himself at the bay window that intruded onto the pathway and watch her passage from store to store—and would be immediately alert to any contact between her and Daniel Rockburne.

No, she wouldn't be wanting the carriage.

On the other hand, if she chose to walk in the rain, by nightfall Shingle Spit would add yet one more eccentricity to her list. Not much of a choice, after all. Before she could reconsider, she quickly stepped out into the drizzle. "I believe I shall walk, Meadows."

"Lawks, Miss, not without your umbrella!" Meadows clucked her way back to the umbrella stand, then trotted back out to unfurl it over Harmony's head. "Take this, now." She slapped the handle into Harmony's hand. "Are you wearing boots?" Without waiting for an answer, she hiked up Harmony's skirt to check on the crucial matter, then stood back to check her over. She reached around Harmony's neck and flipped up the hood, took one last measuring look, then let her go, shaking her head as Harmony escaped down the steps.

"Poor motherless child." Meadows crooned under her breath, an oft-used incantation for justifying Harmony's peculiar ways.

"Poor Meadows," Harmony echoed as the door closed behind her, reflecting upon the many years she'd probably taken off the round little housekeeper's life. After the heartbreak of her mother's death when she was barely nine, Harmony decided to take on the management of Sir Roan's household. Meadows had suffered greatly over the upheaval, pestered as she was by endless questions beginning with "Why?" and the impatience of a too-clever child.

Once Harmony had made sense of household tasks, she turned her sights upon the village and the mysterious business of shopping. Doggedly—and filled with fear of strangers—she'd followed the housemaid as she traveled from shop to shop, mouthing to herself the precise words and manners she used. Not content until she'd done it on her own, she usurped the coveted task and, addicted to the heady respite from her work, managed to stretch the expedition to a full hour.

"Dawdling," her father had called it. "Pesky" said some craftsmen who found her too often at their elbow. "Impertinent" complained the grocer whose addition was slower than hers, and "Brilliant" sighed the vicar who appreciated her intelligent conversation.

For the present, she thought with a shudder, she cared not how they labeled her so long as it didn't begin with, "Here lies . . ."

She marched steadily through the coppiced woods that stood upon her father's land, then followed the bend as it neared the cliffs, soothed by the widened panorama of ocean before her. The sea churned, darkened by heavy clouds overhead.

She squinted her eyes against the rain and looked to the right. The village waited straight down the hill near the cove, its roofs reaching toward each other across the cobbled stretch of road. Dark puffs of smoke from The Wreck's chimney melted upon contact with the rain, while across the street, the bakery's smoke rose triumphantly to mingle with the impenetrable leaves of an overhanging yew.

She swung her gaze back to her left—and found sunshine highlighting Castle Rockburne as it sat atop cliffs that curved along the coastline. A hesitant rainbow hovered above the waves, wondering where, Harmony thought whimsically, to drop its pot of gold. Perhaps upon the castle, with glittering coins filling the moat as they bounced off the sun-glazed edifice.

Rockburne. She halted, the name burning hotly as memory filled her, flushing her skin, slowing her heart, making her ears ring. *Oh, Zeus, she'd been kissed by Daniel Rockburne.*

And then, stunned by the kiss, she'd babbled like an idiot, spewed out half-formed thoughts as they bounced against the walls of her mind—anything that would hide her true thoughts from Daniel—and herself. Thoughts? . . . no, that was not exactly what she'd hidden. Sensations, surges of feeling that threw her reasoning power to the winds, that even now, remembering, made her yearn . . .

For a moment, the kiss had been enough, more than enough to savor, to wonder over, to remember later. Then he'd retreated. Rightly so, the proper thing to do. It would have been enough to satisfy her for a long time—had he touched her only once.

The first kiss had pleased her, so she had smiled in the dark, a private elation. Then, before she could sort it all and give each nuance its place in her memories, his mouth returned and began again. A stranger kissed her then, a stranger whose lips were hotter, whose mouth twisted and slanted and parted hers. A stranger who *tasted* her and left his imprint etched on her lips, sending hot tendrils of feeling streaking through her.

She'd wanted to cry in protest as he pulled away, in fact wondered if some sound had escaped her aching throat. She'd opened her eyes, then Daniel's gaze held her prisoner, captured her will. It hadn't mattered, though, not while she still quivered with such ecstasy . . . then he did the unthinkable.

Gentled her. With his huge hands, he pulled her close—to comfort her, she'd thought. At last, feeling flowed back into her limbs, her hands, her eyelids. He was so strong, she'd thought, he would protect her from everything, would guide her back from the place where he'd taken her. She welcomed his warm breath against her neck, enjoyed a silky thrill as he explored her ear, shivered as he grated his teeth against the edge of her chin. Even as his warm breath bathed her lips, she felt succored, contented . . . safe.

Then, like a shifting wind, she felt a change in the energy between them, a whirlwind that caught them up together, fusing them, shaping what had been benign into a gathering force that defied rational thought. The hand at her waist tightened, powerfully, and pulled her against him. Almost anticipating his plundering kiss, her blood caught fire, welcoming back the marauding sensations that seemed to know their way deep inside her.

No longer were they joined only by lips—she could feel his hard chest, his muscled thighs as he pulled her tight against him. Heavy cloth separated them, but he was too massive to disguise the force emanating from him. His assault was endless. She'd never even imagined such waves of delicious agony, such painful pleasure. She remembered clutching his long hair with the frantic thought that if she were only *closer,* she could stop it. Nothing seemed hard enough, deep enough, painful enough. He'd groaned . . .

Then he stopped. Abruptly.

She, too, had heard the yells from the cliffs, knew why he ended the kiss and smothered the sounds from her ears. It didn't matter, for at that moment, she couldn't think past the shock of separation, the problem of knees that had no strength. Then she realized what had truly happened, *she'd been kissed by Daniel Rockburne.*

Her mind had shut down, had closed those wild feelings into a dark dungeon with no apologies for company. And then she'd regaled Daniel with a frothy, frivolous rendering of the incident. Buried the exotic truth and raised it to the level of a comedy, replaced it with a babbling clown.

Even had she later wanted to liberate the truth she'd entombed, it would have been useless. Heaven knows, all through that restless night, her dream-self had battered on that closed door of memory to no avail. *Until now* when the truth came tumbling out.

Yet, she mused as her thoughts rose to a clearer level, the opinions she'd bombarded Daniel with were truly her own. Writers of the novels she'd read had done a great disservice to kissing. In that, Daniel had done her a great *enlightening* favor, even though she realized a kiss from Daniel must be something of an aberration, wild and unruly like the man himself.

So, what was a *proper* kiss from a proper suitor? Would it leave her feet on the ground, let her mind remain intact to savor the pleasure? And, why was she wondering about such a thing when she had her future of traveling firmly planned? Such a topsy world, being Rockburne's sweetheart, it did things to her *person* that confused her *mind*.

No more kisses with Daniel Rockburne, she vowed. Nothing more than the gracious friendliness that a proper lady would extend to a gentleman who was supposedly courting her. Saul had seen their kiss and had, from all the noise, heartily approved. He certainly would not expect such goings-on in public, and that was the only place he'd find her from now on.

How strange, she thought as her feet began moving down the long hill, were the quirks of fate. After all these years since childhood, to be approaching the village without the old dread of seeing Daniel, without shivers as he watched her with those mocking eyes.

And now to think that he had *kissed her.*

Slowly, she drifted down the long hill into the village, then paused near the vicarage. Had the kiss affected Daniel as it had her? Surely not. Perhaps, if she were lucky, he'd never give the matter of kissing her another thought.

From his vantage point inside The Wreck, Daniel watched the dark shape of a woman approach the village. *Harmony.* Ah, you see? There was nothing graceful or lovely or sensuous about the woman huddled in the black cape, plodding slowly down the hill. And if seeing her sent his blood racing, why it was only the danger involved, the challenge of fooling everyone. He must have lost his mind last night, and this morning's reaction to the sight of her was a lunatic's hangover. It was a damned nuisance, something he'd get over. Probably today when he got a good look at the bedraggled mess the rain had made of her.

He followed Harmony's progress toward the village. He would let her do a little shopping, then "accidentally" run into her and they would talk for a few minutes. Saul would hear of it and be mollified.

He deliberately pulled his gaze from the window and turned to face the interior of The Wreck. Many an hour he'd spent here with his father, celebrating or just passing the time together. He liked the way it never changed, that no matter when you came there was still the same malty smell of ale, still the familiar aroma of wet wool on a rainy day.

Behind the bar, the tall Scandinavian, Matilda Johnson, grinned at him as she, too, monitored Harmony's progress. Her husband, another fair-haired norseman, Elias, concentrated on coins into the box labeled, *To Insure Promptitude,* the oversized capitals forming the phrase TIP from a distance. Three farmers, mourning—or celebrating—the rain, sat on the edge of the stage against the back wall, swinging their legs as they serenaded the room with an ancient drinking song.

> *Farewell, my mistress, I'll be gone,*
> *I have friends to wait upon; . . .*

Daniel turned back to the window and sipped his hot cider, absently listening to the voices behind him as Harmony approached the vicarage. She hesitated, then halted.

Daniel held his breath. It had been years since she'd done that, visibly shed her fear as she approached the village. Was something wrong? He waited—impatiently now—as she went directly to the bakery. Then he stood, dropped his payment upon the gleaming surface and hurried from The Wreck.

" 'Ere, now, Rockburne, watch your step!" Saul's beefy hand pulled him back as the smell of horseflesh and the clang of horseshoes upon cobbles awakened him to his surroundings. Satan's teeth, he'd almost stepped in front of the Roan carriage charging through the street.

"She's headed for the bakery, boy, but you'll have a hard time meeting with her today with Boris coming down the hill. Sure you want to sniff after such a troublesome wench?"

"What're you doing in town, Saul?"

"Wal, I could tell you it's none of your business, which, by damn it certainly is not, but the truth is that I'm guarding my interests." Saul stepped backward, dropping his hand from Daniel's shoulder with a huge grin on his ugly face. "Can't stay away, can you Dan'l?"

"I told you she's going to London before long, and she's already getting weepy over missing me." Daniel almost laughed over the expression on Saul's face. Harmony was a genius, indeed, for the sad tale he'd spun the coarse smuggler had captured Saul's interest.

"Wal, you'd best be going," Saul said, nudging Daniel's shoulder. "Right now, you've got a lady waiting for you and I'm not going to be cheated of seeing you outsmart old Boris. He watches that chit like a cat with a mouse, and you'll have to be fast to put one over on him."

"Damn it, Saul, what d'you mean, he *watches* her?"

"Ho, where the hell have you been, Rockburne? Everyone knows he does it. Question is, what does he mean to do when he finally pounces?"

Daniel felt his anger curl around him like a snaking flame. His fingers itched to strangle Saul, right after he threw Boris off a cliff and locked Harmony up in a closet for safekeeping.

Saul smiled, shooing Daniel away with his hands. "Now go. I didn't get m'britches wet in this damned rain for nothing."

The bell on the tea-shop door jingled on its suspended brace as Harmony stepped into the tea shop. She usually waited for this particular indulgence, saved it as a halfway mark, but today she needed something warm inside her.

Mrs. Pollard, a dark-haired lady whose well-lined face would warm the heart of a portrait painter, turned at her entrance, her eyes lit with pleasure. Hurrying forward, she put her arm around Harmony's waist and pulled her toward the fireplace. "Poor lamb, you're chilled to the bone." She confiscated Harmony's umbrella and handed it to her husband as he, too, lumbered forward to greet the newcomer. Harmony blinked in surprise. Such an effusive welcome!

While Mrs. Pollard's fingers were busy unfastening Harmony's cloak, her ex-pugilist husband pulled a chair back from a round, cloth-covered table. "Sit you down here where it's warm, Miss Roan," he said. "We'll have you dry before you know it." Mrs. Pollard rushed to the back room of the shop.

Obediently, she sat, her thoughts spinning. Was her appearance so bedraggled? Did they fear she'd collapse in their shop and bring Sir Roan's wrath down upon them? Mrs. Pollard returned and swathed her shoulders with a knitted shawl that enveloped her with a lovely warmth.

"Tea," said Mrs. Pollard to her tall husband, "and bring hot cross buns from the oven and a dab of butter on top." He nodded, and pausing only to lean Harmony's umbrella against the brick siding of the fireplace, he hurried to the back room to do his wife's bidding.

"Cream and sugar," Mrs. Pollard threw after him to complete the order, then returned her attention to Harmony. "Now, let's get your cape draped over this chair. We can't have you going out wet—" She stopped as the alley door screeched open and shut. "See to that, will you?" she called to her husband, settling Harmony's cape to her satisfaction before the fire. Then at the sound of heavy footsteps coming through the back, she stopped to look for herself.

"Mrs. Pollard," her husband said, "look who's here." Their glances met and, in unison they turned to beam at Harmony.

In an instant, she knew who had entered. Knew also why

they'd showered her with such fond attention. Thoughts and emotions whirled, turning her perceptions upside down. Because they believed she was Daniel's girl, *now they liked her?* A smuggler had elevated her value to these shopkeepers, turned their pleasant formality into a cozy warmth?

Oh, why did she not own more than two dresses, one grey and one brown? And why had she worn the brown that made her look like the veriest mud dab?

Without thought, without permission, her head turned toward the door. She wasn't sure, but she thought her lips were smiling. The sound of her wildly beating heart drowned out the rest.

Oh, Zeus, this was terrible—in daylight, he was even *more* . . . everything . . . than she remembered. More attractive with the green fisherman's cap matching his eyes, more compelling with the bold outline of him filling the doorway. And the tense expression on his face—concerned, protective, his eyes examining her to make sure she was all right. The thought came to her that nothing could be more stirring than a man looking at a woman with that solicitous expression.

She stood to show him she fared well as he stepped forward to close the space between them. His hand lifted toward her and, without thinking, she deposited hers in his open palm. It fit so well, snug with room to spare as his fingers closed around her hand. *Exactly, what she'd promised herself not to do.*

He recovered before she did, squeezed her hand briefly, then dropped it and turned his smile toward the tea shop's proprietors. "Pollard, Mrs. Pollard. Thank you for seeing to Miss Roan. Who," he added pointedly with a scowl, "has no business walking all this way in the rain."

He looked at her then, smiling at the glower that had sprung full-fledged upon her own features, and stirred her anger up a little hotter. "All those brains, and not a speck of common sense."

The Pollards chuckled fondly. It took her a few seconds to comprehend what he was about, then wondered if she truly understood his motive. Deciding to go along with it, she mused aloud. "I was thinking about something I read recently. It reminded me of you, and I was halfway here before I realized it was raining."

Surprise flitted across his face, accompanied by a quizzical, uneasy lift of his eyebrows. Good. She didn't like his smug belief that he could put words in her mouth or maneuver everyone in the room to his liking.

"Shakespeare," she said with a crooked smile to let the Pollards know it was all in fun:

> *"That man that hath a tongue, I say, is no man,*
> *If with his tongue he cannot win a woman."*

Mr. Pollard laughed aloud and nudged Daniel. Surprise still sat upon his face, then a new thought seemed to cross his mind. He suppressed it, and the bit of humor that evidently accompanied it, swallowing hard and biting his lower lip. "Challenging words, indeed," he mused enigmatically, and with that, he dismissed the subject and turned to Mrs. Pollard.

"I'll have coffee—and one of everything." The proprietress nodded, then disappeared through a doorway to the back. While privacy surrounded them, Daniel ushered her back to her chair, saying urgently, "Why *did* you walk in the rain?"

She sat in the chair he held for her. "If I brought the carriage, Boris would see us." Before he could do more than nod, another unpleasant thought occurred to her, "Is Boris one of your men?"

"No," he returned briefly, "but Boris just drove your carriage into town. Almost ran over me."

She stood. "Oh, no. I must go—"

"Sit down. He'll stable the cattle and then stop for a drink."

She sat on the edge of the chair. "He'll see us together."

"Harmony, calm down. I came in the back. He can't see through the curtains, and when you go out the front door, I'll go out the back."

She shuddered. "I hate him."

Daniel, having draped his coat over a fireside chair, lifted his head at her words. "You do?"

She nodded, concentrating on tugging at her gloves, but too agitated to successfully pull them off. "Why?" Daniel lowered himself into the chair beside her and took over the job. She stared at him as he dragged off her gloves, alert to the change in his tone, far too low and deadly for the innocent question.

Watching his expression closely, she formed her reply. "He's cruel—to animals and the other servants."

"Is that all?"

She sent him a sharp look. "Is he your enemy?"

"Not yet. Answer the question."

"Well, if you must know, he frightens me, reminds me of a wild animal on a leash. I always worry that the leash will break, and he'll turn that cruelty on me."

"Tell your father, Harmony."

"I have, but my father likes him, especially when he's in one of his moods." She could tell immediately that was the wrong thing to say to a man of such a protective nature. *Time to change the subject.*

"Did you talk to Saul?"

"Aye—and he practically blubbered over our sad plight."

She smiled. "Then, he's not so bad after all."

"Don't relax your guard, Harmony," Daniel said, all amusement gone from his face. "One false move, and he'll strike."

"You're right, Daniel," she said, sobered by the truth. "I keep wondering how can anyone truly believe we are sweethearts."

Daniel carefully straightened her gloves and laid them on the table beside him. "Because you are so far above me?"

"Did I make it sound like that? I didn't mean to. No," she said, tipping her head in contemplation, "because our interests are so different. What would an *adventurous* man such as yourself have in common with a cowardly scholar like me, and just as Saul said last night, a smuggler would be too smart to ally himself with Sir Roan's daughter. And if we planned to marry, then where would we live? If we married, I would want to spend time in London, to see the museums, go to plays . . . and you would need to be off on your boat. Then there would be children, and we would disagree . . ."

As she spoke, his face gradually relaxed, then began to show an almost unbelieving amusement. "Do you always do this?"

Heat flushed her face. "Analyze everything to extinction?"

He chuckled. "Let me just give you a simple answer to your question—Romeo and Juliet."

She waved a dismissing hand. "Oh, that *nonsense*. It's my very *least* favorite of his plays, for who could ever believe . . ." Then she paused. ". . . oh, but how clever of you to think of that, because others *love* the play. So . . . it's the *impossibility* that makes it so fascinating to watch, wondering what will . . ." She broke off as he grinned at her doing it all over again.

Mrs. Pollard came through the door with a tray of dishes in her hands. "Here we are now, our best." She placed a setting of delicate rosebud porcelain before Harmony while her husband followed with their pastries and pots of tea and coffee on another tray. They chattered as they arranged the table, instructing each other like two noisy children.

A smile grew on Harmony's face; she couldn't help it with the Pollards using up a year's allotment of conversation in one morning. Daniel caught her at it and sent her a quizzical glance. "What?" he asked when they were finally left alone.

"This feels so strange. They're usually so dignified with me, so reserved." When he didn't seem to understand, she explained. "I suppose it's because we're . . . that is, because they've heard about . . . us. I didn't realize you were so popular," she finished, red-faced and wishing she'd kept quiet.

He'd sprouted a grin during her awkward explanation. "That surprises you?"

"Well, considering the way you've always treated me, I assumed you were unpleasant to everyone." She poured their beverages slowly as her mind analyzed this unreconcilable comparison—and to hide a blossoming anger at his long-ago treatment of her.

Perfectly aware of her changing mood, Daniel studied her

over the rim of his cup as he sipped his coffee. When her clever mind compared his warm relationship with the Pollards to the abuse he'd meted out to her, full comprehension would finally hit her. He hadn't long to wait.

A red flush crawled up her neck and warmed her cheeks. *"Why did you do it?"*

"Do what?"

"Deliberately scare me to death!"

Daniel chuckled, noting with a sinking sense of destiny, that bedraggled or not, she still fascinated him. She was so . . . *alive . . .* so intense about whatever idea filled her thoughts at a given moment, as if seeing the world in the tiny, concentrated pictures one might see through a telescope.

As for her present curiosity, he wondered if he were wise to tell her the truth. No matter, he could never resist such a prospect. "I suppose it was an infantile game at that."

She rose to the bait. *"Game?"*

"Well, not at first. You see, I was used to your sort treating me as something quite beneath them, stepping aside when I passed. Then when you began shopping with your maid, you *didn't . . ."*

"Because I did *not* shun you, you deliberately frightened me?"

"That's not the way it happened," he said easily. "I knew you would come to it, and was ready to pay you back for your snobbery. I began by watching you, looking for my chance." He devoured a pastry in two bites, then raised his cup to his lips and emptied it. Disciplined with proper etiquette, she reached for the pot to refill his cup.

"But," he mused aloud, determined to keep her fuse glowing, "the opportunity never came until the day I discovered what a fraud you were."

"Fraud!" The pot froze in midair. Her hand was shaking. "What did I ever do to make you think that?"

"Actually," he began, holding his cup out for her attention, "it took me quite awhile to figure it out. Weeks. I sat on the burnt-out stump between the inn and the church . . ." She nodded as she poured and returned the pot to the table. ". . . listening to the soldiers gossiping when they were allowed to leave the fort. I was spying for my father," he explained. "It was a wonderful occupation for a boy. Except for the books," he added, waiting to see which clue she would chase.

"Books?" She leaned forward, curiosity foremost.

"My father made me read books from our library while I sat there."

"What do you mean *except for the books?*—was it difficult being distracted from your reading?"

"Not at all. It was bad enough that it damaged my brain," he said straight-faced, "then I had to tell my father about each book. That made no better sense, for he could barely read himself." He inhaled slowly to keep his features even, watching her face openly expressive—belief warring with suspicion.

Flushing once more, she leaned back in her chair. "You've changed the subject, Daniel. Tell me why you called me a fraud."

He grinned, enjoying her indignation, determined to keep her dangling as long as possible. "You'll have to understand how it came about," he explained. "First there you were, a wee, straw-haired mouse, accompanied by your maid." Then, when you grew tall enough to see over the counters, you came alone. I'll never forget your first independent trip to the village."

"A *mouse?*"

"D'you want to hear this or not?"

"Oh, yes, *indeed.*" She folded her arms across her charming bosom.

Distracted, he paused, then began again. "Well, in you sailed like a prim little housewife, going first to the butcher's to order the day's delivery. Then, out you came again white as bleached linen."

She'd stiffened as he spoke, and her eyes cloudy with recollection. "Go on."

"I knew immediately what had happened—you'd rattled off some amazing bit of calculation and someone had shown their pity for your strangeness, hurting your pride with a look or word you were too smart not to understand. You didn't see me then. You stood there with your chin wobbling, glancing back and forth while you wiped away your tears, fearful that someone might see you with your feelings showing."

"Then I saw you."

"Yes," he smiled in reminiscence, "and Lord, did the emotions fly." His smile widened. "Your nanny must have scared you with tales of evil smugglers, for you practically fainted on the spot."

"She did indeed," she murmured, arranging the crumbs on her plate into a tight little square. "She said you were a cruel smuggler and . . ."

". . . and there I was so close to you—big and mean and ugly."

"You practically growled at me. I was terrified."

"I was trying not to laugh."

"What?" She stood abruptly, the dishes rattling as she jarred the table.

Daniel looked up at her with an innocent shrug. "I scowled to keep from laughing. Then when I saw you lift that little chin and scowl back, I realized I'd done you a good turn, for off you went marching to the next shop, bravely nodding to everyone you met."

She leaned forward. "You were *laughing* at me?"

"Well, by then I knew what a fraud you were with all that show of confidence, that stately calm you showed to the pitying inhabitants of Shingle Spit. So," he explained, "every time we met I gave you a fresh shot of courage just to keep you going."

"You gave *me* courage?" She braced her hands on the table and lowered her gaze level with his. "As a *favor?"*

She was furious, that much was obvious, but surely in a moment she would see the humor of—

"Hssst!" Mrs. Pollard whispered loudly from the doorway. "Boris is on his way, looking in the shops for Miss Roan."

Eight

Daniel jumped to his feet, while the Pollards rushed forward. "Sit you down, Miss Roan," Mrs. Pollard said in a managing voice. "Dan'l," she barked softly, "get you to the kitchen now, and take your coat with you."

Harmony's gaze flew to Daniel. In one chilling instant, a fierce warrior stood before her, barely holding himself in check, clearly hating the fact that he must retreat, no matter how sensible it might be.

"I'll take your tea things." Mr. Pollard whisked Daniel's dishes onto the round tray he held in one hand. "Go to the kitchen, m'boy, and pour yourself some coffee from the pot. You can hear everything from there and step in should you feel the need."

Whatever demons he'd been battling now well in hand, Daniel turned at the sweet lady's prodding words. "Thanks, love," he said, bussing her cheek with a kiss, then turned to go.

"Dan'l!" Mrs. Pollard stopped him short. When he gave her a questioning look, she tipped her head toward Harmony.

"Ah," he said with a mischievous grin. He returned to the table in two great strides and scooped Harmony up into his arms. Without giving her a chance to comply, he swooped, claiming a kiss that warmed her to the tips of her toes. Zeus, she thought as the kiss hit bottom, each kiss seemed to begin where the last one left off. Before she could recover, he set her onto the floor, kissed the tip of her nose with a triumphant air and strode swiftly across the floor to the kitchen door.

"Well!" she whispered, partly indignant, mostly bemused as she dropped into her chair.

With a cautious glance toward the back of the shop, Mrs. Pollard leaned toward her. "They're a lusty lot, these Rockburnes, for all their sins," Mrs. Pollard murmured softly. She arranged the remaining tea things in a grouping near Harmony's cup and saucer. "Good providers, though, and faithful when they pick a mate. You're a lucky girl. Except for Neville, who was a changeling, they choose once and that's forever."

"Oh, but . . ." Harmony just stopped herself from setting the situation straight.

Mrs. Pollard stopped and gave her a hard stare. "Yes?"

"I'm sure he's had girls before me."

"Bedmates, yes, for as I've told you, their blood runs hot. But not a sweetheart he's betrothed to." A frown creased her forehead. "You're not toying with him, are you?"

"I never would," Harmony said truthfully, feeling her way along. "But I've never, uh . . . been courted before, so I cannot gauge either of our feelings with any accuracy."

"Ah, poor motherless lamb," Mrs. Pollard said softly, echoing Meadow's earlier words, "of course, you can't." She paused, then sat gingerly upon the edge of the chair Daniel had left ajar. "D'you want some advice?"

"I could use a great deal of advice, Mrs. Pollard."

"Well then," she said, "I'll share my own mother's own wisdom, given when Mr. Pollard came walking out with me. She said, 'This life's a hard one, full of dangers for a female and her young. Choose a mate who'll guard you,' she said, 'one who'll stand betwixt you and danger—be it sharp swords or hard words or killing poverty—for such a man will always rouse your senses and warm your heart.' "

"And a woman's *thoughts?* " Harmony felt close to tears for some reason she couldn't fathom.

Mrs. Pollard studied Harmony's face for a brief space of time.

"If you don't put too high price on your thoughts—that is, if you'll put them on the table where Daniel can see them in the light—I believe you'll be surprised to discover that he can match them and offer you greater coin in return." When, bemused with translating the image, Harmony didn't immediately answer, Mrs. Pollard posed a question. "Has he told you of his travels, first with his parents, then after his mother died, alone with his father?"

"No, he hasn't."

"Well then, think on this, Miss Roan. All these years in Shingle Spit while you've been reading about life in books, he's been all over the world, learning about life as it really is, seeing polished and rough. Wouldn't sharing those tales keep you both in conversation when you need it? Then will come the babies, if God grants them to you, to bind you tight. If not, like my man and me, there's others who'll need your love—like our Dan'l. It's the *giving* love that warms you, not the getting."

She stood, giving the table a quick swipe with the edge of her apron. "It's a great blessing to spend your life with a mate who values you above all else, Miss Roan. I'd like to think that Dan'l won't miss out."

"I promise you that I will never hurt him, Mrs. Pollard. I want him to be happy as well."

She pushed Daniel's chair forward and plucked the teapot from the table. "Well, then," the older woman said in a louder, but still gentle voice, "I'll just freshen this brew."

Still shaken from the impassioned conversation, Harmony sipped the last few drops from her cup, her gaze drifting aimlessly across the expanse of lace-covered windows that fronted the shop. She felt like a new chick, hatching out of her sterile egg—seeing a larger world, watching people move and think and feel—not inert shadows, but more complicated, dimensional. This entire morning had been overwhelming, full of twists and turns, new ideas, new conceptions of life itself.

She had always seen the Pollards as frightening adult figures, foreign to her own experience. She had mentally criticized her father for calling them *ignorant villagers,* but in truth, her own sorting process had followed much the same line, dividing *them* from *us.*

Yet, Mrs. Pollard—and her husband as well—loved Daniel, thought of him as their own. Childless, they had extended their love toward a motherless boy, a resilient link that did not falter as he grew from child to man, as he became someone who defied the law, who dealt revenge to his father's killers, who still relentlessly sought the evil force behind that cruel act— who would certainly exact a final retribution. Nothing would ever sever that link between the Pollards and Daniel. *What, she wondered with a sudden chill, could ever sever the tie between parent and child?*

"There you are." Boris's harsh voice shattered her thoughts as the door rattled open. "I told Sir Roan about your walking in the rain, and he's sent me for you."

Harmony's gaze slipped to the doorway, inwardly shuddering at the sight of Boris's triumphant expression. How did one keep such a dangerous animal on his leash? *Not, she knew, by cringing.*

She lifted her chin. "I shall return when my errands are completed, Boris. If I wish to ride back home at that time, I shall let you know."

He strode across the floor and grabbed her arm. "Your father said to come *now.*"

"Take your hands off me," she said in a low voice, afraid what violence might occur should Daniel catch Boris hurting her. Panicked, she scrambled out of her chair, tipping her tea onto the table—all the time tearing at his loathsome fingers. Oh, what more would he do—

"D'ye think you're too good to obey the likes of me? Well, yer father thinks different, and from now on . . ."

One moment she was helplessly caught—in the next she was free.

Daniel plucked Boris's fingers from her arm and his massive arm wove tightly around Boris's neck. "Bid Miss Roan good-bye, Boris." Wild-eyed, Boris kicked and struggled, barely able to breathe, much less speak. As Boris's futile efforts slowed, Daniel looked into Harmony's eyes. "Are you all right?"

She nodded, not sure which frightened her most—Boris's attack or the thought of what would happen next. She remembered the fate of Daniel's father's killers. "Wha . . . what will you do with him?"

Daniel's face gentled. "Find him new employment."

She gave him a stern look. *"Tell me, Daniel."*

"Tonight," he said with a dark expression that made her shiver, "this brave coachman who likes to attack helpless young ladies will be found drunk in a seaside inn where the press gangs collect their quota. And, then," he said giving Boris's neck a sharp jerk, "he'll be lucky to survive in a ship full of bullies." With an ease she could not quite believe, he marched Boris out the back door.

This was the man who had kissed her only moments before?

Mr. Pollard came into the room. "Here you are, Miss Roan," he said cheerfully, as if his shop had just hosted a fine bout of fisticuffs, "Another nice pot of tea while your cape dries." Clearly brightened over the encounter, he wiped up the mess as if nothing had happened.

Harmony exhaled slowly as Pollard poured the tea. "Thank you." *Daniel had seen her in trouble—and simply made it go away?*

"You're of an age," Mr. Pollard said heartily, turning her cape to dry. "You could be married up north and safe from the likes of Boris."

"It sounds wonderful," Harmony returned, trembling as the alluring image took shape . . . *safe with Daniel,* his hand reaching for her, pulling her to him, his protective warmth surrounding her as they traveled northward. Daniel's promise to care for her always, her promise to cherish him. Daniel's intensity committed to . . . to a love so strong that no barrier could penetrate, no enticement could influence his immovable steadfastness.

They choose once, and that's forever.

A great, inexplicable longing filled her. *Foolish girl, don't go where you cannot stay.* She stirred in her chair, tried to evade her thoughts, but the image unfurled in the warmth of her imagination, held her rooted. *Just a glimpse . . .* a lifetime of Daniel's melodious words sending shivers through her. Nights in his arms, days with him laughing at her side. Seeing life through his eyes—imagine a young man deliberately scowling to give a frightened child courage, amused, yet caring for her pride and dignity—what new insight might she gain with such a mate? After seeing life from *within,* how enchanting might she find it, seen from *without?* She ached as if fevered . . .

"Are you too shy to ask him, though?" Pollard's voice scattered her thoughts. Flushing violently at how oblivious she had been, she shook her head and focused on his question.

"I cannot pursue my own life until I have my father situated in London."

Mr. Pollard stilled and his hands gripped the chair back. "London?"

Quickly, she explained. "My father's works are to be published in London this season, Mr. Pollard, and since I am his clerk, he expects me to assist him."

Pollard relaxed somewhat, but wasn't as easily soothed as his wife. "And how long before you'll be leaving for London, Miss Roan?"

"A week, perhaps two."

"And then you'll be back here with our Daniel?" An impertinent question, Harmony knew, but she understood the concern behind the words.

"As soon as I can. When summer begins, society goes home to the country." When that didn't please him, she jarred him with a jolt of the truth. "This is my father's lifelong dream. Daniel understands that my wishes will necessarily come behind my father's. It wouldn't do to disturb his peace of mind just now."

That convinced him. "Will Dan'l will be going to London, then—to visit his grandmother, as it were?"

She hesitated. Daniel would never go to London. Everyone knew he hated society, even the infinitesimal drop of gentry here in Shingle Spit drew his scorn. "I believe he's dedicated to pursuing his father's killer just now, Mr. Pollard. It won't be long, though, before I'll be home and free to see Daniel again."

"Well then." Mr. Pollard beamed at the tidy solution. "All's well."

All's well? She was only now realizing how her ill-advised jaunt on the beach was to ripple through her life. She wouldn't be making travel plans this season. Instead, she would be coming back to Shingle Spit to steady Saul's suspicions. She might have been amused at Saul and the smugglers watching her and Daniel from their balcony seats on the bluff—but she'd also seen the very real apprehension on Daniel's face in the hut that first night and this morning as well.

Saul *was* dangerous, and Daniel needed his help—and hers. Instead of the life she had envisioned, she had a long, danger-strewn road to be traveled.

"All's well," she echoed to Pollard, for on another level it was, indeed. The threat of Boris was gone, a boon well worth suffering her father's certain wrath over. True also, that this morning's interlude had overturned half the conceptions of life, but she had received back a bounty of understanding.

What jarred was deceiving good people—and slipping into a life that wasn't real. And having to give it up at play's end.

Yet, what was the alternative? Even should she capture Daniel's true regard, did she want to live forever in Shingle Spit, an item of contention between father and husband? Did she want to give up a life of travel and discovery and writing to be the spouse of a smuggler? Did she want her children to be raised in such a harsh environment?

Zeus, Harmony thought, surging to her feet, *all this emotion over a few simple kisses?* She was a foolish girl in a tizzy over her first bit of romance—false or no—and more affected than she should be because it was Daniel Rockburne, who did everything more powerfully than most men. What she should put into the pot of facts was, that for Daniel, it was a few kisses in many, and he certainly wouldn't be spinning daydreams over her.

Mrs. Pollard stuck her head into the tea room. "Dan'l said to tell you he'll see you here tomorrow."

Sir Roan sat at his long paper-covered table, fingers covered with ink, his spectacles firmly entrenched in permanent grooves alongside his narrow nose. Without looking up, he struck. "I sent Boris for you an hour ago, Harmony, what have you been doing?"

Watching Daniel drag Boris off to a press gang. "I . . . I always do the marketing in the mornings, Father."

"I want you to send the servants from now on."

"Father," she said quietly, slipping into a conciliatory manner, "I cannot work without sunshine and fresh air."

"I say let's have done with your constant defying of my word. From now on, you are to let Meadows do what I pay her for, and you are to remain in the house where you belong."

Was he serious? "And I say that I cannot be confined in that manner."

"I should never have let you go to Bath with your damned aunt." He leaned over his papers and the interview was over.

The next morning the house hummed with the news that Boris had disappeared. Her father had gone to bed with a temper headache and every time someone else raised the subject, Harmony's insides twinged. When she entered the kitchen, she was surprised to see the coach leaving the stable yard. She leaned out the open Dutch door. "Where is the coach going, Cook?"

"To the inn, Miss Roan, to fetch a messenger from London."

How very strange. "Who's driving?"

"A new man, Caulder by name—turned up at the stables when Sir Roan was tearing the place apart and your father hired him on the spot." At Cook's strange tone, Harmony turned to stare at her. With a knowing grin, Cook relayed the news. "Seems one of Rockburne's men has turned coachman."

"Rockburne's man?"

Cook gave her an arch look. "Seems your sweetheart wants you looked after."

"Zeus, you know about that?"

"Did you think you could keep it secret?" She patted Harmony's shoulder. "Rockburne's a kind, gentle man. You couldn't do better."

You should have seen him yesterday.

Uneasy, she wandered back through the kitchen. Who was the messenger? Someone regarding their removal to town? Her father had long since sent instructions to Roger Stanford, their man of business, requesting he rent a house. What more was necessary?

In previous seasons, her father had accepted invitations from friends who were only too happy to have the honor of housing the great man. This year was different, however, for Harmony was to be included. She would finally see for herself all the wonderful sights of London.

For now, she thought with uplifted spirits, she would just trot off to the village—blessedly sans the threat of Boris—and enjoy herself.

Harmony found Meadows in the foyer. "As soon as I see what the messenger is about, I'll be going into the village. Do you have my list?"

"What on earth . . . ?" Meadows turned, her face crimson. "Sir Roan said you wouldn't be going," she whispered. "I sent Becky with our order. She left not thirty minutes ago."

Stunned, she could only stare at Meadows. "What . . . what did he tell you?" Surely Meadows had misunderstood.

Meadows twisted her apron with tense fingers. "He caught us at our dinner. He said that you wouldn't be going to the shops any longer, that you were to remain in the house."

In front of all the servants? "Was he in one of his rages?"

"No, Miss. Cool as the first snowfall."

Harmony reeled as a wave of humiliation filled her, tore at her composure. She wanted only to escape, to spare Meadows, whose eyes were even now filling with tears.

"Why don't you leave, Miss, now that you have Daniel? He'd take you north, should you ask . . ."

"Meadows," Harmony said fiercely to banish the lure of her words, "you know I cannot. Do not worry over Father. He's overwrought—he's worried that we will not finish our work on time. I'm all right," she lied, knowing she must escape lest she break down here where all the servants could see her.

She stepped away and collected her pelisse from the rack. "In the meantime," she said with a mischievous grin that brought an answering sigh of relief from the housekeeper, "I'm staging a small rebellion and taking a brisk walk."

Forcing her legs to move, she made it to a rock near water's edge before her own tears fell. Furious, she snatched her handkerchief from her pocket and mopped up the betraying evidence of weakness. In truth, she wanted to howl her eyes out, then storm into her father's room and scream her outrage.

But she would not, for she had been at this point more than once in her life. The trick was to minimize any interchange with others, for those embarrassing moments tended to torment her at night, replaying themselves endlessly as she cringed in the dark.

She knew the drill, knew the pitfalls, knew how to recover with the fewest wounds. Admit nothing. Share nothing. Handle it alone. Find a solitary place to recover. Formulate a solution to give her purpose.

She followed the step path to the beach, determined to find some peace along its windy shores.

Daniel sat nursing his ale, his attention upon the window facing the road from Sir Roan's. The figure sauntering down the hill was not Harmony, blast her cowardly soul. This was no time for her to become missish, sending Becky in her place for the first time in years. That alone would set Saul's imagination afire, and at the worst possible time.

Daniel waited until Becky approached the inn, then threw his coins down near his glass. Ignoring Elias's questioning smirk, he left the inn. He managed to cross Becky's path out on the pathway, rather than trapping himself in one of the shops. She simpered, squirming like an overjoyed bitch long before she was close enough to speak with him—another annoying matter for which he would hold Harmony accountable.

"Well met, Daniel Rockburne." She gave him a suggestive wiggle of her hips. "What brings you to town this morning?"

He ignored her question. "I should ask what brings you here, Becky. I don't usually see you here this time of day."

"I'm marketing." She rattled the leather purse in her hand. "Want to walk along with me?"

He groaned inwardly, knowing that he had no choice if he wanted to gain the information he needed. "I'm on my way to collect Newgate. I'll go that far with you." He shortened his steps to hers.

She pouted. "No further?"

"Quit flirting, Becky. You're too young for me."

The pout disappeared, replaced with a mulish scowl. "Am not."

"And too pretty to frown," he added to soften her up.

"D'you really think so?"

"Reminds me of a female kitten at the castle, had all the tomcats tied up in knots. Is that why you're really here, to drive the lads wild?"

"No, Old Roan's decided Miss Harmony's not working hard enough—she's supposed to stay home and keep her nose out of household matters from now on." She stepped over a sleeping dog sprawled on the pathway. "Makes sense," she said with a toss of her head, "she's not the homey type, if you know what I mean. Too plain for dressing up and too serious for marrying."

You should have seen her after a kiss. "I'm just here, Becky," he said, motioning toward the livery stable. "Good day to you."

He left quickly, striding angrily across the street. Juno bounced to his feet, his tale wagging violently until Daniel snapped his fingers to release him.

"Satan's teeth," Daniel cursed, what was he to do now, with Harmony locked away beyond his reach? Moments later, he was atop Newgate—Juno loping alongside—venting his frustration with a furious gallop toward the cliffs.

Juno ran along the cliffs to torment the creatures lesser than his magnificent self. A flock of fulmars, protesting the interruption to their clifftop breeding, rose squawking into the air. Startled, a pair of pipits floated out on a downy pillow of air, cheerfully singing all the way down.

Daniel looked down toward the beach and spotted Harmony sitting on a rock overlooking the ocean. Rather than call Juno back where he would only frighten Harmony, Daniel decided to let him have his fun. He rode Newgate carefully down the track.

"I thought you were locked in the tower," he called as they reached the bottom. "Yet here you are, trespassing once more."

She rubbed her sleeve across her eyes, then turned around to face him. Her eyes were red and swollen and her voice rough with hastily stemmed tears. "How did you hear? . . . Becky?"

"Aye." The sight of those tears made him wild with fury. With greater difficulty than usual, he clamped down on the useless emotion, assuming an outward calm while around him life went on, oblivious to his rage. Roan did not deserve such a bright, lively creature in his life. He dismounted, leaving the well-trained Newgate behind him. "What happened? Did Roan hear about us?"

She shook her head. Blast, she wasn't going to tell him. Wouldn't the little fool ever tell him when she was in trouble, ever ask for help?

"I'm fine, Daniel," she said—then laughed shakily as Juno flew past Daniel and leapt up on the rock beside her. Heart battering against his chest, Daniel rushed forward. "Juno, get down!" Damn it, if he hurt her . . .

Harmony laughed aloud. "Oh, you love!" She threw her arms around Juno's neck, promptly tumbling off the rock with her arms still clutching the enormous dog. Daniel dove into the fray, raising Harmony her to her feet. "Don't you have any sense at all?" he bellowed, "This dog could kill you!"

Still grinning, she extended her hand down to the mastiff. "We're friends, Daniel . . . see?" She wiggled her fingers and Juno looked up at Daniel, adding his whimper to the explanation.

Ignoring the dog, Daniel let her words sink in while his heart slowed to a steady, thudding cadence. "Friends . . ." he managed. "You know this dog? . . . Where?"

"On the beach, when I walk at night. Haven't you missed him?"

"When did you—"

"Since he was a pup, I suppose, although this dog must have been born full-size, for he's never been small—"

"You've been *playing* with him since he was a pup?"

"Yes," she crooned, kneeling to scratch Juno's neck and nuzzle her face against his.

Daniel ran his fingers through his own tangled mane. "No wonder he's been such a misery to train, with you spoiling him every night."

She tossed him a gleeful smile. "He's *trained?*" She cocked her head and studied Juno with an air of disbelief. "Trained for what?"

How delightful, Harmony thought, to see the great man flummoxed for once. How delicious to balance yesterday's rather frightening Rockburne with this *speechless* version. She liked *discovering* him, seeing new facets of this rough diamond that was Daniel Rockburne. Watching him, she waited with sparkles of excitement dancing in her throat, knowing that Daniel would retaliate for her slur on his attempts to gain Juno's obedience. But how?

"Well, then," he said, extending his hand to her. "Since you are such a daring adventuress . . ." Curious, she looked suspiciously at that innocently outstretched hand. What scheme was he hatching now?

She plucked out the operative word. *"Adventuress?"*

"I'm offering you a ride home on Newgate."

Her gaze slid to the enormous stallion, his wild eyes and evil look, and her amusement died an instant death. "Absolutely not," she said, backing away.

"Give me your hand. I'll let you pet him."

"He'll bite."

Daniel frowned. "He won't bite you . . . kill you perhaps, but he wouldn't bother with a few fingers."

Harmony gasped, never moving her frightened gaze from the satanic beast. Then Daniel made the mistake of laughing.

She took her time responding, and in that time Daniel watched her very politely crawl back into her old familiar shell. "I came out here, worried about telling you that I'm housebound," she said, lowering her voice to hide her seething emotions. "Now that you know, I'll go." With that, she turned and marched away.

Blast, Daniel thought, he'd done it again, let his crude sense of humor offend her, when he needed to do just the opposite. He considered letting her go, giving her time to cool off after his witless trick. But then, how was he to see her again?

"Damn!" He vaulted onto Newgate's back and started after her. "Come on, Juno. We're in big trouble."

Newgate's hooves beat a staccato rhythm on the hard-packed trail, signaling his whereabouts to Harmony who stiffened and increased her speed.

"Damn fool girl."

Nine

One moment she was safely on the beach, the next flying through the air as Daniel swooped and tossed her up before him. Harmony's heart thundered in rhythm to the devil-stallion's hoofs, preventing all sensible activities—such as remembering how outraged she was and properly demanding her release.

Or how *personal* two on a horse would be.

Why had her cherished novels never imparted facts—rather overwhelming facts at that—such as the feel of a warm male hand against one's middle, the heat of his chest against one's back, or the unique scent of such a closely held man clad only in coarse homespun?

She gasped as Daniel nudged Newgate to a gallop. Zeus, she thought with a touch of panic, neither had they addressed a heroine's fear of unexpected velocity, or the wicked elation of such accelerated wind flowing against one's face.

"Relax," Daniel said into her ear—lips touching skin and his toe-curling voice making her want to close her eyes and lean against him, if only to hear a melodious word of approval when she did. Fighting the temptation, she tensed and sat up straighter.

"If you don't lean back," Daniel murmured, "you'll break Newgate's stride. You wouldn't want to cause a spill, would you?"

Heart lurching, she fell back against him, horrified that the stallion was so very delicately tuned, that her silly resistance might effect their outward propulsion as Newgate hurtled down the beach on the tide-packed sand. Why, the magnification of such numbers, she calculated swiftly, would put their very lives in danger.

"Good girl," he crooned in her ear. His voice, like a tuning fork, vibrated its lyrical tones through flesh and bone, stirring her blood as Newgate's hoofs sent them flying at breakneck speed. Even Daniel's lighthearted chuckle sent her thoughts flying.

Oh, this man was dangerous.

Daniel stretched his fingers across Harmony's belly, lost in sensation that conjured up the kiss they'd shared. Soft femininity beneath her dress . . . how surprising that such a bluestocking would wear no stays. In truth, how delightfully surprising he found the entire unveiling of Harmony Roan.

How very surprised he was to find himself in love—and fiercely protective of her smallest comfort. How greatly satisfying had it been to pluck Boris out of her life, to know that even with Harmony's vast learning, she still had need of his aid.

Sleep had eluded him last night, as it always did when obstacles stood between him and what he wanted.

Champions vying for Harmony rose up, weapons in hand. Clever, sophisticated opponents dressed in courtly garb—their weapons, *books* filled with reason and logic—shaking their elegant heads while they eyed his blades and pistols with disdain.

Beside them—claiming loyalty to Daniel—stood fierce warriors, their weapons the call of adventure, *freedom*.

Why not simply slay them all with a mighty stroke, he thought, for headless foes no longer mocked and jeered. But reason prevailed.

Those damned *books* would only multiply endlessly, spouting wisdom from men whom even Daniel revered, and he could waste a lifetime *arguing*. As for his own less-learned warriors, those clever fellows blew the scent of the sea his way, called to his mind spectacular voyages and mighty struggles, reminding him in hearty voices that *marriage was the enemy to liberty*.

Although Daniel preferred the swift arm of might, he had often stooped to outsmarting his enemies. So, he had circled, surveying for weakness, probing for the soft spot, contemplating which of their own weapons might be used against them. And then, knowing that his own shrewd mind would solve the problem, he retired and slept like a conqueror who had already feasted in his enemies' banquet hall.

He had not been disappointed—awakening this morning to find a plan slowly forming—a diabolical wedge to shelter Harmony from Roan, a plan using *books,* Roan's own weakness, and another source of power that surprised even him. In the meantime—he would simply seduce her.

"Mute, are you now?" Harmony taunted, coming far too close to the truth. The sound of her teasing broke the spell and gave him back his power of speech.

"I've behaved like an idiot, Harmony. If I promise never to torment you again, will you forgive me?" When she remained silent, he wiped the slate clean. *"Twice* guilty, twice an idiot."

Harmony ducked her head and smiled. Imagine—the great Daniel Rockburne actually groveling for his sins. A moment to relish . . .

She looked about her, marveling at how adventures with Daniel made her feel so *alive,* every sense awakened, sharpened, savored. Even this frightening ride along the beach she found exhilarating. Herring gulls scattered at their approach, squawking their displeasure as they screamed and swooped over the water.

Daniel wasn't about to let her drift away now. He tightened his fingers against her. "I'm not a gentleman, Harmony, but I've apologized, and if I remember the rules right, a lady is obliged to answer."

Harmony sighed. "You're right, of course." She rested her fingers lightly on the hand holding her against him. "I haven't much of a temper, but you . . . you've always seemed so dangerous that I don't expect you to . . ."

"Tease?" He chuckled. "All boys like teasing little girls."

"You call that teasing?" she asked, clearly dismayed. "You deliberately frightened me, Daniel. Why?"

"Why?" He stopped short at the question. Why, indeed did he delight in stirring her up? "Not to hurt you, Harmony," he explained tentatively, not quite sure how he could soften what must have seemed cruel to her. "Rather, it's an age-old custom between male and female. Remember when you were young and boys threw worms down the back of your dress, and netted eels to chase you with?"

"Heavens, no," she protested, shuddering. "Never tell me they do such a thing!"

"Of course, didn't you . . . ?" He paused as the truth hit him. "You did not play with other children, did you?"

She stiffened against his implied criticism "There's nothing wrong with that. I believe many youngsters have no playmates in the nursery."

"You never played?"

"At age two, my governess began tutoring me—with an old leather-bound horn-book, the Criss Cross Row. It's not unusual," she insisted, "for ambitious parents to see children reading and writing at an early age. I was somewhat precocious, I suppose, for by age four I knew my letters and entertained myself with learning languages."

"Good God! I suppose your father was delighted."

"My father?" she said absently, missing the derision in his comment. "Oh, he listened to my reports during our evening interview, but he was far too busy for more than that token attention. He was either traveling to consult with his literary associates or entertaining them at home." A faint smile touched her lips. "But, after he discovered my language abilities, he decided to tutor me himself."

"Discovered?" He was intrigued. "That must have been an entertaining moment."

"Well," she said, her eyes alive with a mischievous gleam, "when I was five, a Russian peddler came by the kitchen door, pulling his little cart of treasures. I was there eating my porridge—that's where I ate when Father was away, and he was spending that summer in Edinburgh—and this poor peddler could barely make himself understood, so I tried speaking with him in French. He knew more French than English, but still it was not *his* own tongue. When I found out where he was from, I was so elated that I dragged him into the house and began pestering him for more information."

"And in one hour I suppose you knew everything he knew."

"Oh heavens, Daniel, of course not. It took me months. I wanted to impress my father when he returned home and was so determined that I bullied Meadows into housing the peddler for the summer while I studied Russian."

"And when your father returned . . . ?"

"Oh, it was wonderful." She fairly purred the words. How starved, Daniel thought, she must have been for her father's attention.

"He came home in October, bringing along his cronies . . ." She sighed happily, reliving the splendid moment. "Father always showed off my reading progress to his friends when they came. That evening, he handed me one of their papers—a complicated piece that used a lot of unusual words—and told me to read it aloud. I was so eager to impress, I glanced over it quickly, and translated it into Russian instead."

"And he was overjoyed?"

"Heavens, no. He was furious because he thought I playing a trick, shaming him by jabbering nonsense. "Do it properly," he yelled.

"That made me angry," she explained with a frown, "for I had worked so hard to please him. So, announcing beforehand what I intended, I refused to look at the paper and repeated it back to him in French, then Portuguese and Spanish—then Russian once more."

"And . . ."

"I silenced the room. It was a wonderful moment. His friends spoke first, telling him how fortunate he was, how brilliant he was to have sired such a prodigy. When they pointed out how helpful I could be to his work—"

"What, exactly, does Roan do that he considers work?"

Harmony lifted her chin with a censuring rebuke. "Don't be snide, Daniel. His work is very highly respected. He studies and translates the old philosophers, religions and traditions, after which he writes papers that make them understandable to our society."

"An abridged version for lazy minds," he murmured, "then they are all experts. No wonder they like him so."

She scowled at his irreverence. "Lately, though, we have been translating works of the *ton* into various languages and having them published in those countries. Evidently," she said with a tiny shrug, "it's something of a coup to see one's work in foreign publications, for he's become quite in demand."

"And how much of that work do you do?" he asked tightly, suspecting the truth of the matter.

The light left her face. "Don't make him into a monster, Daniel. I am fortunate to have an outlet for my gift. Why else was I given such ability unless it is to help him?"

"Surely you do not believe that."

She paused, then, after making several false starts which seemed to discomfort her, settled on a soft reproof. "I know the villagers dislike my father, and I can understand why they do. Then, too, you must harbor a more personal antagonism for him because he told Sedgewick to hang you and your father. But he wasn't himself then."

Very carefully, Daniel composed a reply. "Are you saying that had he been calm, he would have let us go, or given us a fair trial? Without your interference?"

She shook her head. "You're right, I should not be making excuses for him." When he remained silent, she sighed. "I'm doing this badly. What I want to say is that if we are to discuss my father, you must realize that whereas I do see the bad in him, I also see the good. I cannot help loving him and I'm happy to help him."

Daniel bit back his answer. He'd despised Roan all his life as did everyone in Shingle Spit. He'd often wondered how such a charming creature as Harmony had sprung from the loins of such a man, but had not dwelled on the relationship between father and daughter.

So, as a barrier to winning Harmony, Roan was a far more formidable obstacle than he had supposed—an enemy to whom logic and reason meant nothing, whose singular purpose was to devour what was useful to him and to slay everything else that moved in his territory—a cunning enemy, for he had won the loyalty of the woman Daniel wanted.

Had Roan been an animal, he would have simply baited him with poisoned meat . . . but Harmony loved him. So how did he disarm such a vile creature when his objective was so intricately intertwined with Harmony's? How did he don a dragon-slayer's mantle and fight for her love? If only her dragons were fanged, fire-breathing monsters, he would charge without questioning.

How did one battle the reflection his love saw in the faulty mirror fashioned by her father? Could he, *should he,* reveal the dragon who had kept her immured in his cave—her hero-father— for what he really was, alter his maiden's willingness to forgive her father's blatant cruelty without destroying that which was an integral part of her innocence?

Lest his opinions tumble unbidden into the conversation, he dismounted and reached for her. "Shall we walk the rest of the way?"

"Daniel," she said, falling into his arms, "don't be angry over my father's influence in my life. You're no different than me, you know."

"No different?" He fought to tamp down the fury that arose at her ridiculous words. "How can you say—"

"You weren't *born* a smuggler."

"I *like*— "

She stepped back. "Exactly." They stared at each other across small space, each loath to disturb the fragile peace hovering in the air between them. Her soft smile inviting him to follow, she turned to stroll along the path. "Tell me of your childhood, Daniel."

Twisting Newgate's reins loosely through his fingers, he sauntered alongside her. He would prefer to remain silent, but rather than continue arguments and confrontations that took the light from her eyes, a sharing of experiences might not only soften the harshness between them, but work to his favor. "My mother was a duke's daughter . . ." When she nodded in that eager way she adopted when fascinated, he willingly continued.

"She fell in love at first sight, as did my father. She defied her parents and married him, for she was of age. He quit smuggling for her . . ."

That caught her by surprise. "How did he live?"

"He had amassed a hefty sum already, and her parents honored her dowry. They traveled . . ."

"And left you here alone?"

"Heavens, no. He smiled at her obvious concern. "I went with them. Then when I was twelve, my mother died in childbirth—in London, with a famous society doctor attending."

Harmony's fingers fluttered to her chest. "Oh, how terrible."

"My father hated society after that . . ."

"Understandable," she said fiercely. Then she threw him a perplexed glance. "How did he like society *before* that, when he was a smuggler?"

She was quick. And not afraid to blast away at his logic. "Our family was already ostracized because of my grandfather's despicable actions, so there was no question of mingling with the *ton*. After my parents married, though, he was well enough received."

"And after her death, you traveled with your father . . . a sort of grand tour?"

He laughed aloud. At her quizzical frown, he explained. "The vision of a tour such as ours—surrounded by elegant servants and valets—just struck me as humorous." When she seemed uncertain what he meant, he explained. "My father was out of his mind with grief, so I took him away from all his memories. We sailed where we wanted, and he began to heal. He drank. He fought. It was a rough life."

"Ah," she said, smiling as she, too, caught the vision. "Will you always be a smuggler?"

The abrupt question stopped him, made him uncomfortable. "Will you," he countered, "always be your father's helper?"

Eyelids lifted with surprise, then very quickly, a mischievous grin followed. She clutched her chest and fell against his shoulder. "A hit!"

He blinked in surprise, entranced by her awakened sense of fun, by how quickly she adapted to cheerful laughter after a lifetime of solemnity. "Perhaps," he said, "we should let these questions lie dormant for a while. To prevent conflict when we are pretending to be sweethearts."

She shrugged amiably, then without warning, struck again. "My father said you refuse to use your title."

"Satan's teeth, Harmony," he said, reeling from her outrageous probing, "are you out for blood today?"

"Another touchy subject, Daniel?" She grinned again. "I believe I have found a method for your long-overdue retribution. You tease and torment me—I quiz and prod and generally make your life miserable."

When she found him speechless, she added, "You'll never know another peaceful moment, *Lord* Rockburne."

Ten

Speechless indeed, he could only stare at her. Laughter threatened, indeed gurgled in his chest, but as if dropped onto a deck from the foremast, he could not catch his breath to utter a sound. She was enchanting, this chameleon, this elusive woman-child who had slipped so effortlessly beneath his guard.

Daniel could not resist. He slipped his arm around her shoulder and buried his face in her windblown hair. Indeed, he thought as Harmony innocently raised her chin to give him greater access, he had no intention of resisting. The sooner he bound her to him mind and body, the sooner love would follow. He wanted her, but he wanted *all* of her, willing—nay eager.

"Is Saul watching?"

He almost laughed. His logical little love required a reason for everything. He envisioned a lifetime of *explaining*. "Aye, most likely. He was on our trail in the rainy village yesterday, so who's to say what he's up to this bright day." He pulled her round to face him, kissing his way toward her mouth. He liked the way her breath caught with each passing touch. "D'you mind this, Harmony?"

He caught the whispered, "no" in his mouth as she lifted her face into a kiss without hesitation, a purring kitten with all the little sounds she made.

"Saul's probably wondering if you still love me," Daniel murmured, "you should be embracing me back."

"Oh dear." She slipped her slim arms around his chest. "Is this sufficient?"

He bit back a grin. "That's fine for show, but the secret is to put your mind into it as well. Just let yourself think how much you love me . . ."

He broke off as she followed his example and began nuzzling his neck. He groaned, fighting to keep his mind on the task at hand. "Say the words aloud if you want to do it right."

She pulled back, frowning. "Words . . . ?"

"If you loved me, what would you say?"

"Oh . . . I can't get you out of my mind, I think of you . . ."

"Yes?"

"I think of you first thing in the morning . . ."

"And I," he returned with perfect honesty, "think of you when I awaken in the night, wishing you were in my arms . . ."

"I think of you when I look at the stable . . ."

He leaned back. "What?"

"When I look out my window, I can see the stable—and remember that Boris is no longer there."

He chuckled and pulled Harmony's head against his chest with stroking hands. With every utterance, with every kiss, he was more resolved to have her. What would his father have done? *Mastery, be it man or beast, begins with trust,* James used to say.

Harmony would never be able to let go of her father's hand and reach for his, until she trusted him, *wanted to be with him.* And, Daniel thought with a wicked grin, *repetition* was the secret to learning, as James used to say. Of course he'd been referring to the troublesome Juno, but before Harmony took her little jaunt to London . . .

A shout penetrated his musings. "Roan's gone wild, Rockburne. He's dismissing all the servants . . ." Caulder, the new Roan coachman pounded down the path toward them.

Harmony stepped away from Daniel, her face drained of color. "What upset him?"

"Messenger came from London. Seems Stanford, yer man of

business, has spent the last month in bed, and yer house in London's not ready for you." Daniel took the man a little way off, where a brisk conversation ensued, well punctuated with Daniel's furious oaths. Finally, Caulder nodded and trotted back down the path.

"Oh, Zeus, I forgot the messenger was coming." Harmony stepped forward, but Daniel grasped her arm. "I'll walk you home."

"Oh, no, you cannot—"

"To the edge of your land. We need to talk." He draped his arm back over Harmony's shoulders as they moved forward. "I think I'd better know what started all this, Harmony."

She hesitated briefly. "Just a little tiff last night and my father stirred up the household. It's nothing serious I cannot fix."

"You're a terrible liar," Harmony. "You forget I saw you bawling your eyes out this morning." The blasted girl was far too independent.

"All right . . . Father humiliated me terribly, but with good reason. I have been arguing with him, defying him over little things . . ."

"Defying him?" This was hopeful news. "Such as . . . ?"

"He sent Boris and John to drag me home when my aunt was dying, but I refused."

Daniel grinned. "That must have shocked him."

"I wasn't there to see his reaction, but he didn't send them back."

"And . . . ?" He wanted the story whole.

"Pierre."

"Pierre?" he snapped back. Who the hell was *Pierre?*

She grinned. "Ah, Pierre . . . he's a Frenchman who has commissioned my father to write a walking tour along the coast. He's a sour-faced weasel who has flattered my father into doing it without payment, then wants all the credit while I do all the work."

"That makes you smile?"

"Well," she said, sharing her mirth with him, "I'm afraid I

staged a small rebellion over that, although my father doesn't know it. Any Frenchman who follows my route will find himself going round in circles or . . ." Daniel chuckled. ". . . or falling into the river."

As she went on to tell him the rest, Daniel laughed as he pictured the hilarious repercussions, barely able to believe Harmony had actually executed such daring nonsense. "Any other inciting rebellions?"

"No . . . I think the worst is that we argue a lot, something we never used to do. Yesterday Father insisted I keep to the house, but I told him no. Then, last night he caught the servants at their dinner and told them that I was not . . . allowed out of the house. I found out this morning from Meadows. He never said a word to me."

Anger rose, a crimson sheet of fury that almost blinded him. "He's a madman, Harmony," he ground out.

She halted, placing tentative fingers on his arm. "Not if you see it from his viewpoint, Daniel. He's anxious over getting his work done and perhaps a little frightened I will leave him."

"He made you cry," he bit out through clenched teeth, knowing even as he spoke the words that his approach was once again faulty.

She dropped her fingers to her side. "I wish you had not seen that, it was a private moment."

You're only alienating her by attacking, you clumsy fool. This is not a battle of force—use your brains! "Harmony," he said gently, "I'm sorry."

"For seeing me cry?" Confusion laced her voice.

"No, for . . ." *for doing it all wrong* ". . . for reacting so harshly about your father. I should trust you, see it from your viewpoint."

"You should?"

"Of course," he said, feeling his way along, "I cannot keep bludgeoning you every time you take your father's side. Indeed, my own father gave me some unpleasant moments."

"Oh, Daniel, *truly?*"

He could drown in that expression, Daniel thought, that glowing look of approval, of dawning hope. *"Truly,* Harmony. Why, after my mother died, he went berserk. It took me years to bring back the father he'd been before."

She sighed. "No one understands, Daniel. Sometimes I don't understand myself how I can love him when he is so difficult. It's just that I have warm memories of our working together, of how proud he has been of me. Even now when he seems to not care about my happiness at all, I cannot desert him. He needs me."

"Probably the strongest tie of all, being needed." How very tightly Roan had her snared.

"Well," she said in a lighter vein, "once I have him settled in London, that will end."

Not a chance in the world. He smiled and offered a platitude that comforted neither of them. "It couldn't get worse."

Harmony rushed to her bedchamber to freshen up after her ride on Newgate. It was a mystery, she thought while washing, how perfect chaos could flourish in the disapproving silence that blanketed her home.

She pulled the pins from her hair, still in a daze over how drastically things had changed while she was gone. She'd left this morning to contemplate her dilemma—forgetfully leaving behind another problem brewing in the shape of the London messenger—and had come home to find her little world under an evil spell. A spell in which she'd metamorphosed from the dedicated, if somewhat strange, heart of the hearth into *betrayer of the household.*

She looked into the mirror. How could she have forgotten the messenger was coming? She'd gone off nursing her wounded feelings, and look what happened.

In the throes of his tantrum, Sir Roan had dismissed half the servants and suspended the remainder's wages until they proved their worthiness to serve him. For hadn't they, he accused, secretly conspired with his daughter in permitting her to leave the house when he had clearly forbidden it? If not for their treachery, Harmony would have been home to stand buffer against the messenger's unacceptable news.

How the servants had managed to contain his wild explosion within the confines of Roan's bedchamber where he'd retired with a sick headache over Boris, she'd never know, for he liked to embroil the entire household in his spells.

She brushed her hair and pinned it back so tightly it hurt. How strange human nature was. While the servants had shielded her father, who was the villain in the drama, such practicality had not been extended to her, since she had somehow lost her power to stem Roan's cruelty. Without that saving grace, all their submerged suspicions of Harmony had rushed to the fore. She could see it in their faces—hadn't she always been just a little strange? . . . just a little too odd for their tastes? . . . didn't blood breed true? Even John, the valet, described the day's events with an edge to his voice, for he had borne the brunt of Roan's outburst.

She sighed and slipped on a clean dress. Any moment now her father would confront her. Oh, Zeus, it loomed like a pit of writhing snakes. Her father was perfectly capable of enacting the entire scenario all over again to make sure she paid the full price. And she knew in her heart that all her rebellions—all those bits of mutiny she'd recounted so humorously to Daniel— were finally going to take their toll.

Why had she thought she could get away with even the slightest resistance to her father's will? Because he hadn't immediately retaliated? Well, just as she had become more daring, her father had grown more cunning. What, she found herself thinking, would he do next?

In truth, she was badly frightened. Whatever he plotted was a simmering pot of misery, and she was the intended victim. *And it wasn't the anticipated suffering that distressed her, but how she would react to his attack.*

She wondered at the tea shop yesterday what could possibly

sever the bond of love between parent and child, thinking how steady was the Pollards' love for Daniel. Now she assigned that worry to herself—what would it take to sever her love for her father? It seemed impossible, but *what would it take?*

Oh, she hated what was happening to her safe little world. Her life's equilibrium seemed to have grown increasingly shaky since her aunt's death, and that fragility had accelerated enormously in the past few days. The winds of change were blowing, altering every facet of her life.

And the deep-down truth was—no matter how the adult Harmony found the outside world exhilarating—the frightened child inside her didn't want to change. She wanted the solidity of her childhood when her father's love and admiration were the sublime reward, when the solid rock upon which she stood was her own love for her father. She wanted to be content with the life he'd mapped out for her. True, she'd planned a gentle change toward her aunt's way of life—but in the future when it wouldn't disturb anyone.

She didn't want the servants shunning her, finding her flawed and undeserving of their respect. She didn't want Saul's suspicions to be a constant threat to her and Daniel.

Daniel.

She sat down on the stool, contemplating how very changed the girl in the mirror truly was. By every rule by which she'd been reared, she should be ashamed, contrite over disobeying her father's wishes, for after all, that very rebellion had sparked the rather frightening changes in her father over the last few days.

Instead, after all these years of submission, indeed, *willing compliance* to her father's will, she felt her spirit soaring toward something else that began the night Daniel found her on the beach.

If she were truly contrite, she might be blaming Daniel . . . for distracting her, for enticing her. For blinding her to the consequences of her actions. For showing her laughter and teasing and fun. For leaving her with a longing that could never be fulfilled. For opening her to those dangerous winds of change.

But how could she find fault with Daniel when the heart of that girl in her mirror was secretly filled with joy?

The door slammed open, hitting a table in the corner. Harmony jumped up, her heart pounding so hard she could not breathe. Dizzy, she reached for the bedpost to hold her up while her father, fresh out of bed it seemed, glared at his victim.

As judge, he wouldn't deign to sit for a sentencing, and Harmony didn't dare do so. She managed the courage to twine her fingers tightly around the bedpost, since her knees had forsaken the responsibility of holding her upright and were instead blancmange beneath her skirts.

"You've heard about our reduction of staff?" He surprised her, for she'd expected him to attack immediately. She nodded . . . and waited.

She literally ached to point out how many years the half-dozen servants had served him faithfully, but she didn't dare. Admitting mistakes was not even a possibility to Sir Roan.

Roan seemed disappointed at her silence, and tried to stir her into speaking. "Don't try hiring them back, Harmony, for I won't change my mind."

Again, she nodded. Then, finally seeing how furious her silence made him, she relented. "I understand."

It wasn't enough.

"What do you have to say about the trouble you caused yesterday?"

The trouble I caused? "I'm sorry I missed the messenger." Had the servants ever confessed that she was gone from the property?

His eyes glowed hotly, and she could tell that he was determined to have the confrontation he wanted. "I've been patient," he said, then raised his voice a notch. "I've let you back-talk and argue with me, thinking you would get it out of your system. But it only made you worse."

He watched her so closely she thought her teeth might crumble from holding her features immobile. She knew he wanted her to weep and plead—but, as much as she yearned to give him what he wanted and have peace again, like a kitten trapped on a high limb, she dared not let go and suffer the inevitable fall.

She looked at his once-dear face now creased in the mask she dreaded and asked herself why she couldn't give him his triumph. Was it so much to ask, this capitulation? What was wrong with her?

"Your stubbornness has cost a lot of good people their employment, Harmony. Aren't you ashamed?"

Answers hovered in the air, waiting to be spoken. A simple *yes* would satisfy him, or at least serve as a beginning, but even though she belatedly knew she *had* jeopardized servants' positions by leaving the house, to admit it would bestow upon her father unlimited permission to imprison her at will.

Unfortunately, just as her mind vowed silence, her tongue chose that moment to free itself. "I admit that I should have remembered that the messenger was coming, and I regret they lost their jobs. However," she said, as Roan's eyes widened in amazement, "you cannot ask them to be jailers. Their positions only require they cook and clean and care for our needs."

As his face reddened, she continued, knowing she was absurd to attempt logic at this time, "What were they to do, Father? Tie me up? Lock me in my room? Hold me by force?"

"If necessary!" he stormed.

"They have no right to do that, Father—in fact," she added as a new thought occurred, "you do not have the right to hold me prisoner either. I'm almost an adult now, or have you forgotten that in a few weeks I shall be of age?"

Furious, he grabbed her by the shoulders and shook her. He had never touched her in anger before, and inside, her heart was breaking. *Didn't he know what he was doing to her . . . to them?*

He leaned forward and pinned her with his stare like a bug in a display case. "I know exactly how old you are, Harmony Roan. In one month we shall celebrate your birthday in London, and before that *uneventful* day, I want to see this very unpleasant girl you've become *disappear.* I want the sweet child back—the one I used to love," he purred softly.

He stood upright once more, all business now. "And while you're erasing those unpleasant flaws from your character, you can busy yourself by putting our London house in order. You will leave in two days."

"Goodness, Father! Yesterday you threw a fit over my leaving the house, and *now* you want me to go to London?"

Furious once more, he glared at her. "Yesterday I needed you here. Now, you will be more useful in London. It's bad enough that I will have to post the changes of my work to you instead of having you home where it's convenient, Harmony. Do not add whining to my troubles."

He stood quietly while he gathered his thoughts. "I shall give you Mr. Sanford's direction and written authority to act in my name. It's more than any other daughter is entrusted with, and you should be grateful."

"I shall need a chaperon."

His face turned purple. "Must you always argue, Harmony? Haven't you learned your lesson, or must I dismiss a few more servants?

She opened her mouth to answer, but her common sense finally kicked in and she nodded her acquiescence in absolute silence.

Eleven

The morning sun warmed her back as she slipped into the stables. Immediately, Caulder strode forward. "Something's amiss?"

As if the words had come from Daniel's own voice, she smiled. "I have a note for Rockburne. Can you get it to him?"

"Meeting to say good-bye, are you?"

She laughed. "Have we no secrets?"

Caulder shrugged good-naturedly. "News, blight or bounty, it blows in the wind." He frowned. "Don't know what he'll think about your going to London alone."

"How did you discover that?"

"Not hard to cipher when no one in the household is allotted the task."

"Of course . . . well thank you, Caulder," She wandered back out into the sun, then, taking a deep breath, ran a mental calculation of all she had left to do, deciding they could wait just a moment while she caught her breath. She lowered herself onto the bench against the stable wall and lifted her face to the sun.

All morning she'd been filled with a frenetic need to *move*, to get things done. *And to outdistance her thoughts.*

Last night's clash with her father was absolutely off limits, of course, as was the cynical thought that in his tantrum, Roan had *not* dismissed Meadows and John, conveniently the two servants necessary to his own personal comfort. If she wasn't careful, she might begin thinking like Daniel . . . or Beatrice.

How she wished Beatrice could be there waiting for her in London as they had planned. What would the dear lady do in her situation? *Board a ship—and take Daniel with her.*

Abruptly, she stood. Thoughts like that were far too tempting, and although her father was being a perfect beast, she had no intention of jumping her present ship before his future was well and truly moored. And as for that, she'd better get moving.

Daniel read the note while Caulder stood nearby, worrying his cap into a snarled ball of yarn. "Leaving tomorrow, is she?"

"Aye."

"What else, Caulder? You're fairly bursting with news."

"You haven't heard, then?"

"Caulder . . ."

"The old devil's sending her alone—no maid, no woman to give her proper station. And I get only Willy from the stables for the trip."

"Satan's teeth! Does he want to ruin the girl?"

Caulder shrugged and waited for instructions. "I'll send along a maid," Daniel said. "And outriders. They can catch the coach outside of town."

"Aye."

Harmony yawned and stretched. She should have gone to bed many hours ago, as had their guests, but she was rising before dawn to begin her trip and all must be done tonight. She tucked her father's latest instructions into her leather satchel and laid it on the library table. She had sent her London direction to her aunt's servants, Sorrel and Biggins. Only one small task to go. "I shall need funds to run the house and to purchase a London wardrobe. And I shall need the papers on the rental house."

Her father's head rose sharply. She was surprised to see a flushed embarrassment upon his face. "Sanford has the papers, just get the key from him. As for cash, there is a pouch in my

desk drawer for the trip. Take half and I shall bring the rest."
Then his eyelids blinked—*a sure sign of guilt.*

Normally, she would have relented and ceased pursuing an unwelcome subject. Now, however, she was driven to discover what he concealed. She leaned forward. "Have you overspent again, Father? We can borrow on my inheritance—then pay it back when your books sell."

She watched his eyes—his blinking eyes. "Your inheritance?"

She sighed. He didn't want to talk about it, but she needed to know. "If I am to leave tomorrow, I shall need the papers and the money. If you have overspent, then we shall use my monies."

He dismissed the problem with a wave of his hand. "I believe that my banker has commingled it with my own funds."

A shiver of alarm shuddered lightly through her. She took a deep breath, telling herself to remember that this was her father and that he loved her. "Father, a banker is not allowed to do such a thing without your permission. I shall have him investigated."

Sir Roan's jaw came forward, a forerunner to a blustering attack. "Leave well enough alone, Harmony. I am perfectly capable of overseeing our finances."

Harmony fell back against her chair, blurting out the alarming thought that flooded her mind. "You took my inheritance, didn't you? You used it . . . what did you spend it on?"

He stood and leaned forward, towering over her with a wild glaze in his eyes. "As I told you, I'm refurbishing a house in London."

"You used my money for fixing up a rental house?"

"If I wish to borrow my own daughter's money to invest in our future, then it is not your place to question me. I provide you with a place to live and put food on the table—and have borne the unwarranted expense of your selfish trips to Bath every year—one might consider this money simply a repayment of that burden."

She risked a dignified reply. "Aunt Beatrice financed my visits."

He glared at her, sat down, and opened a book. "Sharpen a pen for me." He was lost once more in his own world, and the discussion was closed. A spell barely averted, she thought with relief. *Or had that threatened tantrum been simply a tool to shut her off?*

In a daze, she walked to the small table in the corner and gracelessly fell into the chair. As she executed her father's small request, her brain raced back over his remarks, the logic contained therein, and the motivation that drove him. As the significance of Sir Roan's diatribe sank in, her world tipped just a little sideways.

Beatrice had been correct.

As things stood, she could never reveal her true, larger inheritance from Beatrice, not as long as her father lived, for without apology, he had already spent Beatrice's clever *decoy.* Should he discover the real fortune, he would gain control of it, and would thereafter pour it down the same black hole, dedicating it blindly to the god of literary fame. Books, travel, research and his indigent friends would devour it whole—all for nothing, and nothing for her.

While some part of her mind refused to believe it, her intrepid intellect analyzed and acknowledged the truth. Rather than finding her aunt's judgement of her father harsh, she knew now that it had fallen far short of the mark. If she did not find some solution, she was trapped in the life her father chose for her. Unexpected tears filled her eyes. Blast, she was *not* going to cry at the first hurdle.

"By the Gods, Harmony, cease that endless sniffling and get to work. We have two letters from Pierre to answer."

"I sent it off to his address in Alfriston this morning." *With all the delicious mistakes.* "How can he claim authorship when all he does is pop over here once and order it done by me?"

"Harmony! I do not know what has come over you, but your insolence is unacceptable. Apologize at once."

When she remained silent, he looked at her with that focused stare that always made her feel like he'd nailed her to the wall. "You do realize that your rebellious attitude will not endear you to Lord Beckman."

"Lord Beckman?" What had Father's patron to do with her?

Sir Roan sighed deeply. "Lord Beckman has expressed an interest in you, my dear. Surely, I told you about it."

"No . . . no, you didn't." Horrified, she knew she had to say something—anything—to nip this in the bud, before he closed his mind on the subject and it became hard-shelled fact. "I do not wish to be courted by Lord Beckman, Father. Please do not encourage him."

"Nonsense, it is the perfect solution. He wishes to sponsor our work and is especially enthusiastic regarding your translations."

"He can surely do that without *marrying* me."

"Try not to be more obtuse than necessary, Harmony. The point is that your marriage to Lord Beckman will seal his sponsorship, yet I will not have lost you, for he has graciously granted you permission to continue working with me after you are wed."

By the time he finished, her entire life, past, present and future, had shifted—from what she now realized was a myth of her own making—to the raw, ugly truth. She had believed she was managing her father all these years by assuming more and more of his own work and diffusing his disastrous tantrums. Reality, however, was simply that she had made herself a willing slave.

In all fairness, any normal person would probably accept such voluntary cushioning of his life, but her father's innate selfishness had flourished like a strangling plant, winding its tentacles around her before she realized how firmly snared she had become.

She had often thought herself lucky having uncommon skills, for it made her father love her more, brought them closer. Now she suspected that pleased amazement at her skills, the hours spent together—that had been for *him,* not for her.

What should she do? What *could* she do?

She could jump off the cliff, but her father would probably throw a tantrum and then forget to bury her. She could disappear, but eventually Aunt Beatrice's solicitor would come asking for her, and Father would only be too glad to have her money.

She could storm into Beckman's bedchamber and demand that he undo the despicable agreement—but a lady could never do such a thing. It would have to wait until they all came to London.

She took a deep breath. One thing she was not going to do was waste her valuable time arguing with him. No, her wondrous brain—*traitor it had shown itself to be all these years*—might as well start thinking clearly, and find a solution for this terrible mess.

No more slipping back into a fog of denial, no more making excuses for her father. No time to mourn what she'd never had. Loving him, she could not prevent, trusting him would be disastrous.

A swift, fierce rush of emotion burned through her, scorching all the weak *what if* rationalizations and leaving them behind as useless ashes. Something uncurled inside her, something fierce and frantic that knew it must stay one step ahead of her father's plans, for she would have no warning.

Her imagination jumped ahead, flowed into the world of possible scenarios that her father might concoct. Lock her up? Drug her and see her married in secret without her permission? Abduction, ruination?

Zeus, it sounded like a gothic tale.

Placing her father's sharpened pen before him, she announced. "I am finished for the evening. I am going to go for my walk and then I shall retire for the night."

"You may walk, but for fifteen minutes only," he said, absently turning a page.

* * *

Rain clouds threatened as Daniel and Juno waited at the bottom of her cliffside track, while two of his men stood a chilled guard on the hill above. They would probably be glad to see the end of these nighttime rendezvous so they could go back to spending their evenings drinking in the toasty inn.

He raised his lantern and studied her face. "Something's wrong. What is it?"

She shook her head as if to clear her troubles away. He wrapped his arm around her, pulling her head against his chest. "Tell me." He knew there was more.

"You'll only want to do something about it, Daniel, and I can't have my father dragged off to the slavers."

"I wouldn't do that, Harmony."

"You'd do something worse."

He swung her around to face him. In the lantern's light she could hide nothing. "Do you trust me?"

She looked surprised. "Of course, I do."

For a moment he could not speak, so open and believing was her expression. "I won't harm your father in any way," he managed. Then to cajole a smile from her, he added, "Unless you tell me to."

Her face softened, the only encouragement he needed. "Just start talking." He pulled her close to his side and strolled slowly down the beach.

"He spent my inheritance."

Daniel swallowed the harsh epithet that rose to his lips. He wanted Harmony to talk, and calling Roan names wasn't the way to do it. "I thought he didn't know about it."

"Not the ninety thousand—a smaller amount my aunt used to decoy him, to test him, to show me that he wasn't trustworthy."

He whistled. "Clever lady."

"You would have liked her."

"You needn't worry about having an inheritance, Harmony. The man who loves you won't be stopped by such a foolish item as that."

"I haven't told you everything—he's made plans to marry me to his patron."

He stopped. A deadly calm stopped him cold, sharpened his mind. Automatically, he surveyed the empty landscape and checked the pistols in his pockets as if an enemy were near. "When?"

"No date. He had it all planned and forgot to tell me about it until tonight."

Forgot to tell her? A powerful fury hit him, tightening his chest and painfully cording the muscles in his arms. How like Sir Roan. He ought to turn Saul loose on him. No one deserved to be fodder for a marauding shark more than Harmony's father. He wanted to pick her up in his arms and carry her away from it all, whisk her off to safety. She didn't deserve such callous treatment, nor should she be at the mercy of two heartless men who only wanted to use her for their own selfish reasons.

A whimper escaped her lips.

"Sorry," he gasped, quickly releasing her shoulder from his clenched fingers. She'd have bruises in the morning.

"I was sure Roan would never let you go, Harmony. What is he planning to do without you?"

"Oh," she said bitterly, "he has no intention of doing without me. That's why he chose his sponsor—he would get a permanent connection by marriage, and they would keep me working."

"So the man loves you?"

"No," she sighed, "He doesn't think of me that way. Their plan is to keep me from marrying anyone else, so I will be handy—"

He choked. *"Handy?* He doesn't want to bed you, then, just keep you *handy?"*

She gasped. "Daniel!"

"Believe me," he said in the most reasonable voice he could muster, "men do not marry to secure the services of a translator. They don't stick their necks in the parson's noose unless they want something important like a healthy dowry, a breeder for their nursery, or a woman they love and want in their bed."

"But Lord Beckman—"

"Beckman? My damned snake of a cousin is your father's patron?" Satan's teeth, he couldn't believe it. Robbie was exactly what he'd called him—like the snake his grandmother's vicar droned on about, he was too damned sneaky to do his own dirty work, he had to get Harmony's father locked in before he asked her.

He'd made Daniel's trips to London a misery, going through the motions of being pleasant to impress their grandmother, while managing little scenes where Daniel became the scoundrel.

He knew Robbie, and he damned well wasn't after Harmony for literary reasons.

"I didn't think you would like it."

"Is he here again with that gaggle of geese at your house?"

She choked. *"Gaggle of geese?* Oh, dear, if they could hear you speak of them like that—"

"What the hell are they doing here?"

"Actually, it's an important time for them. My father has asked them to review his work before taking it to the publisher. Then I shall make the changes—"

"Will you marry him?" Not as long as he was around to stop it.

"Absolutely not."

"Good girl. What did your father say when you told him no?"

"He . . . just stopped listening to me."

All the while they were talking, a plan had been forming. A new plan to supplant the old. Fast. Decisive. "I'll take you away from it, Harmony. Come with me now and you'll never have to worry about Roan or Beckman again."

Harmony's heart pounded so loudly she could hear the pulse in her ears. "Where would we go?" Oh, she was so tempted . . ."

"We'd go to Scotland and marry."

"You'd do that for me?"

"Aye. Will you come?"

Here was her chance to make that compelling illusion a reality, and oh, how she wanted to just *go*. "I cannot wed until I am of age, Daniel, and if you were caught, my father would use every power within reach to destroy you."

"D'you think I cannot protect you?"

"I know you would die trying—that's what has me worried. Not only that," she said, coming back to earth with a great depressing thud, "I am within inches of fulfilling my promise to my father."

"At your own peril," Daniel retorted as the wind kicked up.

"Your man, Caulder is taking me to London. He could bring me to you if I needed to escape."

Daniel knew the moment she hesitated, her damned *brain* would decide for her father. What he wanted to do was abduct her, keep her in his bed for a week and then ask her if she wanted to go toddling off to her father. He could guarantee she wouldn't choose life in a library over the love he could give her. Blast, if this had only happened later, when he'd had time to make her fall in love with him . . . "How long before your birthday?"

"It's the twentieth of June—a month away."

"Will he try to push the marriage through before then?"

"I don't know."

He pulled the cowl of her cape over her head and tucked her under his arm. Walking toward her stretch of beach, he tried to be reasonable. "I'll think of something Harmony. I'm not going to let you handle this alone."

"You cannot keep rescuing me forever," she said loudly to penetrate the noise of the wind. "You could waste your whole life getting me out of messes."

"Aye." He'd realized that long ago. As they reached the bottom of her track, he pulled her into his arms. "You can rely on Caulder. If you get in trouble, tell him and he will bring you here to me."

"I know," she said, as dark clouds masked her view of his face, "and thank you for everything . . . for Saul and Boris, and for giving up so much of your time." *And for kisses and laughter and teasing.*

Tears filled her eyes. Her throat ached with the need to weep. She swallowed hard, forced the emotion down. She couldn't allow him to see her tears, for then he would take matters into his own hands. She stepped back out of his arms—and not realizing what she meant to do, he let her go easily.

She wanted to hold her lantern up, to look at his face, to just soak up *one more memory* to take with her on her journey.

But she didn't dare. Oh, why couldn't she just stay here with this man? She just wanted to spend her days talking to him, riding on that blasted horse. She *liked* his teasing, she wanted to hear him *laugh at her.* To feel his fingers on her face, in her hair.

She didn't think she could bear leaving, for who knew what might happen. He might find the assassin and not need her any more—or, God forbid, be slain himself.

She could not endure the rest of her life without seeing that dear face, hear that rumbling voice. So she did the only thing she could.

"Thank you, Daniel," she whispered.

She ran all the way home.

Twelve

Beside him, Juno whined, unhappy that he could not follow Harmony. Daniel touched the mastiff's head in commiseration and turned back toward his own beach. "Come on, Juno, we have a lot to decide."

Juno bounded forward down the beach, stopping to root around in a pile of tidal debris. Furiously shaking his head, Juno tugged on a stick of wood, and finally pulling it free, trotted back to offer it to his master. Obediently, Daniel threw the stick out into the waves, then walked on while the tenacious dog waited for it to float in.

Love was tough on men. No wonder they spent half their lives avoiding it and the other half moaning about what they'd lost. Harmony had been gone two minutes and already the beach seemed like a lonely, deserted island.

Daniel kicked the sand, sending a glorious spray into the wind that flew all the way to the cliffs. He damned well wasn't going to stand around moaning about what he'd *lost* because he didn't intend to lose anything. He'd let her go finish her blasted project for Roan and that's the last leeway she'd be getting. After that, she was his. But tomorrow ... . well, tomorrow he'd take a guard of men and accompany Harmony to London and assign a maid the task of chaperoning her. Harmony had no idea what kind of trouble a single woman with no maid could find herself in.

He would quit worrying whether Harmony loved him or

not—she loved him enough for now, and she could catch up later.

Meanwhile, he would put his plan into action, and if that devil Roan didn't fall into place, Daniel would turn the heat up so hot that he would be begging to cooperate.

His cousin would be crawling around somewhere in the middle of the mess, acting like a gentleman, when all the time, he was just a spoiled little brat gone bad—just like Roan—for Robbie, too, would strike out blindly to any opposition, not caring whom he hurt.

He wasn't surprised Robbie and Roan had found each other, for they had each discovered a way to fill their heads full of other people's ideas and then acted as if that made then superior. They had taken it a step further with Harmony, letting her do the hard work, then basking in the glow of her brilliance. No wonder they didn't dare let her go. Like the parasites that they were, they would greedily sap everything from her until there was nothing left.

To his gloating cousin, Harmony must be a golden source of everything he loved—a priceless, unique beauty and a source of power and admiration reflected toward himself. How he would love *controlling* such magnificence—the ultimate thrill for Robbie.

Juno's wet nose against Daniel's hand alerted him to his duty. Once more Daniel tossed the stick into the waves. Damn it, his father should be here. Daniel would gladly admit now that the curse was not an idle whim, something a man could ignore. He'd always thought it would come like a blow to the head or a pain in the gut—something a man could fight—but, no, it came veiled so alluringly that a man wanted to leap joyously into the trap. James had described it to him, but Daniel had discounted it, believing James's grief had embellished the curse with an other-worldly magic.

How had his parents, so opposite in background, overcome the barriers that must have been thrown up against their union? At least his mother had loved his father, while Harmony remained still unawakened, seeking only to serve her father, to live in her books and in her blasted brilliant mind.

A few feet ahead, Bernard coughed. Damp night air did not agree with him. "She's gone," Daniel said quietly. "Let's go home."

Bernard snorted. "I'm glad to hear that. You're not even alert these days, Rockburne, you're wandering around in a lovesick daze." When Daniel refused to rise to the challenge, Bernard shook his head, then stepped quickly back to avoid the charging dog. Daniel laughed as Juno shook water into the air, then offered him the prize.

Smiling at the mastiff's dancing eagerness, he reached for the dripping stick. "I'm taking some men and following Harmony to London tomorrow."

Bernard folded his muscled arms across his chest with a look that told Daniel what he thought of that nonsense. "Your girl is as snug as a tick on a hound, Rockburne, and no one has a price on *her* head."

"Let me tell you what Roan's done and you'll change your mind." As he did so, Bernard's assorted grunts expressed his disgust over Roan's latest villainy. "Why don't you just take her away, Rockburne?"

Swearing, Daniel gave Juno's stick a mighty heave into the water, then frowned as the stick disappeared far out to sea. "Sorry, Juno."

Leaving the mastiff behind, they walked along the water's edge. "You asked her, didn't you?" Bernard asked. "Why wouldn't she go?" As Daniel once more explained, Bernard's grunts denoted his opinion of females in general and their universal lack of sense.

By the time they reached the track to the castle, the wind was blowing flat across the beach. They pulled their caps down to protect their eyes and ears. Daniel led the way up the track with Bernard following close behind.

"Juno?" Daniel shouted, staggering as the dog leapt against his legs, poking his precious stick triumphantly into Daniel's hand. "You actually *found* . . ." Then he heard the faint crack of a rifle, and a zing of hot fire turned his leg into a burning inferno. He fell to the ground, tumbled a ways, finally landing on his back.

Not the blasted leg again.

Juno flew up the track in pursuit, as Daniel pulled the Mantons out of his pockets. He heard a shout from above that sounded like Saul and heard another shot, but this time he was looking upward and could see the puff of smoke before the wind whipped it sideways. He fired at the target, praying fiercely that this time he'd found his father's killer.

"Blast it, you're shot again, Rockburne." Bernard shoved the spent pistol back into Daniel's pocket and threw Daniel's freed arm over his shoulder. Stretching his strong arm around Daniel's waist, he asked, "Can you still shoot?" Daniel's nod earned him an admiring grunt.

Above them, Juno's barking mingled with heated curses and a loud shout of pain. As they neared the top, Bernard crept ahead to reconnoiter the clifftop. "He's down," he reported, hoisting Daniel up to a standing position at the top of the cliff. As Daniel spotted the fallen man, he felt an exultant thrill streak through him, filling his limbs with unbelievable energy.

A few yards away, the assassin lay crumpled on a blanket littered with weapons—a breech-loading Ferguson rifle and two pistols, with another clutched in his hand. Daniel's men had arrived, torches lit, and were making bets over the killer's chances of living. The unpredictable Juno stood at alert with his head hanging over the cliff, barking into the wind.

Daniel turned his gaze on the killer. *Let this man him live long enough to talk.* And talking, it seemed, was just what the villain had in mind. "Well, Daniel Rockburne, here we are again."

"Who the hell are you?" Daniel called as he moved steadily forward toward the speaker, shaking off Bernard's support.

The killer laughed. "You don't recognize me? Well, neither did my mother," he said, turning his head to reveal a ghastly

scar over one eye. Then he chuckled to himself. *"Sedgewick,
don't you remember?"*

"Sedgewick? Satan's teeth, man, it's been years . . . you've
been waiting all this time . . . out of revenge for that night?"

Sedgewick's lips curled in a sneer. "You always were a stupid
ass, Rockburne. I've been in the peninsula all this time, or you'd
be dead long ago, damn your misbegotten luck."

In a venomous rasping tone, he explained. "I'm a younger
son, Rockburne. My brother purchased my commission so I
could make a fortune in India. But," he ground out bitterly,
"instead, I ended up on this benighted coast, then *disgraced*
and sent to the peninsula.

"How do you think I got this scar, Rockburne?" Sedgewick
laughed, revealing a mind not quite intact. "Two days before
Ciudad Rodrigo a herd of black swine wandered in front of the
lines after acorns, and the starving men went wild. Men were
captured, I was wounded—but was it a glorious charge for the
Times to report to my family? No, I got *this—from pigs!"*

He fastened his glittering gaze on Daniel's face. "I had you
in my sights tonight, Rockburne, but like the great ox you are,
you fell and my bullet missed your heart."

"So, you were the one who hired Lark and Flemming."

Sedgewick issued a weak cough. "That's right, and a fine fee
I got for it, too. When they botched the job, I decided to finish
you myself. But you know," he said raising his pistol, "I would
have done it for free."

He fired, but he was a hair-trigger too late. No one spoke
while Daniel's bullet found the heart of his father's killer. *But
not the assassin who hired it done.*

Bernard roped an arm around Daniel's chest. "No sense you
bleeding to death beside him, Rockburne." Pain shot up his leg,
and the sky began to whirl.

"Hey," a voice called from the direction where Juno stood,
"Saul's down here on a ledge. Someone help me get him up."

"Bernard," Daniel gasped faintly. "See to Harmony's safety—
but don't tell her about this."

* * *

Harmony was just brushing her hair when someone knocked on her door. "Come in," she called, surprised to see Meadows, already in robe and sleeping cap, enter her room. "Is something wrong?"

"No, Miss Roan, but the wind is making me nervous."

"I didn't know you were afraid of the wind, Meadows." Curious, she watched Meadows prowl around the room, then finally stop before the window. She followed her and looked outside. "There are lights in the stables, Meadows."

"Perhaps the horses are nervous, Miss."

Poor woman, Harmony thought, all this dismissing of servants had made her afraid of her own shadow. "Would you like me to ring for some hot chocolate?"

"I've done that already. The maid's on her way up."

"How nice," Harmony said faintly. "Is there anything else I might do for you?"

"The footman is bringing a cot up too, Miss Roan. If you don't mind, I'll just sleep in your dressing room—in case the storm makes you nervous as well."

"Thank you, dear Meadows. That would be just the thing."

Thirteen

If I could just sit up.

Daniel strained to roll over. Damn this weakness, he thought, unable to stop the agonized moan that escaped as the stitches in his calf threatened to tear. Satan's teeth, who could have believed that a simple gunshot wound could be so blasted painful . . . or so apt to bleed, he amended, as the sheet turned red where it rested on his leg.

"You've been rolling around again," growled Bernard, stomping into the room with a tray of dishes. He lifted the sheet and issued one of his disapproving grunts.

Daniel flipped the sheet back into place. "It's barely a scratch. It just likes to bleed."

"The damned bullet nicked the bone, Rockburne, and if you rip the threads loose with your blasted impatience, it'll turn septic." He leaned down close to Daniel's face. "And if you do that, I'll turn my mother loose on you."

Daniel groaned. "Your blasted mother's been draping cupid's bows on my bed."

Bernard glanced at the decorated bedposts and grinned. "Let her have her fun, Rockburne. There's not a soul in Shingle Spit who hasn't gone maggoty over your romance."

Daniel tipped the covers off the dishes and sniffed the hot food. "What's going on at Roan House?"

With a wry smile, Bernard shook his head and buttered a piece of dark bread. "Meadows spent the night in her room and

Miss Roan left at dawn, surrounded by your men. I hope that meets with your approval."

"Did you to send a maid?"

Bernard swore. "Sorry . . ."

"Blast it all, I forgot to tell you last night . . . do the men know not to tell Harmony about this?" he said, glaring at his wounded leg.

Bernard's smile grew. "No one is going to jinx this romance, Rockburne."

Daniel scowled. "What about Saul? Has he awakened yet?"

"Not a sound."

Weary from almost two days on the road, Harmony went directly to the ailing Roger Sanford's house. Between the protective tenacity of his housekeeper and his own maddening belief that Harmony belonged back home with a bit of embroidery, she was quickly losing her temper.

He coughed and glared at Harmony as if she were the sole cause of his discomfort. "You cannot have the keys to the house, Miss Roan; it's not ready yet, just as I indicated in my note to your father."

Harmony stood stiffly in the stuffy bedchamber, barely able to see their man of business by the single candle's light. The smell of medicants and ill health accompanied his frequent cough, rendering the chamber as unpleasant as his sour disposition.

"Then return our money and I shall rent another place."

"I cannot do that, as I explained to your father, for I've already expended the funds in buying draperies and wallpapers and such."

"Then" she said in a gentle tone, "let the next renter of the property pay for that and refund our money now."

Another fit of coughing sent him sitting upright, after which he wheezed deeply and fell back upon the wrinkled pillows. "Better get your facts straight, Miss Roan. Your father *bought* the house.

Had I been able to fight this ague, I would have seen the job done by now, but as you know, servants will play when the master's away."

"He *bought* it?"

"Why are you here invading my privacy, Miss Roan? To make my life a misery, like all females do? I vow if your father knew what you—"

Because I bullied your stubborn housekeeper into letting me in. "My father sent me, Mr. Sanford. My father does not handle problems—I do. I always have, and I am commissioned to do so now."

He coughed again. "I know that you handle the mundane correspondence for him—any dunce can see the difference in the handwriting—however, for *serious* correspondence, he writes directly to me as any sane man would. Look on that desk," he said pointing to a dark corner of the room, "you will see letters in his handwriting. Then perhaps you will leave me alone."

Lifting the candle from the table and carrying it to the corner took only a moment, but to a lady who had received far too many surprises from her father already, the trip seemed akin to a jaunt to the guillotine. *Her father had been corresponding privately to Sanford?* It was true he handled the money, which was necessary, for a female's signature in such matters held no power. But she had thought all this time she was composing all his correspondence.

She placed the candle on the corner of the table. Surely, nothing sinister awaited her here; she was simply anxious. With shaky fingers she leafed through the stack of papers, and to her horror, *there were several items of correspondence in her father's handwriting.* She divided her own handwriting from her father's, then began to glance through her father's letters—and stopped when she saw her aunt's name on more than one letter. What on earth . . . ?

"There," Sanford croaked, "are you satisfied?"

Glancing quickly to ensure he was not observing her, she folded the entire stack and slipped them into her case.

Applying the manner she used when her father became unreasonable, she handed him the item she had held upon entering the house, wishing to make an efficient and speedy visit. "Dear Mr. Sanford, please accept my apologies. You are correct, of course, and all this could have been avoided if I had handed you my father's letter at the onset." That much was true.

He glanced quickly over the document. "Hmphh! Why didn't you say so? The funds for finishing the house are in my office, as are the key and the remodeling papers. Get them from my housekeeper, she knows where everything is."

"Thank you," she murmured, and wove her way out of the furniture-littered room, propelled by a strength that had blossomed during her trip to London. She hadn't a clue where this newfound backbone had come from, but as every obstacle arose—from the insulting innkeepers who rented only the lowest rooms to a woman who travelled without a maid, to the thoughts of her father's treachery—she had felt the new courage strengthen her.

Each time she faltered, the thought followed that she'd be pegged out for torture before she'd go whining back to her father with tales of her own incompetence. What she needed, she often thought, was one of Daniel's fierce *medicinal* scowls to keep her going.

She went searching for the housekeeper, determined to gain her cooperation. She adopted the same cajoling expression she had used with Sanford. "Your employer wishes you to give me the key and the monies for Roan House and the papers concerning the house." The housekeeper gave her a haughty sniff and marched into Sanford's bedroom to verify Harmony's request. Upon returning, she did not even bother to admit the instructions were correct. Off she went to another room, and came back with the items in question, which she dropped into Harmony's hands as if touching her would contaminate her own spotless fingers.

Another time, Harmony might have let it go, but this new Harmony was made of sterner stuff. "Tell me," she said in a firm voice, "are you this unpleasant to everyone, or am I a special case? And if so, do me the courtesy of telling me why."

The housekeeper was perfectly willing to do just that. With her nose raised, she asked, "Where is your maid, madame?"

"My maid . . . ?"

"Or your chaperon?"

"Are you telling me . . . ?"

"Mr. Sanford is not accustomed to dealing with females who are no better than they should be."

Harmony felt sick. Why, though, was she surprised? Innkeepers had behaved with the same insulting manner. "Perhaps," she said in a low tone that didn't even tremble, "you should check with your employer after I leave. Ask him who I am, and of what importance my father holds in his list of clientele. If I must return, I will not be so insulted." She left the woman blinking with surprise.

Harmony's knees were shaking when she left the house, but her hands—and case—were full, and her heart pounding with the success of her perfidy.

Caulder hopped down to open the coach door for her.

She slid onto the bench. "Please wait until I read these papers before going elsewhere." Obediently, he closed the door behind her and stood with his back to the coach. *Thank you, Daniel.*

Resisting the impulse to read the contents of each paper randomly, she put them in chronological order. Then she began.

The first paper concerning her inheritance didn't surprise her, although the amount of the bequest was even more generous than she had imagined. Perhaps there was something left over after purchasing the house?

The second paper dealt with the purchase itself. She read it through twice, then sank back into the corner. There would be no monies left over—instead, her father had indebted himself to obtain it. The town house was in Grosvenor Square, a place even she knew was above their means. Lord Beckman had purchased it in tandem with her father, and they were indebted for the remainder of a ninety-nine-year lease that began in seventeen fifty-three.

Doggedly, she tucked that document to the bottom of the pile and pulled the stack closer to read the next one. Tears blossomed when she saw her aunt's name in her father's handwriting, but not from sentimentality or grief. Pure, unadulterated fury filled her at the words. "Ascertain through whatever means you deem necessary what disposal the deceased made of the remainder of her wealth and the house . . ." She read the rest, forced herself to commit to memory her father's instructions, especially the part where Harmony was to be kept ignorant of the proceedings and findings alike.

On she went, coldly reading every word. Soames, her aunt's solicitor, evidently was far too canny to give out information regarding his client's transactions—even with the promise of a generous "gift" and the reminder that, "after all, the woman was no longer concerned with her earthly possessions."

She found Soames's address embossed on his letterhead. Opening the door, she gave directions to Caulder. The surprising strength that brought her from Shingle Spit to this place surged through her once more. She had braved Sanford's ill humor, daringly taken papers and challenged the housekeeper who thought her a slut. She had survived. *She had courage.* As the coach moved forward, she smiled.

"Saul's awake and up?"

Bernard shrugged. "Brass-faced and full of sauce, claiming he wants the reward. Wait until you hear his story."

Daniel couldn't help smiling as a surge of battle-energy flowed into his muscles. Ignoring Bernard's instant scowl of disapproval, he swung an arm out to the mahogany French secrétaire beside the bed and snapped the cupboard door open. As it fell down to create the desk he used on better days, he selected one of the loaded Mantons that rested on the lowest inside shelf and slid it under the sheet. "Bring him in."

Bernard strode out to the sound of the cupboard door slamming closed. Daniel fingered the pistol absently, his mind on the coming interview.

"Dan'l!" roared Saul as Bernard and three of his men pushed him into the room. "Call off yer men, I'm here on my own, and heartily insulted that you think I'd sink so low as to ambush you. Hell," he said, shaking his arms as the men dropped their hold and stepped back, "the day I want you dead, I'll be looking straight into your eyes."

He was a disreputable sight as usual. Boots that seawater and stable muck had softened to swaddle his thick legs in dark folds and creases. Loose pants that had once been lightweight nankeen, now so greasy and stained as to be almost waterproof. The usual black seaman's coat, held closed with wooden buttons, two of which were broken into smooth half-moons. Eyes red with drink and lack of sleep, beard and hair dank and snarled. "Did they tell you I found the killer?"

"Nay," Daniel drawled, "only that you were found near him."

Saul stilled and gazed into Daniel's cold eyes.

No one spoke as Saul finally realized he was looking death in the face. His Adam's apple bobbed as he swallowed and fell silent. Finally he took a deep breath. "So ye're judge and jury with no witnesses for arguing, eh, Dan'l?"

Daniel's head tipped a fraction as he contemplated Saul's words, more impressed with the smuggler's dignity than he could have imagined. Courage, he admired. Courage deserved a hearing.

"First accusation, Saul," Daniel said. "You promised to snuff out Miss Roan and me should she prove to be untrustworthy." Unconcerned, Saul nodded, earning him a growl or two from Daniel's men.

"Second, she sent Becky to the village for the first time in years. To a buffle-headed cretin like you, that's proof that she's through with me, and reason for you to act."

"Third, you were on the hill with the killer, with your gun not fired and I didn't hear your shout until after I was shot."

Saul sunk his hands into his pockets, and a lopsided sneer appeared as he relaxed into an unconcerned slump. "Ar'ye through?"

"Aye, I'm through."

"Then, listen," Saul said, shuffling to rest on the other foot. "I admit being there. I'd been tracking you, but just for my own information and jollity. Unlike some other people," he said with a pointed look at Daniel, "I wasn't about to act until I knew I had reason—and I already knew about Roan's saying his gel couldn't leave the house."

At Daniel's frown, Saul explained. "I'm a careful man, Rockburne, and I figured trouble would start with the little gel, not you, so I had my own informer in Roan House. I'd only do *you* to death if I knew *she* was going to peach, and then I'd have to kill you both."

He shifted once more, this time with a grin. "Then, too, watching you two courtin' all over creation has given me more laughs than watching a dancing bear."

Daniel gritted his teeth as Bernard and his men chuckled, but Saul wasn't through shocking him. "As for the killer, I almost stumbled over him on top of the cliff."

"If you saw someone aiming at me, then, why didn't you stop him?"

"Ho, did I say I saw him aiming at you? Wal," Saul sputtered, "I did no such a-thing. First clue was when I heard the shot and recognized him. I fought with him, but your damned dog jumped in and butted me over the side—that's when I yelled. I fell and knocked myself out, but I hear tell that you knew where to shoot. So," he said with a cocky grin, "I figure that I not only saved your life with my yelling, but warned you where to aim your gun."

Bernard chimed in. "So you were close to him, but didn't see him until after he fired. What interests me, is what did you mean you *recognized* him?"

Saul shifted again, this time with a nervous shuffle that couldn't make up its mind which foot to land on. "Wal, happens I talked to him the day before—and before you let that temper roar, Dan'l," he said quickly, "hear me out. You see, he'd come asking if I wanted to slay you, and I said I'd have to think about it."

Daniel didn't know whether to leap out of bed and wring the simpleton's throat or to give into the laughter that sputtered inside him.

"Now," Saul said, shuffling again, "I figured if I was going to kill you m'self I'd might as well get paid for it—but if I decided not to, at least I'd be able to tell you about his offer, and you could capture him yourself. That way, I'd get the reward from you, and the truth is, I rather fancied keeping you alive over seeing you dead."

He nodded as if to validate his tale. "So, you see, Dan'l, I could have lied, or I could have let the fellow go just to keep clear of you, but the truth is that, where the time might have come that I had to *kill* you, I've never *lied* to you."

Daniel glanced at Bernard whose expression assured him that he had heard the story right. According to Saul, he was an honest smuggler out to make an honest bit of gold, no cards up his sleeve, but out on the table for all to see.

"So," Saul said, moving his hands from his pockets to clasp them behind his back, "what do you say, Dan'l? Are we friends or not?"

Daniel slowly drew the pistol from under the sheet. He waited while Saul turned ghost-white. "You know, Saul, when you first threatened my woman, I was willing to let you live—only because you could identify my father's killer for me. But now . . ."

Fourteen

"Waiting room, indeed," Harmony muttered bitterly, squirming on the torture-instrument masquerading as a hall chair. She'd been here an hour, while other clients trooped in and out as if they owned the place. Why had her aunt chosen such a man for her solicitor? No matter, her patience was at an end. Rising to her feet, she marched through the door to stand before the receiving desk.

The young clerk, a thin man who was all angles and pointy features, glanced up, but with a dismissing glance, returned to the document he was laboriously copying. She moved closer. "I have been waiting an hour to see Mr. Soames. I do not wish to wait any longer."

He lifted his pointy nose just long enough to let her note his importance—and her lack of the same. Before he could return to his writing, she leaned across the desk. "Young man, you march into Mr. Soames's office and tell him that I will only be here long enough to take my inheritance out of his care and place it elsewhere. I am sure he can spare me five minutes for that."

He was startled, at least she'd accomplished that. He even sent his gaze traveling over her person—tired features, drooping hair and faded dress—then a feral smile spread across his face while he deliberately went back to his work.

Knowing he was no use to her, Harmony looked around the room to see what other avenues were available. The clerk laboring beside the young tyrant sent her a fleeting grimace of sympathy, but obviously fearful for his job, quickly looked away.

Across the room, a pleasant, white-aproned woman, perhaps twenty-five years of age, had turned at the sound of Harmony's voice. As Harmony watched, she quietly abandoned her task to slip through the door upon which Mr. Soames's name was embossed in gold. Something about her alertness and furtive movements caught Harmony's attention, and she suspected she might have found the gateway to Mr. Soames.

A moment had not passed before the woman returned, and giving Harmony a quick smile, swiftly made her way back to the tea tray.

The door left ajar by the maid now opened. A tall, gray-haired gentleman strode through, his gaze darting quickly over the room, past Harmony, then back again. He frowned. "Miss Jones?"

The clerk finally found his voice. "A Miss Roan, sir, come to discuss her inheritance, *she says.*"

Mr. Soame's face flushed. "I am so sorry, Miss Roan—"

"A little too late for that, Mr. Soames," Harmony said, while he turned chalky gray. "I have been kept waiting in your little torture chamber for an entire hour while your *petty* clerk ignored and insulted me in turns. I have not been offered even a glass of water, or directions to your ladies' parlor." At this, the maid turned to stare.

The others were horrified to a man. Harmony could not believe that she had uttered such a bizarre statement. But, if she knew anything, she knew that to apologize was to lose all ground.

So, she attacked. "How much commission do you realize on an inheritance of ninety thousand, Mr. Soames?"

While the clerks remained frozen with shock, Soames recovered. Bowing, he made amends. "If you are anything like your dear aunt, Miss Roan, you will forgive my error in calling you the wrong name. As for keeping you waiting, please believe me that I did not even know you were here until Mrs. Noble called it to my attention."

He waved his hand toward the maid. "Mrs. Noble, please see to Miss Roan's comfort if you will, then escort her back here to me." The maid bustled across the room, dipped a bow, and led her from the room to, thank heavens, the very elegant ladies' parlor.

After showing her the amenities, the maid bade Harmony wait for her. Moments later she reappeared with the coveted tea tray with enough for two extremely hungry ladies.

The maid sank gratefully into the chair opposite Harmony. A winsome lady, Harmony noted, with sea-green eyes and hair the color of ripe wheat, softly pulled back from a finely boned face. Quick movements, but graceful like an excitable doe in an open meadow. She chuckled, a mellow sound that surprised Harmony, and began pouring with well-trained grace. "I am Laura Noble, widow. Thank you for that lovely moment," she said simply.

Bemused, Harmony reciprocated. "Harmony Roan, spinster. I should be thanking you. Had you not delivered me out of there, heaven knows what I might have done next."

Then they both began to laugh.

Harmony studied the young woman for a moment. "Is Soames a competent solicitor?"

"Very competent—brilliant really. It wasn't his fault that you were treated so badly. It's that toad, Mr. Dennis, but since he's Mr. Soames's nephew, he thinks he's God. And," she said with a sigh, "to us, he is."

"Dennis," Harmony said aloud, while Laura's eyes narrowed.

"Please don't make trouble for us, Miss Roan. Mr. Soames was bending Dennis's ear when I went back for the tray."

"How badly do you need this job?"

"Very badly."

"Does Mr. Dennis have power over your employment?"

"Yes," she whispered.

"Hmm," Harmony mused. "Tell me what you do."

A full half hour elapsed before they wandered back to the office. Soames still stood where Harmony had left him. Dennis stiffened at Harmony's entrance and Soames looked properly contrite, Harmony thought, and the interlude had given her back her equilibrium.

"Mr. Soames." She extended her hand as if he were visiting in her home. "Your dear Mrs. Noble has made me see the error of my ways, and I do apologize for raking you over the coals."

Eyes alight, Mr. Soames bowed over her hand. "Please forgive me, Your name should have been at the very top of my mind, but . . ."

Harmony cut him off. "Enough, Mr. Soames. I dislike hearing apologies almost as badly as I hate to offer them, and believe me, I have great experience doing just that."

Relaxed, he smiled. "Too gracious."

Mr. Soames bowed her toward his office. "Will you come through now?"

"Thank you," Harmony replied, her blood singing with energy. "I do have several concerns."

"Well," he said in a reassuring manner she liked, "now those concerns are in my hands."

"Now, Dan'l," Saul said, "didn't I give you what you have been asking for? Didn't I help you get him? And," he said, slowly as if Daniel might have forgotten, "isn't it true that I'm a man of my word?"

"Well, Saul, I don't recall your saying precisely that you might not decide to kill Miss Roan and me sometime in the future."

Saul opened his mouth to reply, but Daniel wasn't finished. "I don't like Miss Roan being fearful for her life, Saul. Not only that," Daniel added, waving his pistol for the pleasure of seeing Saul's eyes widen, "I don't like having you following us around spying on us."

Saul's chin rose at the insult. "Did you bump yer head rollin' down that hill, Dan'l? I just *told you* I wasn't going to kill you, but if you didn't catch on, I give you my word now—and I *never* change my mind."

Then he shrugged. "As for the other . . . I can't promise not to *look* if I happen by when you two are carrying on afore the rest of the world."

Daniel couldn't hold back a chuckle. "It's true that you've never lied to me. Saul. And it's true that you didn't say yes to the killer, and since your story might have a warped bit of truth to it, I guess the reward belongs to you. However," he added with a grim smile that clearly made Saul nervous, "I do have another proposition to make."

Instantly stilled, Saul frowned, "And what would that be, Dan'l?"

"I'm quitting the gang and going to London after my girl. I'm offering you my job if you want it."

"Gawd," Saul said with a fatuous grin on his face. Romance clearly had softened Saul's brain, Daniel thought—and his as well, if truth were told.

"You'd better think twice before you start counting your cut, Saul. Whoever wants our deal enough to kill me will turn his sights on you. Do you want that worry?"

"Ho," Saul said, puffing his chest out to show how brave he was. "He'd better not tangle with me."

Soames's lips twitched. "You're going to inspect my books?"

"Absolutely. I have handled my father's affairs since I was nine years old, and until this year, have managed to keep him in line."

His smile widened. "You remind me of your aunt—"

"I'm nothing like her. An ugly duckling to her graceful swan."

"Well, Miss Roan, you know the ending to that story." He opened a cabinet and handed her a package. "This is for you." At her quizzical look, he added, "From your aunt. She says you are to open it when you come to see me, but are to follow the instructions before opening. Would you like to be alone?"

"Let me see . . ." She opened the envelope pasted to the top. The note was brief. *If you need help of any kind, Soames will help you in any way. He is Completely Trustworthy, and an Absolute Dear!*

"Mr. Soames, do you know what is in here?"

He nodded. "Cash—a thousand pounds. For emergencies, she said. In case you needed it before you came of age. Do you?"

Harmony left the package unopened on the table. "May I tell you a story?" At his nod, she gave him the papers she had pilfered from Sanford and began her tale. As she catalogued her unpleasant voyage of discovery, including the necessary items of her interlude with Daniel, he looked through the papers, nodding as if he were not surprised.

"What did you tell Sanford about Beatrice's money?"

"I told him the truth—that she had left everything to you, which she did. I did not tell him about your hidden trust which included the house."

"Thank you. Not everyone would be so trustworthy. My aunt was fortunate to have you on her side—as am I."

Harmony opened the package and counting out half, pushed the rest toward Soames. "Will you keep this in case I need it in a hurry? And," she added, "I plan to travel after I come of age—with a chaperone and servants of course. Could you find some travel information for me—Scotland, Ireland, or the Netherlands? I prefer to not stir up my father at this time."

As he agreed, he scribbled something on the back of his card. "This is my home, please feel free to contact me at any time."

As they left the room, Soames handed Harmony's file to his nephew. "Your first duty as filing clerk will be to put Miss Roan's file away. Please see that your personal things are transferred to the back room before day's end." Dennis stood, horrified and clearly furious.

Beyond him, Laura turned at the wonderful news, watching Harmony with a touching sweetness.

"Don't forget, Mr. Soames," murmured Harmony. "You promised to increase Mrs. Noble's salary. Deduct it from my account."

"Don't worry. I'll see that she has everything she needs."

Harmony hesitated, reviewing all that Laura had told her about this office. She was a maid of all work, from scullery duty to preparing tea. What a mundane occupation for someone so cheerful and full of life.

Someone whose company she had truly enjoyed.

An idea formed, a tiny bud ready to blossom. "On second thought," she told Soames, watching Laura's face, "may I take her with me?"

Fifteen

Harmony stared in awe. *How had her father dared to buy this house?* Grosvenor Square was, she thought with rising hysteria, a neighborhood far too grand for a bad-tempered scholar and his daughter-turned-thief from the tiny village of Shingle Spit.

Further investigation only substantiated that opinion.

The stables, fragrant with sweet, fresh feed and hay, were an argument for Sanford's good management, and with a squirm of chagrin, Harmony repented having thought him without *any* good traits at all. Caulder's team was present as was its cheerful master.

The house was better—and worse—than she had expected. For some reason, the work was progressing downward from top to bottom. The bedchambers were finished, and were splendid—decorated in a collection of soft pastels to capture a sense of sunlight and breezes in a city that she understood often forgot that such a thing existed.

The public rooms downstairs were another matter entirely.

Barely a floor could be trod across in a straight line, some only at one's risk. Workmen had accomplished a great deal, but finished nothing. Everywhere was the debris of their industry, as if the house had been deserted by fleeing villagers—plaster-spattered scaffolding, ladders of every size, buckets half full of dried wallpaper paste or paint, brushes curling into grotesque mummified corpses.

Laura looked confused. "Where are the servants?" They had

investigated every corner of the property, and had it all to themselves.

"Hmm." She had neglected to get that particular information from the ailing Sanford or his housekeeper, but since they were nowhere in sight, she must do something. "How does one hire servants in town?"

"I'm sorry, Miss Roan, but I don't know. I've only just come to London, and found my job through an acquaintance."

Then a horrible thought occurred to Harmony. "Mrs. Noble, I believe I owe you an apology."

"You do?" Her eyes sparkled at the novel idea.

"Well, I'm pleased that you seem so cheerful, but the truth is that I just absconded with you and never bothered to even ask you if you wanted to work for me. It's just that I've never been in a position to control any part of my life before, and you seemed to be in the same position . . ."

"I cannot imagine you *not* in control," Laura replied.

"Do you regret my having taken you away from Soames's? I do not recall either you or Soames resisting the idea."

"Miss Roan," Laura replied with a grin, "Mr. Soames would have given me to the slavers to retain your goodwill."

Harmony felt sick. "You did not wish to leave?"

"Heavens, Miss Roan, I was willing to follow you to the ends of the earth, just for the exhilaration of watching you put into action what I was powerless to achieve." Then she looked worried. "This wasn't just a whim on your part, was it? If I inadvertently offended you as Mr. Soames did . . . ?"

"Wait a moment," Harmony said, rushing into the house. She couldn't believe she had inspired such anxiety in the poor woman. She opened her bag and counted out a year's salary, then rushed back down to the gazebo. "Amends," she said briefly. "I'm sorry I made you worry. but this is my first experience of that kind, and I didn't handle it very well. Actually," she said sighing, "I feel as if any moment the real Harmony Roan will appear and send me to my room without any supper."

Laura stared at the coins in her hands. Then she began to laugh softly. "Well, Miss Roan, thank you for letting me be part of such an important day. Just tell me what you'd like me to do."

"I'd like you to call me Harmony."

"Are you serious?"

"Would it make you feel uncomfortable?"

"A maid using her mistress's given name?"

"Oh, no . . . Laura . . . I've hired you as a *companion*."

That night Harmony knew she was dreaming, but never remembering her dreams, she dared not awaken lest, upon sleeping once more, she could not find her way back . . . for she was fleeing and must not break her concentration and lose the ground she'd gained in her flight to freedom.

She was climbing a hill, running, actually, easily outdistancing her pursuers. Obstacles appeared—frightening, grotesque things— but she simply veered off like an agile deer and went round them. She was young and healthy and could conquer the world.

At first she'd been escaping alone, then gradually others began clutching at her—her father and his associates who screeched with fright as their feet slipped. After awhile she could see that she was not going to make it, for each time she lunged ahead, her muscles became weaker. And the more ground she lost, the more frantically would her dependents cling to her. *If only, she thought, they would help themselves, they could all reach the top.*

Then, suddenly, she saw Daniel above her, and—horrors of horrors—he was falling, would pass her by without even touching. Oh, Zeus, she thought, if their hands could only grasp and cling, they would both be saved.

But she could not maneuver quickly enough. While she, unnoticed, was sinking under the weight of those screaming for her help, Daniel was plummeting to his death. *Give me strength for one last try.*

Her fingers were bleeding now, and her toes stung where she dug them into the tufted earth, but she turned off the pain and went straight for Daniel as he, too, twisted his powerful body to reach her. Neither had she time to avoid the loathsome obstacles, and so, shuddering, she closed her eyes and pulled herself over them—losing her dependents one by one as they recoiled in fear.

After awhile, her own fear of them waned, turning into fury. And fury turned into strength. And then she used the blasted things for stepping stones. Lighter now in her solo climb, she went faster and faster, almost soaring now as Daniel's hand neared hers, she knew how fragile was that magic rhythm of body and mind. *And she knew failure would only come if she let herself dwell on the impossibility of it all.*

Bernard, laden with a string-tied package, strode into the room with a smile on his face—and immediately roared at Daniel. "What d'you think you're doing sitting up?"

Daniel, seated snugly in a wing-back chair, rolled his head sideways to see his accuser's face. "Letting my muscles know I'm alive."

"No need to hurry the process, Daniel. I've agreed to go check on your woman, and our bargain was that you behave yourself."

"Aye, and the stronger I get, the sooner I shall join you. What's that you're carrying?"

Bernard handed the parcel to Daniel with a flourish. "From your lady love, via your men who travelled straight through to deliver it."

Frowning, Daniel ripped it open. "What the . . . this is *money.*" He shuffled through it, looking for a note. "*£200 for my dismissed servants. Please look after them.*" He crumpled it in his fist. "She sent all this cash—with smugglers? The woman's a menace."

"Help," Harmony mumbled, "we're being invaded!" She rolled off her bed and ran to the rear window. Workmen's drays filled the mews, and laborers were making themselves at home in her garden.

The floors and walls vibrated with the tromping of boots and bellowing voices. She donned her wrapper and hurried to the door, intent upon rousing Laura. She found her in the hall, perfectly groomed, coming toward her with a tray of fresh strawberries and clotted cream. "Good heavens, what a treasure you are."

"You have no dishes," Laura said, indicating the mismatched pieces on the tray. "Just a few cracked bits left behind."

"I suppose I must start a list," Harmony replied, scampering back into her room. She cleared away a collection of knick-knacks—a pair of miniature blackamoor figures and an Indian snake dancer on a pedestal from the round table near the corner window, thinking how wonderful it would be to collect her own foreign oddities in person.

Laura hummed happily as she arranged their breakfast. "Somehow the workmen discovered we had arrived," she said. "One burly fellow asked me if you had any money, and when I told him you were not only wealthy but generous with it, he gave a great whoop and brought in his troops." She chuckled. "However, we may have to climb down a tree to get out of the house."

Harmony laughed. "Have any servants arrived?"

"No one has heard of any expected servants."

"Satan's teeth," Harmony muttered—then clapped her hand over her mouth as Laura stared in horror. "Sorry," she whispered, "I've been country-raised." *Keeping bad company, more like.*

Barely hiding a grin, Laura rushed around flinging all the windows open, then returned to serve the rare delicacy. "In London, wonderful things just come to the door, Miss . . . Harmony. Peddlers come singing and calling out their wares."

Harmony smiled, and at first bite, moaned in delight. She was going to like London.

"In what endeavor are you engaged for your father?"

"My father is a scholar, and I am his scribe," said Harmony.

"And translator," she added, somehow needing to reaffirm her own abilities, not for Laura's ears, but for her own.

Then she noticed something odd.

"Why are you not eating?" She glanced over the table and found only one plate—hers. Heaving a great sigh to show her exasperation, she piled more berries onto her plate, and when her portion matched the serving dish, she plopped cream on that helping and pushed it toward Laura.

"When I let down my skirts and put up my hair, I was pushed out of a cozy kitchen and made to eat alone in the dining room. Now that I have acquired a companion, I no longer wish to be lonely at the table. And for your gross neglect," she said, handing Laura the serving spoon, "you must use this most inelegant utensil."

Laura sank down on the chair and took the proffered spoon. "Well," she said simply and began to eat. It was a comfortable silence, Harmony decided as they practically inhaled the wondrous food. And because they sat near the side of the house that had no walkway between, they were close enough to the neighbor to have a lovely view of their climbing roses along the fence.

And close enough to hear conversations, she thought noting to herself that London gardens were no place for confidences. After a moment of eavesdropping, she realized that what she heard was a rather heated confrontation. And weeping. She rose from her chair and looked out the window. Without apology for snooping, Laura joined her.

"M'girl won't be trouble to you," the woman servant insisted.

"Servants don't bring their brats to Preston House," said the arrogant butler.

"But I've been housekeeper here for three years . . . and m'mother's passed on, and my Rosie has no place to live."

"If you keep sniveling, Bessie, I'll send you on your way without a reference." With that, the hardhearted butler left her alone in the garden.

Harmony's heartbeat sped faster. "Hmm," she mused, watching the abject figure weeping her heart out.

Laura cleared her throat. "Don't do it, my dear."

"We need a housekeeper, and what would it hurt?"

"The aristocracy don't like people interfering with their servants."

"She won't be their servant long."

"She hasn't made up her mind."

"But when she does, we won't know it, and she might be on the streets with a child to feed."

Laura sighed. "Can I stop you?"

"I don't think so."

Sixteen

Harmony dawdled as she descended, in wonder at the lovely house. Laura jaunted down ahead, humming as she went, precipitating a sudden outburst of whistling and salutary comments. Alarmed, she turned back to look for Harmony. The laborers' friendly greetings fell silent as Harmony joined her and the two girls traipsed down the stairs together. In her elated frame of mind, Harmony found herself wishing she might have been *noticed* as well.

As for running the watchful gauntlet as they descended, since ladies were taught from birth to *not see or hear* unmentionable things about them, they reached the garden without mishap.

By the time they made it to the fence, the distressed housekeeper's weeping had trickled down to whimpers and sniffs, but still had the power to elicit sympathy from her intended rescuers. The first problem, Harmony decided, was the leafy barrier between them. While the brick wall only reached her chin, fruit trees along the interior boundaries had been left unpruned to run amok and now presented a tall, prickly barrier of suckers and untamed branches.

"Bessie," she hissed as loudly as she dared. Immediately, the sniffing ceased, and Harmony wondered if the distraught housekeeper would think she was being hailed from her own house. "I'm in the garden beside you," she added blindly, feeling more foolish every moment. Laura, the gudgeon, watched and wrung her hands.

"Who are you?" came the hoarse reply. "I thought the house was vacant."

"I'm the new owner . . . and I'm looking for a housekeeper."

"You may bring your child," added Laura.

"Can you come round through the mews?" Harmony asked, anxious to be finished with the business. Expecting an answer, Harmony hesitated, feeling like a Punch and Judy handler whose characters talked back, but only at their own pleasure. "Can you come now?" When Bessie didn't answer, Laura and Harmony looked at each other, and with tacit agreement hurried back toward the mews.

The gate between the garden and the stables opened. "Are you the ladies of the house?" The housekeeper had arrived.

As for Bessie, it was clear from the way she skirted around them, that she was somewhat leery of ladies who did their hiring over the back fence. Harmony led the way to what she thought might become her favorite spot—the gazebo—and promptly got to the point.

"I am Miss Roan and this is my companion, Miss Noble. My father will be arriving soon. We need to hire servants, and although I'm sure there is an easier way to accomplish it than eavesdropping, we were touched by your predicament."

Bessie listened to Harmony with half her attention on the message and the other half examining the unfashionable ladies in the gazebo. "You've *rented* this house?"

"No, my father has a purchased the lease, just recently, which is why the renovations are being done."

Bessie's face cleared, and Harmony realized that the housekeeper had doubted their ability to afford life in London, much less pay her wages. "Then," Bessie said, all attention now on Harmony's face, "is it true I may bring my Rosie with me?"

"Yes." This from Laura who seemed determined to negotiate for the child in question.

"When do you need me? May I come at once?"

Laura looked at Harmony for an affirmative answer. At Harmony's nod, Laura took over. "You'll be our first servant, and since we desperately need a housekeeper, you'll be welcome at once."

"Your *first* servant?" A strange expression hovered, but then, all wreathed in smiles, Bessie bounced to her feet. "I shall report for duty in an hour."

"Here she comes," Laura said from her vantage point in the gazebo. She and Harmony had spent the interim enjoying the relatively quiet spot in the garden. "She has someone with her, but it isn't a child." She leaned out through the opening to get a better look and as Bessie reached the stable, Laura flopped back down on the seat. "You're not going to believe this, Harmony."

"What?" Harmony replied, scrambling across to lean out the same opening. "Oh, my goodness." She swept Laura a conspiratorial look of surprise, then waved at the visitors. "Over here, Bessie."

"I'll bring Rosie later, but this is my sister, Tessie," the housekeeper said, stopping at the bottom step. Standing side-by-side, they were mirror images, red hair and freckles with robust bosoms that gave Harmony a definite twinge of envy. "Tessie is a pastry cook."

"Twins," Laura whispered. "Twin sisters."

"Is it all right, bringing Tessie? We always work together."

Quickly masking a dawning smile—for she'd been smoothly out-maneuvered—Harmony welcomed Bessie's sister. Intending to exit the gazebo, she stood. "Shall we go inside and show you—"

"Oh, no need, Miss Roan," said Tessie. "I know the house upstairs and down. My sweetheart, Moffett, used to work here. He's working two houses over, and misses this place; he'd worked here for ten years when they sold the lease."

Harmony and Laura exchanged glances, both worried about the tiny pebble of compassion they had so innocently rolled down the hill. Laura found her voice first. "What was his position?"

"Butler, Mrs. Noble, and with Moffett to supervise the men, and my sister over the women, you'd have a good beginning."

"Of course," Tessie added, who as her sister, had quickly deduced the ladies' inexperience, "you'd have to offer him a bonus to come on short notice."

Two days later, Harmony's descent down the staircase was accomplished to the lovely sound of *silence.* Once Harmony had transferred a sum of cash to Moffett, miraculous things began to happen. The new butler, whose managing ways cast a tall shadow over the twin sisters' meager efforts in maneuvering Harmony, had inspired the workmen to finish by working in shifts, day and night, in order to be ready for Sir Roan's anticipated arrival.

The man was a whirlwind of efficiency. Harmony liked the idea of having an efficient henchman at her service, just as Moffett had liked the bonus she'd surprised him with the day the laborers bid them good-bye, leaving behind a refurbished home she loved down to the smallest detail. So different from her home in Shingle Spit, every room glowed with sunlight and spring-garden colors.

As she reached the foyer, the door knocker rapped an imperative tattoo on the brass plate. Moffett immediately appeared.

"Who are we hiring now?" she asked, smiling as he drew near.

"At the front door?" His eyes rolled in friendly reproof, but when he opened the door, two more servants had clearly arrived.

"They're turning the sooty gravel over in the back, so we had to come round," one apologetic man explained. Moffett waved them in, and turned to Harmony. "Peter, your new doorman and Charles, groom of the chamber."

Harmony's eyes narrowed. "Where did they come from?"

"Across the square," they answered cheerfully.

That gave Harmony a warning twinge, but she had an even more imperative question. "But what do we need with—"

Moffett stopped her with a warning look and sent the men

back to the kitchen. As they left, she lowered her voice. "I do not mind you looking after our needs, Moffett, but that doesn't mean we need such a complex staff. And," she added before he could reply, "you may call Peter a doorman if you wish, but he'd better be willing to do more than open doors. As for a *groom of the chambers,* I have no idea what such a person would do."

"Miss Roan," he said, aghast at her ignorance, "he will greet visitors, take charge of the visiting cards and either announce them or declare the family 'not at home.' And," he added quickly lest the lady find those duties not enough, "he makes sure the fires are lit and the room lighting is maintained; he will open and close the house, and stock the writing desks—"

"Goodness, Moffett, what will the doorman be doing? Standing there sucking his thumb?"

While he stared openmouthed at this, the first touch of anger from her, she had another thought. "How did you get them, Moffett? You didn't steal them, did you?"

He raised his narrow chin an inch—a guilty inch. "They are simply coming home, Miss Roan."

Her anxiety grew. "In Shingle Spit, the small town I come from, such actions are considered piracy."

"This is London. If you want respect—" he began, but was stopped by the sound of yet another knocking. He shook his head and opened the door.

Then frowned at the stranger standing there.

Harmony had difficulty placing the man as well. He was neither servant nor aristocrat. Built broad as a boxer, with an air of command, he looked her over with an almost personal interest. Had they met before? She looked beyond him and saw something she did recognize—Daniel's stallion, Newgate.

For a moment, she thought she might faint, so frightening were the implications that raced through her mind. Daniel never let anyone ride his horse, everyone knew that. So, if this man was here—

"Daniel?" she whispered, her hand extended toward Newgate.

"Lord bless you," he said with a worried look, "Daniel's all right. Sorry that . . ." He looked back at the horse. "I gave you a fright."

She didn't quite believe him. "He never lets anyone ride Newgate."

"Well, the beast needs the exercise with Daniel injured—"

"Injured?" She *was* going to pass out . . .

"Just a bullet wound," he said in an attempt to calm her.

His words were lost entirely as he disappeared in a cloud of brilliant white stars.

Seventeen

She awakened with the deepest sense of humiliation. She had never fainted before, and to find that she had lain helpless before these people, looking who knows how disheveled . . . and that bitter smell at her nose! Close by, she heard Laura's voice. "She's coming round."

"Rockburne will kill me."

"Laura," Harmony pleaded, raising a hand to her nose, "please take that away." Laura removed the burning feather and began mixing a white powder in a beaker of wine. "For the pain," she announced as she stirred it briskly.

"It will make me sleepy, and I have no time to sleep, Laura."

"Doctor's orders." With surprising coordination, Laura lifted Harmony to a sitting position, and with a clever pinch of Harmony's nose and a judicious tip of the glass, Bessie and Tessie got the noxious stuff down.

Before Harmony could protest, a backlash of pain from the movement exploded in her head. "Good God," she whispered, fighting a rising nausea as the pounding slowed, "did my head hit something?" Lifting her fingers to her head, she found it swathed in bandages,

"The door," Moffett reported. "You hit the door."

"And my knee," added the stranger.

"And the ground," Laura said, watching the stranger. "She bled on the pathway."

"A great deal of blood," he replied solemnly, as if to indulge Laura's penchant for accuracy.

Moffett winced at their indelicacy, clearly annoyed at the others usurping his explanation. "The doctor came and bandaged you—"

"And left, with her not even awake," the stranger growled, clearly disgusted with the absent doctor. "Rockburne's going to kill me."

"Who," Harmony said behind clenched teeth, *"the devil are you?"*

Bernard sighed and moved closer to the bed. "Bernard's the name, Charles Bernard. Rockburne's steward. And, Miss Roan, I'm sorry I explained it all wrong. Rockburne's fine. When you feel a little better, I'll tell you all about it."

"Bernard." Harmony mouthed the word. She'd heard of Bernard, back when all those rumors of Daniel were finding their way to her. He was the man who saved Daniel's life and captured one of the assassins. And stayed at Castle Rockburne.

"Please, everyone," Harmony said, looking at the little crowd in her bedroom, "may I be alone with my visitor?"

When protesting murmurs began, Laura cast a sweeping glance over Bernard's broad shoulders, then took a few seconds to study his face. He returned the inspection with an amused interest, which made her scamper in the other direction. "I'll leave the door open," she said, shooing the others out before her.

Harmony motioned to the chair nearby. "Tell me everything."

Bernard hesitated, looking from the bandage to her face that was, no doubt, sickly-white. Finally, he folded himself stiffly into the chair. "Right then," he said gruffly. "Here's how it happened. After you said good-bye on the beach, Daniel and the killer shot each other. The killer's dead and Rockburne's up on crutches and feeling fine."

Harmony sat straight up and stared at him. *What did he say?* Like thick pudding on the boil, a dozen questions bubbled up at once. Finally, one stuck. "He was shot the night before I left?

He was *wounded* when I left for London?" She pressed her fingers over trembling lips. "All this time I've been worrying about a *house,* and he was *hurt?* How badly was he hurt? Tell me everything."

Bernard frowned. "I just did."

"Bernard! Where was he shot, who did it, was he hired or the real assassin?"

"Oh." He looked relieved. "Rockburne was shot in the leg— by a fellow named Sedgewick who hired his father's killers. He was paid by someone else, but we don't know who."

"Sedgewick? She was so surprised at that news that it took a moment to put the rest of the pieces together. "So the man who wants him dead will just send someone else, only Saul can't identify this one?" Bernard shrugged as to say that was the way the tide came in, and no one could change it. *Men,* they were incomprehensible. "But Daniel is going to be all right," she said slowly, "or you would not have left him."

Bernard nodded, relaxed and leaning back, his hands resting easily on the arms of the chair. She might have thought he was truly at ease if he weren't watching her so carefully. Could he see how foolishly she wanted to race back to Rockburne Castle and see Daniel for herself?

"Saul . . . is Saul still worried I shall betray Daniel?"

"No, Miss Roan, that matter is settled. He's got Saul's promise to leave you both alone, and his promise is good—"

A knock on the open door interrupted them. "Miss Roan?" Laura said. "A messenger has just come with a package from your father. Do you want it now?"

"Yes, thank you. Bring it here, will you?"

Laura entered with a careful vigil on Bernard, circling wide around his chair as if he might be dangerous. Bernard observed her lazily, amusement barely hidden, as she handed Harmony the packet and rushed out of the room with the same nervous avoidance.

Harmony tried to untie the string, but her fingers wouldn't work. Blast the doctor's tonic! "I'll do that," Bernard said, leaning forward and making short work of opening it. She thumbed through the papers. Changes, she thought, and a letter.

She sat up. "Excuse me while I read this . . ." It was a short note, but the news was not good. "My father's coming," she said aloud. "He's bringing all his guests to stay *here*—and he's coming in two days! How am I to get everything done? We need more servants, and food, and linens—we don't even have proper dishes." Zeus, it was impossible to even think about, especially with her brain half-foxed.

"It's so blasted *hot* in here." She pushed the hair off her forehead—then remembered that what was falling down over her eyes wasn't hair, but a very tender bandage that didn't like being touched.

She needed *air*. "I shall open the window," she announced, maneuvering herself onto her feet and several steps forward before teetering to a halt. Her poor, drugged body hadn't liked that swift motion, and it was protesting with a definite *woozy* feeling. And, her tongue was going to sleep.

Bernard stood at once. "Miss Roan, you should rest, let me open the window for you."

"Would you?" she said, grateful that she didn't have to walk across the room when she could barely stand where she was. She'd better get to bed. She turned, only to find that the bed was *moving*. Bernard stepped forward to help her, but she waved him away. "Don't help me—hold down the bed."

"Right," he said with a chuckle, but he supported her elbow anyway. She felt better once she was tucked under the covers, except that all her emotions were tumbling out, babbling all her secrets.

"I'm in trouble here, Bernard," she called as he swiftly let fresh air into the room. "M'father and Beckman are galloping down the street, and here I am, dragging along behind them, getting all bumped and bruised while they're having a fine time."

"Is that right, miss?" he said, returning to his chair.

"You see, Bernard, the problem is that some of the people *like* me and some of the people *want* me. My father doesn't *like* me but he *wants me*—so he sold me to Lord Beckman. D'you know what I went for? Half a house and Beckman's hand in marriage . . . *and* fame and fortune . . . *and* m'father keeps the rights to all my work forever—not a bad price for a country girl from Shingle Spit."

She thought he might laugh at that, but all he did was growl. "Rockburne asked you to go away with him—why didn't you?"

She grinned. "Rockburne *likes* me, but he doesn't *want* me."

"Rockburne's your betrothed, girl. You could hie off to Scotland and marry the man," he growled again, reminding Harmony of Mrs. Pollard's suggestion. "He'd take you in a minute, should you ask."

"I'd like the trip," she said, floating into the air. "I've never been to . . . Scotland . . . and I already know the language."

"Is that right?" His words were correctly spoken, but his amused expression belied his agreement. Not understanding it, she extended her hand to speed him on his way before she fell asleep. "Thank you for coming."

Properly ignoring her hand, he bowed with great solemnity. "Rockburne sent me here to take care of you, and as of this moment, you see before you your new steward." For some strange reason, she relaxed and welcomed the sleep that beckoned.

Eighteen

Golden hay flew into the morning sunshine as Daniel limped forward and slapped the riding whip against his leather boot. "What do you mean, Bernard took Newgate to London?"

The cringing stableboy could barely speak. "Said you'd kill yourself . . . said it would keep you home . . . said a soft coach would do if the need was great." He backed up and grasped the top bar of the empty stall. "Said you wouldn't budge until he came to get you."

"Who gives the orders here?" he asked coldly.

The boy's eyes widened. "You do, m'lord."

"Get the coach ready. Two coachmen, four outriders. *Now.*"

Harmony felt a little like a conspirator, and her accomplices numbered three—Moffett, who thought his place as butler held authority in this situation, along with Bernard and Laura—and their task was to bring the household up to snuff in the short time remaining before her father arrived with his guests.

"That's it for servants and supplies," Moffett said, ticking off the last of his fingers. "What's left?"

"A good cook," Bernard added. "Who is the best?"

"The *best* is across the square, but—"

"Get her." Moffett gulped and fell silent. Bernard emitted a disgusted grunt. "I'll get her myself, Moffett, give me her direction."

"Moffett?" Harmony had to ask. "Am I going to be inundated by irate neighbors for stealing our neighbor's servants?"

"Not at all, Miss Roan, this sort of negotiation is handled in the butler's pantry. If anyone should be so ill-mannered as to complain, you will never know of it."

By the next morning, she knew better than to trust Moffett's word. Not only had every hour been peppered with irate voices emanating from the butler's pantry, their *parvenue* mistress was branded the villain of the piece. Zeus, she thought, what if her father learned that she had imperiled their entree into society? It didn't bear contemplating.

What she could not understand was why the servants themselves were not concerned. Was there not some kind of status among servants, some layer of society into which they wished to fit? But, no, their faces were cheerful. They nodded to each other in great camaraderie, one might even say *smugness*.

With one exception.

Upon hearing a strange noise, she followed it to a window overlooking the square and found Moffett with an expression she never expected to find on his face—stark terror.

His unblinking gaze remained paralyzed into one position, and if she focused on that same point of view, the arresting sight that seemed most unusual, eccentric even, was the imposing matron marching straight toward their house . . . straight in an even line through early morning traffic, ignoring bellowing coachmen who barely missed her, young bucks trying desperately to calm their rearing mounts, and screeching milkmaids whose hanging buckets were swinging wildly as the lady simply pushed them aside.

She was magnificent.

She was coming to Roan House.

Harmony knew instantly who she was. "The cook's mistress," she murmured to Moffett who, in turn, managed a croaking sound that she assumed meant yes.

"Well connected, you said."

"Umm." He was thawing out. *"The duchess."*

"Bring her here to the parlor." When he did not move, she leaned toward his ear. *"Moffett!"*

By the time Moffett returned to announce the duchess, Harmony had worn out several emotions and was working on a rather garbled mixture of fate and kismet in whose absolving arms she'd hoped to escape to during the upcoming interview.

Moffett announced her. "Lady—"

"Yes, yes, yes," interrupted the visitor, "Get out and leave us alone—and shut the door." Then, as Moffett scrambled to obey, she locked her dark gaze onto Harmony's and searched—and found, Harmony was certain—every sin Harmony had ever committed.

While thus transfixed, some wandering part of Harmony's brain took stock of the enemy. Not so tall as *erect.* Dark hair with dark chocolate eyes. Her skin, stark-white with the faintest trace of pink to soften it, clung to her marvelous cheekbones with a tracery of fine wrinkles that betrayed an age that must reach toward the seventies. Perfectly coiffed hair framed a still-beautiful face etched with sorrow, but not defeat.

No dowager's dress for the duchess, Harmony noted, but the latest, most vibrant style. Harmony could not imagine her in anything less.

The duchess took the first shot. "Who are you?" Her voice, low and penetrating, gave no quarter.

"Miss Roan," Harmony began, but the lady waved her hand impatiently to interrupt.

"I *know* your name. What I want to know is what kind of person would move into Grosvenor Square and commit so many bird-witted idiocies in one short week."

It was probably the *bird-witted* that did it. "Perhaps we should exchange names and idiocies, madam, before we begin the battle." It was lovely to see her taken aback. Even lovelier to see a trace of admiration and a reluctant smudge of amusement flicker in those dark eyes.

She hesitated only a second. "Fair enough."

"Would you like to sit—or are we to pace off?" Surprise this time, and more amusement.

Harmony pulled the servants' bell while her visitor scanned the room, then walked to the least comfortable-looking chair in the room, an eighteenth-century oaken relic that allowed her to remain upright while leaning against the solid carved back.

The door opened. Moffett awaited openmouthed at the sight of their formidable neighbor sitting calmly in a chair.

"Tea," Harmony murmured pleasantly, sending the butler rushing out of the room. Exhilarated, Harmony settled herself opposite the grand dame. Having won a few skirmishes with her own father, a dragon of sorts himself, Harmony waited.

Pausing only long enough to weigh Harmony's willpower, the ogress plunged right in. "I am Lady Talbourg. As for exchanging idiocies, to date I acknowledge no idiocies on the scale of yours."

Lady Talbourg—why did that name sound familiar? "Not even strolling uninvited into a perfect stranger's home and insulting her? In my neighborhood, it's considered worse than idiocy."

Lady Talbourg lifted her head as if to sniff the air. "Fair enough once more, Miss Roan. But extending that fairness," she said grimly, "perhaps you might explain why you deliberately pilfered my cook—enticed her with a king's ransom—when she has been with me for over ten years."

A king's ransom? How much did Bernard give to steal such a gem away? And she was just that, Harmony thought, remembering the exquisite meal they had enjoyed the previous night. As for her response, the truth would do just as well as any other.

"I have been sent to London with the commission from my father, Sir Temple Roan, to set things to right before his arrival. He is . . . *a tyrant* . . . an exacting man who does not allow for mistakes, and he is bringing many guests with him. This is to be a triumphant season for my father, for his life's work will be published this season."

Lady Talbourg's black eyes snapped angrily. "This is your excuse . . . a pressing schedule? There are agencies, Miss Roan. One does not need—" Then she stopped and tipped her head as if remembering something. "Roan . . . what town are you from?"

"Shingle Spit, Lady Talbourg. It's a small seaside village on the Sussex coastline. Have you heard of my father?"

Lady Talbourg ignored her question, instead asking her own. "Tell me of your life there."

It was a curious inquiry, but Harmony could see no harm in it. "The village is small, with a coaching inn and perhaps two dozen shops. Our villagers make their living in sheep and crops and . . . fishing."

"Fishing . . . ?" The word begged a better answer.

Harmony grinned. "Well, a bit of smuggling . . ."

"That does not bother you?"

"Not at all," Harmony replied, thinking how differently she might have answered a mere fortnight ago. "In truth, their leader is my best friend."

"How very . . . democratic. Tell me about this friendship."

Harmony chuckled—as much at the strange conversation as with the memories the conversation roused. "Actually, the man was my childhood nemesis. I was frightened of him for years." Lady Talbourg leaned slightly forward, encouraging Harmony to tell the tale whole. "Then recently I accidentally walked into his landing party, and his associate wanted to do me in . . ."

Lady Talbourg's hand fluttered to her chest. "Oh," Harmony hurriedly assured her, "nothing unfortunate happened, thanks to Daniel."

"Daniel," mouthed the lady, her face incandescent. "How did he save you?"

"Oh," Harmony said, blushing suddenly. "He declared we were sweethearts and . . ." she trailed off, suddenly engulfed with memories that only became more precious as she realized how she wished the farce had been real.

She was grateful to have the tea cart rattle its way into the parlor at that moment, and vowed to begin the painful business of jettisoning such useless thoughts. The ceremony of pouring soothed her, and it was not until Lady Talbourg murmured her approval over a pastry that she realized how far her mind had drifted.

And, surprisingly, Lady Talbourg's face held a dash of mischief. "Strawberry puffs. You have Tessie here?"

"And Bessie as well."

"However did you get those girls? I tried for years . . ." Lady Talbourg gasped at her own *faux pas,* and the women stared at each other, each biting back smiles.

In unspoken agreement, tea was enjoyed with only social chatter to accompany it. When they were finished, Harmony rolled it out of the parlor herself and firmly closed the door.

"Finish your story," Lady Talbourg ordered, reclaiming her superior status.

Harmony shrugged, not wishing to think of Daniel any longer. "We kept the pretense up until I moved here last week. And so my wicked smuggler became my friend."

Looking out of the window with a distracted air, Lady Talbourg's voice softened. "Tell me about your Daniel."

How charming, Harmony thought, following Lady Talbourg's glance. She's lonely and wishes to hear a story to while her time away. Harmony went back to the beginning and told her everything—omitting Daniel's cousin, Lord Beckman—embellishing it with all the details that would touch an old lady who remembered a sweetheart of her own.

When she finished, she glanced at the lady, and found tears flowing down her crêpey cheeks. Stunned, she didn't know what to say, and so, said nothing. *Then she remembered.*

Lady Talbourg—Daniel's grandmother.

"He's the most honorable man I've ever met, your Daniel."

The duchess brushed away her tears. "You know?"

"I just remembered his grandmother's name."

"And you . . . ," Lady Talbourg said, with great conviction, "you care for him."

Harmony meant to deny it. Indeed, opened her mouth to do

just that, for there was no purpose to such an acknowledgement. But another glance at Lady Talbourg's face brought the truth to her lips. "I do, but I'll get over it."

"Must you?"

"Can you see us together? My father hates him—actually, he nearly had him hanged years ago."

Lady Talbourg's face froze. "Indeed."

"He's the magistrate," she said simply.

"And Daniel, does he love you?"

Such longing in that old face, Harmony thought. "He thinks I am something of a pest," she said to soften the truth. "And since I saved his life once, he feels indebted to me." Another glance at Lady Talbourg's touching expression made her add one item she had omitted.

"We kissed."

Lady Talbourg's head raised quickly, her eyes alight. "Kissed?"

Harmony grinned. "On a moonlit beach," she said dreamily. "Of course the smugglers were up on the bluff cheering us on."

Lady Talbourg chuckled in delight.

"The kiss, though . . ." and then she could not go on, not even for his grandmother.

"Perhaps," Lady Talbourg said, rising briskly to her feet, "we might continue this conversation at another time." Harmony could see that the lady was badly shaken. She rested her trembling hand on Harmony's arm. "Will you accompany me home?"

"I would be honored," Harmony answered, knowing she had made her first friend in London.

"But," she added hesitantly, "may we use the footway?"

Nineteen

"Oh, your grace . . . look!"

"What on earth . . . ?" Lady Talbourg replaced her pen in its holder and turned toward the window, amazed to see her companion practically doing a jig as she pointed out the window. With an amused smile—one that had often made its way to her lips since meeting Harmony Roan the previous day—she stood and joined her.

From her vantage point, she could see nothing amiss. Everything looked just as it should . . . flowers bloomed in rectangles and squares, the precise geometric pattern her late husband's parents had established the year of his birth. Inside those disciplined borders—in wild abandon—bloomed her own random scattering of perennial sweet william, thrift, and white lilies mingled with annuals of sweet pea, violas and stock.

Lilac hedges bloomed along the walls among fruit-bearing trees, giving her the double pleasure of her own blossoming trees intermingled with the scent of lilac—a triple pleasure if one counted how outraged her friends became when they saw a duchess picking nectarines like the veriest country girl!

"Where shall I look?"

"Near the stables . . . see the coach? Watch the gate, he should be coming through any moment." And then she saw him . . . *Daniel.*

Her lips trembled at the sight. So tall and powerful—so like his father. So full of life—so like her own Caroline.

His very presence breathed life into her garden. As he passed, servants glanced up, looked again, and then in ripples, the excitement began. One after another, they searched for her face in the upper window to see if she knew. Grins blossomed, work stopped. And as Daniel passed, leaves fluttered into the air then drifted slowly down, changing . . . everything.

Her companion started toward the door. "Shall I bring him up?"

She shook her head. "He's using a cane. I'll go down." She hurried to the door.

Daniel maneuvered up the steps, leaning far too heavily on his stick to please him. His grandmother waited on the top step, concern on her face as she eyed his cane. So strong, this valiant lady, so unbending in her dignity, so steadfast in her belief that some day he would relent and take his place in her world.

Each time he came to celebrate her birthday, he vowed that he was strong enough to stand unaffected by her machinations. Vowed that a man whose prowess against the thugs of his world would, this time, rise above the petty irritations she rekindled. Each time he lost the battle and fled back to a world he understood, where the rules were his and propriety was a word in someone else's vocabulary.

Nevertheless, he was glad to see her, to bask for a few moments in her eagerness to be with him. She glanced curiously at his cane, but strangely, said nothing. He reached the top step and leaned to kiss her dry, scented cheek.

"My love," she whispered simply, and turned to lead the way back into the house.

"Miss Roan," Moffett said softly, waiting in the open library doorway to get her attention. "There are *people* on the front door—to see you. Shall I send them to the back?"

"No," she replied, grateful for an excuse to leave the stack of work for a few moments. She followed Moffett to the foyer and gasped in delight to see Sorrel and Biggins on the doorstep.

"Oh," Harmony said, "I'm so glad to see you." Moffett cleared his imperious throat. "Moffett," Harmony said, hugging Sorrell as she entered, "this is my aunt's lady's maid—now to be mine—and her husband, Biggins, who is a coachman."

Moffett watched in amazement as Harmony grasped Biggins' hand and gave it a squeeze. "We came at once," Sorrel began.

"You'll need our help—and someone to keep that Boris in line," Biggins added. Harmony leaned forward and whispered in his ear. As the brief tale of Boris's dispatchment enfolded, Biggins roar filled the entryway. "Tell you later," he told his inquisitive wife.

Responding to the noisy commotion, Bessie appeared at Harmony's elbow. "Bessie," Harmony said, giving introductions once more, "take them to the servants' quarters and give them a nice room, then bring them back when that's done."

Moffett rolled his eyes and walked away shaking his head.

Daniel stirred his tea. To his regret, there were no pastries in sight, but perhaps his presence was too unexpected, and Grandmother had lost her preference for sweets. "I have a boon to ask, Grandmother."

"Yes?"

He balanced the fragile cup on his knee. "I owe a favor to a friend." When a curious smile met him, he went on. "She—"

"She?"

"A neighbor in Shingle Spit who has come to London." As Lady Talbourg nodded graciously, he related Harmony's story. "I thought to take Robbie out of the picture and place you in his stead. It sounds peculiar," he admitted at her startled look, "but I thought if you were to rather forcefully insist Sir Roan accept you as his sponsor—offering an influx of money he could not refuse, funds which I will provide—Robbie would no longer have a hold on either Roan or his daughter."

"Robbie, a rather nasty little boy," she mused with a frown. "He's taken after his father, I suppose. His mother, Rose, is a sweet little thing. Used to invite me to her little literary salons, but I can't like having someone tell me what to think."

"What do you think of my scheme?"

"Excellent plan," she said, surprising him, for he thought she would find the deception distasteful.

"You'll do it?"

She gave him a mischievous glance. "Imagine the pleasure it will give me to do this to the man who intended to hang you."

"Who told you about that?"

"His daughter, Miss Roan did." At his amazed look, she explained. "She is, after all, a neighbor, and I went over one morning to . . . welcome her to London. I discovered who she was, and your name entered the conversation."

"What did you think of her?"

"I thought her a most unusual girl, Daniel. She made me laugh."

"Aye, she does that."

Her eyes shone with mischief. "You love her, then, and this is a ploy to win her?"

"Nothing gets by you, does it, Grandmother?" When she smiled, he ventured another query. "Do you know how she feels about me?"

"She's fighting it, she thinks it wouldn't work." She watched his face. "She liked kissing you."

"She told you that? Perhaps I should just abduct her." He was only half jesting, wondering how shocked she would be. She surprised him entirely.

"Just like your father," she said. "Did you know he came storming into my parlor, demanding I tell him how to get Caroline to admit she loved him?"

He laughed. "My father did that? What did you say?"

"I told him Caroline was so stubborn that he had to let her think it was her idea, that I'd been opposing it so she *would* marry him."

"You wanted the marriage?"

"Heavens, yes. Your father was the first *real man* she'd ever met, and he loved her fiercely. I wanted that for her—and the alternative was one of those tip-toeing poets she was so fond of."

It took him a moment to absorb that picture. "Then, would you give me the same advice over Harmony?"

"From what you've told me, you'll be walking a fine line, but it would be best if she brought her whole heart into a marriage. If she becomes endangered—then I wouldn't wait. But, she is just across the street, and we're here to help her, so there's little to worry about."

"Aye." He sipped the cooling tea, then frowned.

Lady Talbourg rose to her feet and plucked his cup out of his hand. "I cannot imagine why I keep serving you tea." She placed it on the tray and headed for the sideboard. Lifting the stopper out of a decanter, she lifted it up for his approval. "Brandy?" At his grin, she poured a portion into two glasses and resealed the container.

When she handed the glass to him, she lifted hers in a toast. "To confounding our enemies." He joined in salute, then sipped with pleasure. "No pastries these days, Grandmother?"

"In a moment," she assured him with an enigmatic smile. "My cook has decamped, and we have taken to buying them from a neighboring pastry cook who has set up a little business in her mistress's kitchen."

Daniel laughed. "How very enterprising."

A maid entered with a heavily laden tray. "Ah, here they are," Lady Talbourg said, "You must try the strawberry puffs."

As he enjoyed the treats, she filled him in. "Miss Roan has worked wonders with Roan House. When she arrived, the laborers had abandoned it for lack of funds, and she has solved her problems with an unusual flair."

"I can imagine," he growled. "She no doubt showered them with cash, and they will rob her blind. She sent two hundred pounds to me for her discharged servants' care—by my men, if you can imagine!" When the duchess grinned and shook her head over Harmony's antics, Daniel slipped in an innocent question. "Did she seem happy?"

"More tired, I would say, but not suffering unduly. She seems a bit homesick, I thought." As Daniel leaned forward at that news, she chuckled. He had never seen her so happy. "Am I to arrange this sponsoring business through my solicitor, or shall I speak to the man myself?"

"Well," Daniel said, "I thought I might become your ambassador, so to speak, and administer the business myself. That would give me entree into Roan House where I could . . ."

"Shall I invite her over? Will she be privy to our scheme?"

"No, I think our first meeting must be when we initiate our plan. I would rather Roan not know Miss Roan and I are acquainted."

"I understand completely, Daniel. Her father sounds the perfect scoundrel. I shall put my mind to the terms of our association and see if we cannot tie the man in knots."

He grinned and lifted his glass. "To revenge."

"To restoration of all good things . . . and speaking of good things, my dear, your clothes . . ."

They arrived in the middle of the night—her father and his friends—more jovial than usual, having endured the last leg of the trip with numerous stops at inns along the way. To her relief, Sir Roan took brief note of the house's interior, and to even greater relief, he noticed the servants not at all.

Despite the fact that he was castaway with grog, he watched her like a cat, frowning at her midnight déshabillé. She hated the anxiety that churned inside her. And when he leaned down and kissed her cheek—a gesture seldom given even in her childhood—her stomach burned with worry.

She took a warm glass of milk upstairs and, sipping, sat upright in her warm bed to formulate best how to handle her father tomorrow. She must accost him with the truth, for when Sanford discovered her father's letters missing, he would report to Sir Roan—and her father would know what she had discovered—

for her devious snooping, like a mouse sneaking out of the flour bag, had left telltale tracks behind.

Truth to tell, she was glad.

All her life she had handled her father with the lightest touch. When she'd saved Daniel and his father, she had been able to put words into Roan's mouth, to pat and caress and soothe his runaway temper so he wouldn't have to face it himself.

She never questioned her procedure anymore than a night-pacing mother would balk at a little whiskey on a baby's sore gums, or a nurse would question distracting a wild-tempered child with a sweet. Her father was simply throwing a tantrum, and she was using whatever means necessary to quieten him down before he began breaking things—in this case, people's very lives—and he went on his way as if nothing had ever happened.

Her father had changed, though, and so had she.

She finished the milk and placed the glass on the bedside table. Sinking back into the pillows, she stared at the ceiling. Her simple life had gotten so very complex. First, she'd only wanted her father's attention. Then, she wanted to learn enough to dazzle him and his friends. Then she saw Beatrice's life and the idea of traveling—like her father and her adventurous aunt—caught fire, kept her going, gave her something of her own.

Then came Daniel. And Saul. And the betrothal that was real in a strange way to Daniel, and to her if the whole truth must be told, for she'd kept veering off in her thinking—wanting Daniel with her emotions when her brain knew how foolish she would be to choose that life.

What *was* clear was that she no longer had to return to Shingle Spit. Now that Saul was no longer necessary to Daniel's quest, he had put Saul in order. At last, she could escape, to travel, to be on her own. She rolled over and stared at the flickering flame of her bedside candle. *She still wanted to travel, didn't she?*

She reached deep inside her, whipped up the old enthusiasm, gathered all the wonderful pictures of what she would see and write about—and rolled them past her mind's eye. Yes, she still wanted to do it, but what happened to the *joy?*

She sighed. It was, she supposed, muddled up with all that had happened. Then, the only thought left was to decide how to handle her father now that he was here. Should she do as she had always done?—coddle him, see to his comforts? That part was easy, something that gave her pleasure as well. And if he threw a tantrum?—she would be willing to soothe and distract him, to protect his reputation and those who might be hurt by his actions.

As for the rest—his schemes to use her—nothing but complete honesty from now on. She would face him as an adult.

Could she do it?

What would her father do then?

"Stultz," Lady Talbourg said firmly, "Ten Clifford Street off Bond Street." At her grandson's pained expression, she gave him a stern look. "Do you wish to ruin the entire scheme, you need only present yourself in those . . . seafaring clothes."

He nodded, but not willingly. "Aye, I'll do it."

"And Truefitt & Hill on Old Bond Street. He'll do something with that unruly hair."

She looked off into space. "You'll need a stickpin—Rundel's will do well enough . . . and boots . . ."

Sir Roan sent an approving glance around the library, a room to which she had given the bulk of her attention. She had duplicated his own room in Shingle Spit, save for the bookshelves which were sparsely filled but neatly at that. "You've done very well, Harmony."

"Thank you, Father."

He tapped the stack of finished papers on the table. "All finished?"

At four this morning. "Yes."

She ventured a question. "Do you like the house?"

"Very much."

She could not resist suing for another compliment. "Do you like what I've done with this room?"

"Done with it?" He looked around once more, this time frowning. "It seems just as Sanford described it. It will be far more pleasing when they finish the draperies." Noting her confusion, he made an exasperated sound and waved his hand at the windows. "I cannot like this glare, Harmony. Surely you do not mean to leave it like this?"

She tried for a steady voice. "I shall have heavier ones made at once, Father." He blinked at her conciliatory tone and studied her for a few seconds. Then he smiled briefly and waved her to a chair.

After he'd seated himself, he folded his hands over the stack of papers with an air of anticipation. "Lord Beckman will wish to call on you, take you places, show you London."

A sharp jolt of fear hit her at the thought of his certain fury, but she took a deep breath and replied calmly. "I will be happy to see him, but I must tell you that when I speak with him, I will tell him that I cannot marry him."

Instantly, his eyes blazed. "Are you deliberately defying me?"

Very slowly, she counted to ten—in Portuguese. "Yes, I am. You told me Beckman was interested. I asked you to discourage him. You said that it was all arranged, completely ignoring my very clear opposition to the plan. Just because you and Beckman think it is a good idea does not mean I am willing to sacrifice myself to some scheme the two of you have concocted for your own convenience, including," she added with a pointed emphasis, *"buying this house with him—with my inheritance."*

His face turned red and broke out in sweat. "How in blazes did you discover that?"

"Mr. Sanford demanded that I look at your correspondence to prove that you were corresponding with him privately. I saw your letters."

He swallowed and his eyes began blinking. "All of them?"

"You should be ashamed of yourself, Father, going behind

my back to see if Beatrice had more money you could get your hands on."

"She had a fortune. Why d'you think I let you go to her every summer? And what did she do with it all, I ask you that?"

"Perhaps she had it buried with her. You could rob her grave I suppose—I wouldn't be surprised if you did."

He stood and leaned toward her in his favorite intimidating pose. "This is intolerable. Apologize at once!"

Then he began to swear wildly, his voice rising as he let himself go. She almost gave in, almost lied to calm him down. Standing, she rang the bell for John and strode quickly to pour him a glass of wine. He took the drink and gulped it down, his fury raging, but slowing down. She set her hand on his shoulder and rubbed lightly back and forth. When his bunched muscles softened, she sat down beside him.

Satisfied, he nodded. "We are too close to our goal for you to lose it for some frivolous reason." When she did not reply, he frowned. "You do look a bit haggard, Harmony. It won't do to lose him over your looks. Do something . . . *something* with yourself."

She looked directly at him and prayed for an unwavering voice. "I am sorry for making you unhappy, but that does not mean that I will marry Beckman. I will not. You may keep insisting and wish to argue the point, but I shall not change my mind."

He leapt to his feet. "Back to your old ways, Harmony? Arguing with me, making excuses? I thought we had that problem solved . . . no, don't you walk out of here . . . I haven't finished with you . . ."

She rose and walked out of the room, leaving him to John. As the valet rushed down the hall toward her, she remembered something her father had said. *"Do something with yourself."*

So, she did exactly that. She marched around the square to see Lady Talbourg.

Twenty

"And so, Laura, Lady Talbourg will be calling for us in the morning, after which we shall go with her to the shops."

"You just walked over to see her—a duchess—just like that?"

"She asked me to call on her."

"Dear heavens, Harmony, you are dangerous."

"Ahem."

Harmony raised her head from the library table and glanced quickly toward the sound that had awakened her. Laura stood just inside the library, shaking her head at Harmony's having worked through the night. How long had she lain thus? She had fallen asleep in the middle . . .

Oh Zeus, the work. She had not finished the corrections her father had brought from Shingle Spit. Sending a swift, heart-stopping glance toward the clock, she scrambled to her feet.

Sir Roan and his coterie would be just finishing their morning meal and would at any moment be trooping cheerfully into the library. Worse, when Lady Talbourg came for her this morning, he might forbid her leaving. She reached for the incriminating papers.

Too late.

Her father marched into the library, a confident Pied Piper to the younger set who noisily followed him. Sure enough, as he passed her on his way to the end of the table, he sent a quick frown at the small stack of unfinished work before her.

Harmony's thoughts flew. She must leave at once, for if the men followed their usual pattern, they would sprawl in their chairs blowing smoke all over the books and draperies, *talking,* an activity that seemed to require Harmony's rapt attention. Once they started, she would be trapped.

Why, she wondered as the buzz of voices increased, could their guests not go home to their own rooms while in London? Immediately she knew it was a foolish question, viewed with a surfeit of venom because of her fatigue. They, to a man, save Lord Beckman, hadn't a feather to fly with, and had, as usual, given up their rooms when they traveled so eagerly to the generous bed and board of Shingle Spit.

It had ever been thus—not that other, influential scholars did not revere her father—but, Sir Roan liked the constant stroking of his ego. And, truth to tell, she normally liked having them clustered around as well, for it kept her father in a state of peaceful equilibrium.

Ignoring his pointed scrutiny, she gathered up the papers and placed them on the sideboard, preparing to leave the room.

"Dear Harmony, ever laboring in a good cause," drawled Beckman as he strolled toward her, kissing her as usual. How many unwilling brides had been driven, one habitual rite at a time, into submission?

As Beckman returned to take his chosen place at the end opposite from Sir Roan, Harmony took a step toward Laura, trailing her excuses behind her. "If you will excuse us, gentlemen . . ."

As a speedy escape, it might have worked—if Moffett had not appeared in the open doorway. Harmony stayed where she was, tensed for a hasty exit as soon as the butler cleared the way.

Unfortunately, he had other plans.

With a smug expression, he announced their visitor. "The Duchess of Talbourg!" Then, with a great flourish, he bowed the duchess in. Harmony's heart sank, while behind her chairs rattled as the men rose to their feet.

"Ah, my dear," Lady Talbourg said sweetly, stopping before Harmony, "I hope I find you well?" It would have been obvious to a child that Harmony looked a veritable hag, but as the duchess leaned forward to clasp Harmony's hand in hers, she *winked*.

Harmony's crotchety mood instantly disappeared. Suspecting the old darling was up to something, Harmony waited with the same excitement she'd once felt at the arrival of traveling players in Shingle Spit. Was there ever such a marvelous woman?

Lady Talbourg moved forward once more—then stopped before Harmony's father. With a flourish, she raised a pearl-chained lorgnette to peer at him. "Sir Roan," she said, as a schoolmaster might address a recalcitrant boy with a frog in his pocket. "I hear you are something of a scholar."

Sir Roan tried for dignity, but stunned at the unexpected admiration from such a great lady, and impressed with his own admirers bowing with such deference, he could barely speak. "I have that honor."

"After hearing your praises sung so lovingly by your daughter, I have made some inquiries of my own." Then she stopped, stretching the silence to place the obvious question—*what had she discovered?*—onto the high plane of suspense. No one spoke. Sir Roan seemed transfixed by the drama of the moment.

Lady Talbourg dropped the glass and sent another searching glance over his person as if to reassure herself that the man before her was no imposter. "I have decided to *sponsor* you."

For the second time that morning, the room exploded with the young men's voices, all excited as if they had earned the accolade themselves. "So gracious," and "Too kind," and "What an honor," were overshadowed by the agreed-upon, "Too condescending."

Harmony could not resist glancing at Lord Beckman—and was chilled to see a violent fury twist his features. Well, she thought briskly to dispel the strange feeling that crept over her, what man would not be angry in such a situation? Beckman had discovered her father, had poured his attention into bringing Roan into the spotlight, had expended funds toward that effort.

She should be feeling sympathy, not anxiety over Beckman's natural reaction.

She watched carefully as Lady Talbourg, who was quickly becoming Harmony's idol, strode a few feet back to reach her great-nephew. "Robbie, dear," she said, kissing his cheek, "I understand that you have been carrying this burden upon your shoulders. May I offer my thanks for supporting this great man with such wisdom and generosity?"

"Well, I . . ." Beckman began, clearly willing to expound upon his own nobility, but his eyes narrowed as the duchess busily turned back to the others. Neither did he like what she said next.

"I have, of course, arranged all with my solicitors"—this to the awed exclamations of the company—"but have left the rest to be managed by my grandson." Then she frowned and looked round the room, bellowing in her husky voice, "Where the devil has that boy gone?"

Harmony virtually reeled with shock, saving herself only by grasping Laura's arm to steady herself. *Daniel here?*

Daniel—oh Zeus—seeing her like this?

Then the duchess's words sunk in. *The duchess replacing Lord Beckman, thus weakening his link with her father? Daniel administering Lady Talbourg's sponsorship of her father? Daniel entering Sir Roan's home with such glorious influence?*

Even as she sent a searching glance toward Lady Talbourg, she was half-sure she must be dreaming. But, oh, the brilliance of the plan . . . concocted, she knew, by that devious Daniel Rockburne.

And, once again, Lady Talbourg winked.

"That's your cue, Rockburne," said Bernard.

Daniel ran his hand through his hair, annoyed as usual to find it no longer than his collar, and then the damned stuff would *curl* at the neckline. He sent his gaze skimming down over his attire. He felt like a clown at Astley's, but at least he'd convinced

Stultz to forego garish colors and give him something in simple black and white. How on earth had the busy shop managed to deliver it this morning?

But here he was, for all his sins, about to take the stage.

Just a few feet away from his love.

Satan's teeth, how would she respond to seeing him?

It took only a moment to reach the library, his heart pounding more erratically with each limping, cane-aided step. He stopped at the doorway and looked in . . . and there she was, looking absolutely . . . *dreadful?*

In an instant, his calf-love-hesitancy exploded in a fiery blast of fury. He strode forward. "What in the hell's happened—"

Lady Talbourg stepped in his path and, glowering back at him, stopped him cold. "There you are, my dear. Come make your bows to Miss Roan and her father, and Robbie, of course. The others," she said, turning to open a path, "I have not had the honor of meeting. Perhaps Miss Roan would do the honors?"

Harmony knew she was being spoken to, could hear the words in fact, but they were being uttered in some language she had yet to learn. *Daniel.* Daniel here in the room with her, that wonderful face *scowling* as usual. Had there ever been such a wonderful face as his? And that incredible *growl* as he found something wrong? All those nights wishing for just one more moment with him—and here he was . . .

She took a second look. Zeus, he wore civilized clothing, and his wonderful hair only reached his collar—and curled?

Panic struck as Daniel met her at her father's side. This wasn't going to work. Her father would take one look at the smuggler he so heartily disliked and throw a terrible fit. "Sir Roan," Daniel said politely, making his bow.

"Lord Talbourg," Roan said—erroneously, for that was his grandmother's surname. Daniel opened his mouth to correct him, but could see that Roan was too exhilarated to really see him—nor would he probably recognize Daniel at first glance— he was too stunned at this cataclysmic change in his fortune. His previous sponsor, Lord Beckman, might be well known in literary circles, but having the duchess's backing was akin to hobnobbing with royalty.

Harmony gave Daniel her hand. The shock of touching her almost ended the farce. The Rockburne curse may have jolted him, but *he loved this woman*. Still holding his hand, she dipped a small curtsy as he bowed over those precious fingers. "Are you enjoying London, my lord?"

The clever little devil, asking just the question that would be the most awkward to answer. "I am now," he murmured for her ears only, paying her back with the blush she could not halt. He searched her eyes. Did she know she loved him yet? Glowing back at him were treasures enough—for such intense delight and merriment, such *affinity* as if they were alone in this vast room—were good enough for now.

"Here is Lord Beckman," she said, leading them away from Sir Roan's hearing. She lowered her voice. "Behave, now."

"Rockburne," Lord Beckman drawled as they drew near. "How did the duchess ever drag you into this?"

Daniel shrugged. "You know Her Grace. If she gets an idea and you're standing anywhere nearby, you get recruited."

Gloating, Beckman sought to torment. "Must be galling to be the duchess's errand boy. And to cater to Sir Roan who nearly—"

"Lord Beckman," Harmony said in a warning tone, "Do not start that again." She turned to Daniel. "And the same advice applies to you, Lord Rockburne."

Beckman didn't like it, but he was pleased to see her turn on Daniel. "The lady has developed a temper, better mind your step."

Daniel smiled as if mildly interested. Letting his cousin even scratch the surface of his composure would be contrary to his plan. He'd vowed to woo and win Harmony, and that meant playing the gentleman. His *methods* for winning her were not so noble, but, then, neither was he.

Harmony touched his arm to direct him toward a waiting group. "Lord Rockburne, may I present Lord Haughton and his brother, Mr. Lewis?"

"Haughton." Daniel gave the portly earl a bow. "We've met before, when my grandfather passed away. Didn't know you were a scholar."

"I like reading," he said, "and Miss Roan's an angel."

"I'm Tony," his cheerful brother said, pushing himself forward. "I remember you. Handy fives, if I recollect correctly. Dropped me like a rock."

"Did I? I'm sorry if—"

"No, really. Honored to be dropped by a man of your stature. Now that you're staying in town, I'd like to hear some of your adventures."

"D'you know our Miss Roan from Shingle Spit, Rockburne?" This interruption from Lord Haughton whose true literary motives were becoming increasingly clear.

Tony answered for him. "It's a small town, Mark. Bound to be acquainted." He turned to Daniel. "Bet she's broken a heart or two, though. Not a man who can see that smile and not be smitten."

Good God, Daniel thought, was there a man here who wasn't half in love with her? He met the others and had to admit that none of Sir Roan's admirers were foolish or old or unhandsome—nor did they look upon Harmony with simple avuncular admiration. No, he spotted more than one gentleman's eye casting affectionate glances laced with lustful appreciation.

No matter that dark circles underlined her eyes or that her hair looked like a robin's nest, he could see why they lusted. And he realized that—with the exception of their meeting when she was but a child—he had never seen her without some concealing covering. Even in the Pollard's tea shop, she had worn a draping shawl to cover her charms.

Now, however, he could see the truth—even in one of those everlastingly faded dresses, her figure was enchanting.

Abundance was not the keyword, although every curve blared her femininity to the males within eye view. It was the way they flowed from hill to dale that made him ache to hold her, as if each movement were an unconscious dance of seduction. Even the curve of a shoulder invited a kiss in that enticing hollow, as it had on the beach at home.

Satan's teeth, the dress was so old it was obscene, and when she walked, her hips flowed into long, firm thighs, delineating every charm that should be hidden from the lascivious eyes of the men in the room.

He looked away, clanging the gate closed on his lustful thoughts. He had important work to accomplish here today. His future and Harmony's depended on his strength and cunning—and a clear head.

Even now his grandmother was lending her incredibly managing ways on his behalf, and for once he didn't feel like bolting. "Sir Roan," she said, sitting at the table, "this is the agreement my solicitor has drawn up. Please read it, just to be sure that you have no questions."

Sir Roan sank heavily into the chair he'd risen from at her entry. Like the dazed man that he was, he began to read. It led him through legal phrases that took everyone's concentration to understand, and when he came to a part that surprised him, he stopped.

"How much per month?—good God!" He lingered on the enormous amount until finally, Lady Talbourg had to cough to break him loose.

Then he came to a bit he did not like. "Sir Roan will . . . ensure that his daughter will be free to accompany Lady Talbourg to various social events of Lady Talbourg's choosing?

"Your grace," Roan protested, "my daughter has *work* to do."

"But," the duchess said smoothly, "I understand that you are soon to be published, and surely you will allow her a time to rest, and to enjoy the season she was denied when her aunt passed away . . ." As Sir Roan hesitated, mulishly stubborn, Lady Talbourg raised her glass to an imperious eye. "Is there a problem?"

"Not at all," he mumbled, pulling the papers back below his jutting chin. He bent his head to read, but not before he sent Harmony a look that bode her no good.

After that, it got a bit boring, and to everyone's relief, he finally came to the last page. "And," he read aloud with a sigh, clearly pleased to have reached the end with no more unpleasant demands. "My grandson, Daniel Rockburne . . ." Slowly, his head rose, and like an animal scenting the enemy, he searched for the man in question—and found him. "Daniel Rockburne," he said, rolling the name over his tongue as if he had tasted something spoiled. "Rockburne of Shingle Spit?" It was obvious he had not really *looked* at the duchess's grandson.

Daniel had heard that tone before, had seen Sir Roan change before his eyes as his temper raged. Would he do so now? Surely not before his admiring coterie of men—or his new, outrageously wealthy benefactress. With a smoothness that revealed years of practice, Harmony drifted near Roan and laid a soothing hand on his shoulder.

Sir Roan's fingers clenched the edge of the agreement until his knuckles turned white, then in tiny increments, he relaxed. Like a man with an aching fever, he began to read. "My grandson, Daniel Rockburne, will become the student of Sir Roan— or his daughter, Harmony Roan—to become educated in things cultural and literary, so he may take his rightful place in society as the Duke of Rockburne, a title going back . . ."

Roan was clearly incensed. As Daniel prayed it would work, he shared a tense glance with duchess. *How would Roan react?* They'd been like naughty children together, he and his grandmother, planning Sir Roan's downfall and Harmony's emancipation.

Roan's voice rose as he stabbed his finger into the writing and looked up at Lady Talbourg. "Is this a jest, madam? You are actually acknowledging your grandson? He is a criminal, a smuggler who defies the law year-after-year in my own town, just as his father before him."

Not a word was spoken as the company waited for the duchess's response. One of the young men coughed, but quickly smothered the sound. Daniel expected his grandmother to jump in and take up the fight, but she surprised him with her silence.

He looked to Harmony. Her eyes were wide with fear that her father would destroy himself. No matter how he despised Sir Roan, Daniel could not let that happen and, he realized, the duchess knew it.

This was the pivotal point of their plan and the real beginning of Daniel's place in Harmony's life. Relating successfully with her father would break down barriers nothing else could touch.

The resolution rested in his hands.

"Sir Roan," Daniel said carefully, his thoughts scurrying ahead of impending disaster, "as executor of this agreement, you must know that I am here to carry out my grandmother's wishes. She admires your work and likes your daughter. However, it is an offered gift, freely given. If you wish to decline, she will withdraw without any ill wishes toward either you or your daughter."

Roan, a cautious look replacing the wildness in his expression, was at least *listening*.

"On the other hand," Daniel continued, "if you feel your work is important enough to benefit from the cachet Lady Talbourg's name will lend it, and you feel that her generous bounty may be used to benefit your associates . . ." He waved a hand at the others watching so quietly ". . . then you might remember that it was you who acquitted me and my father of any crime when Lt. Sedgewick dragged us from our home with no evidence, but only to benefit his career."

He paused long enough for that information to sink in. "You neither are, nor were you ever part of anything illegal, nor were my father and I ever charged with a crime other than Lt. Sedgewick's own vile attempt to fool you—which, if you remember, you were clever enough to see through."

He could see the relief embrace Sir Roan. He did not want to throw the gift away, that was clear. As for the rest, Daniel could only plead his own case. "If you feel that it would take too much of your valuable time to tutor me yourself," he said, as though reluctantly giving up first choice, "I would be honored with instruction from a daughter of yours." How much thicker must he butter this bread?

Roan didn't like it. One could almost see his mind running around in its cage, rattling the bars, only to find out there was no escape. "She may tutor you, but only after she has finished her work and it is in the hands of the publisher."

Daniel's gaze shifted from Roan to lock with Harmony's own. Such fragility, he thought. How much more was she to endure at her father's hands? What was she thinking behind that bewildered expression?

"And when will that be, Sir Roan?" This from the duchess, who clearly held the power in the room.

"Weeks," grumbled Roan into the table, but before he could elaborate, everyone heard Harmony's clear reply. "I shall be finished tomorrow. The publisher is expecting the package before day's end."

The duchess sealed the agreement. "There, you see? I shall forego our shopping this morning, Miss Roan, in the interest of your dear father's important work. Then," she said, rising with a straight-backed stance that would have made any governess proud, "in two days we shall *transform you* as your father requested . . ." at this Roan's head rose abruptly ". . . and in the afternoon you may begin tutoring my grandson."

She clapped imperiously for everyone's attention. When she had their attention, she gave them the grand news. "On Thursday next I shall hold a reception to announce our wonderful news. You are all invited, of course. We'll have dinner and dancing and cards for the gentlemen . . ."

In the background he could hear the tension of the room dissipate as his grandmother took over, maneuvering everyone into a celebration. Servants were called, refreshments ordered.

Still, he and Harmony searched each other's faces.

And then he moved.

Twenty-one

Daniel strolled toward the doorway where Harmony consulted with the servants. "Miss Roan," he said formally, bending over her hand, "please assure me that you will not mind laboring over so uneducated a brain as mine."

Behind him, conversation halted in mid-word. Almost palpable was the company's blatant fascination with so unlikely a literary match.

Harmony's anguished glance fluttered past Daniel to the others, her color fading as they awaited her reply. Then, and as he had seen her do so many times, she raised her stubborn little chin. "Rockburne," she began, and then clearly remembering how he hated his title, her lips twitched. "My dear, *Lord Rockburne,* please rest assured that no matter how difficult the task, I would be delighted to honor Lady Talbourg's request."

The duchess broke into a coughing spell, while at the door, Bernard suffered a similar affliction. Laura and Moffett had disappeared and were back now with a bevy of footmen bearing trays. At the sight of refreshments, the room's inhabitants lost interest in Harmony and the smuggler duke. Grateful for the privacy, Daniel couldn't resist pressing a kiss against Harmony's fingers. Her lips parted and her breath caught in a charming little gasp.

A fierce thrill of satisfaction tore through him.

He'd imagined a hundred scenarios for this meeting, not all of them ending the way he wanted. He'd seen her surrounded by a swarm of aristocratic scholars, and known he'd lost her—seen her looking upon his rough countenance, and turning away—worse, he'd seen her pity when he followed her into a milieu where he did not belong.

What he hadn't forgotten was this magic between them, one he understood, even if she did not. She glowed when he touched her, and she melted with a kiss. It wasn't much, this tiny ember of passion, but fanned properly—rather *improperly*—it could tip her into his waiting arms.

Flushed, she raised her fingers to what once had no doubt been a proper coiffeur. "I wasn't expecting . . . my hair . . ."

". . . a veritable rat's nest," he drawled, waiting for her response with an amusement he hadn't felt since she'd left.

She didn't disappoint him. Up went the chin. "How unkind of you to . . ."

". . . notice?"

"Comment, Daniel Rockburne! A gentleman would never . . . you're *teasing* me, are you not?"

"Missed it, have you?"

She tried for a casual shrug. "It's not so bad when you know it's a game."

"Want to play another game?" She shook her head—but curiosity hovered in the air. He grinned. "This time we shall be sweethearts and spend our time convincing everyone we are not."

"Did that bullet strike your brain, Daniel . . ." Then her face crumpled, and her fingers flew to her mouth. "Oh, Daniel," she said with an anguished glance toward his cane, "I haven't even inquired—are you hurting? Should you be standing on your wounded leg?"

"It's healing." he said, dismissing the subject. "What about you? Grandmother said you are working too hard."

"I'm fine," she said with the same impatience with formalities when they had so little opportunity to speak. She leaned forward eagerly. "This sponsorship? Was it your idea?"

"Aye."

"I knew it! It's absolutely brilliant, Daniel." She paused. "How long can you stay—must you hurry back home?"

"Oh," he drawled, "I'll be back soon enough." *With you.*

Lord Beckman's rather penetrating voice intruded from across the room. "Harmony, my dear, shouldn't you be . . ." He let his words trail off, letting the rebuke take whatever interpretation the curious listeners might choose.

Instantly alert, Daniel watched Harmony's face as her gaze flew to Robbie's. "Now you can be rid of him," he murmured, pleased when she nodded, then looked back at him.

Her lips curved upward. "I'll speak to my father tonight."

"Indeed, Harmony." Sir Roan echoed. "See to your guests."

Watching Harmony's panicked start of alarm, Daniel suspected that he had underestimated Roan's hold on her. Or else, he thought with sudden clarity, Roan's last tantrum had negated all those small rebellions Harmony had related to him with such tentative joy.

She touched his sleeve—turning to him in time of jeopardy, he saw, without realizing that she did so. "I must go."

"I shall see you in two days. May we talk then?"

"Talk?" She smiled impishly. "My dear Lord Rockburne, you have *work* to do."

The arrival of port at the dinner table was Harmony's signal to leave her father to his evening pleasures. He liked his pipe and his port and his evening papers served like a finale to an opera. The minions were expected to leave him to it.

Instead, she waited. "It's been a lovely day, hasn't it Father?"

"A grand one," he agreed. "Imagine—the Duchess of Talbourg as sponsor. D'you realize what doors are opened to me? Dukes and princes will be reading my books . . . perhaps even the Prince Regent himself." He sighed and opened the paper.

"Now you don't need Beckman."

The paper slammed to the table. "Oh, he's been wonderful," she quickly assured him, "and he's still our friend . . ." Roan nodded with narrowed eyes, for he had heard the pause. ". . . but now we can drop this idea of marriage to keep his sponsorship." Lest he argue, she hurried on. "All the reasons for the marriage are invalid."

"You forget one thing, Harmony. We made an agreement, Lord Beckman and I, that he would let you continue working with me."

"Surely, that should be an agreement between you and me, Father, not a friend of yours." When the mulish expression lingered, she became desperate. *What could she offer in place of marriage to Beckman?* She needed something to hold him off for the three weeks before her birthday. "I've been thinking. I wish to travel and write—why don't we do it together?"

His shoulders heaved and his eyes rolled upward to silently beg patience from the ceiling. "I cannot leave now, Harmony. I am in demand all over town. Didn't you see all those invitations on the tray this morning? I've seen the world, now I want to remain home and reap the rewards of my hard work."

Of course, she thought, she would not expect it of him. *Think, what else might work?* "When I marry, my husband might be willing to live in Shingle Spit and I can still assist you. Or," she said, excited as the thought grew, "you could hire someone to translate for you. With your bequest from the duchess, it would be the simplest thing."

His head began shaking before she finished. "I've provided a husband already. If you chose your own, he wouldn't like sharing your time—or have his holdings halfway across England."

"Father, you're just being obstinate. I am not going to marry Beckman. You cannot force me to do so."

"Harmony," he said with an amused laugh, "girls are married against their will every day."

She ignored the sick nausea that clutched her throat. "But then you would have nothing, Father, for I would simply stop working."

He leaned forward, his forearms crumpling the paper beneath

them. "A woman with children can be coerced into anything, especially if she wishes to keep her children with her."

She swallowed. "You would not do that."

"Don't put me to the test." He leaned back and meticulously returned the paper to a neat, readable state.

She left, but not with the intention of submitting. Did he think he might threaten her and she would do nothing to prevent it, nothing to save herself? No, just as soon as the duchess's reception for her father a week's time hence—for she had waited to see him famous for so long, and her father would not make a move before that—she would leave. She would take Daniel up on his offer, would let him take her . . . then she stopped. She had her own money now, tucked away safely at Soames's office. She would leave with her own little retinue of servants surrounding her. She would *not* tell Daniel of her father's threat, for he would do something rash, like sacrifice his own freedom for hers.

The footman entered the billiards room and waited for Daniel to finish his shot. Daniel looked up then, and smiled at the sight of a note resting on the footman's tray. Breaking the seal, he read it.

Rockburne. Miss Roan is preparing to leave now. Bernard.

A few moments later he arrived at Roan House. When the doorman bade him enter, he could see that Roan and Robbie were just donning outerwear prior to leaving. "Sir Roan," he said, leaning on his cane.

Roan managed a pleasant, respectful bow, but Robbie didn't bother. "What are you doing here, Rockburne?"

Daniel spoke directly to Roan. "I came to take Miss Roan to the printer. I must speak to him as well, and she can introduce me."

"I don't think that's wise," Beckman drawled. "With Rockburne's history of attempted assassinations, it might be dangerous for Miss Roan to be with him in public."

"Not at all, Sir Roan," Daniel said, ignoring his cousin. "I have cut all my ties before coming to London, so I no longer have what the assassin wants. Then too, I travel with an armed guard."

Roan was torn, Daniel could see that. Not, he suspected over the safety of his daughter, but although he understood that the duchess's grandson was in a position of power over him, he hadn't considered that Harmony would be leaving the house with him.

Robbie, Daniel took pleasure in noting, was fidgety with impatience, slapping his leather gloves against his hand while he waited for Roan's decision.

Daniel moved toward Roan, invading the space a gentleman always gave another. "Is there a difficulty?"

Roan backed up. "No, Rockburne. I shall send a maid for her . . ."

"Good morning," Harmony said coming down the stairs, as if he had conjured her up. Daniel turned to greet her, instantly noting how tired she looked. She'd probably worked half the night, while everyone else slept. Behind her marched a footman with a heavy basket in hand, with Laura trailing behind. She sent a questioning glance toward him—*why are you here?*

"Rockburne's come to take you to the printer's," Roan said pleasantly. Harmony's eyes widened, and she looked back and forth between them, amazed at the sight. Daniel grinned.

Harmony caught her breath at that look on Daniel's face, *I'm in your house,* he seemed to say, *and talking to your father.* "Well, then," she said breathlessly, "shall we go?" Laura held back, knowing she was no longer needed. Daniel moved to the bottom of the stairs.

They almost made it.

An impatient volley of knocks rang through the foyer, followed by another before the footman could reach the door. Behind her, Roan and Beckman had reached the entryway as well.

The door opened. The man on the footway looked familiar, as did the gloating expression on his pointy face. *Dennis.* Dennis from Soame's office. What on earth was he doing here?

"I'm here to see Sir—" *He came to see her father. This was even worse!* "Mr. Dennis," she trilled, improvising as she went. "I've told you and told you to leave me alone." Dennis's mouth fell open.

"Father," she said over her shoulder, "this man is a fortune hunter who's been pestering me ever since I came to London."

Roan rushed forward, pushing the footman aside. "Get the hell out of here, you scoundrel!" Dennis fell back, horror and confusion turning him sickly pale. Roan grabbed the footman's sleeve to pull him forward. "If you ever see this blackguard again, take him out and throw him in the Thames."

Dennis scampered out of sight. "Thank you, Father," Harmony said demurely.

Daniel watched it all without a word.

He had her out of the house and into his coach before anyone could begin asking questions. "Now," Daniel said, pulling her shaking hands into his, "who the hell was Dennis, and why did you put on that act?"

She leaned back. "He's a clerk—nephew, actually—in the office of my aunt's solicitor. I thought at first he wanted to give me a message, but I couldn't think why Soames would send him here when we are supposed to keep the trust secret. Then he asked for my father." Shaking still, she sighed. "I must send Soames a note—"

"What did Roan say when you talked to him last night?"

She squirmed on the seat. "He clings to the idea that he needs me to work for him, but it's ridiculous since he could hire someone to translate and scribe for him, especially now that he has the money coming from the new sponsorship. I would be willing to pay that amount from my inheritance forever to just keep him happy."

She sat silent for a moment. "Perhaps it's not just the work that he wants, perhaps . . ." The coach stopped and a look of relief came over her features. She didn't want to tell him the rest.

He knew why she hesitated—that blasted independence and

her determination to keep private matters to herself. Too, she worried about his reaction to her father's infamies.

Well, that was too bad, for after talking to Bernard about her little drunken babbling, Daniel knew she had more to tell.

In moments, they entered Keaton & Sons, a small publishing house with whom Harmony had contracted over a year ago. Daniel carried the basket and followed Harmony in.

The noise of pounding presses assaulted their ears as the foreman took them to his office. While Harmony explained the change in names where the bills were to be sent, Gaunt, the foreman took stock of Daniel. "I'm sorry, Harmony said when she realized her error. "This is Lord Rockburne who will be in charge of the account. Where is Mr. Keaton?"

"Home, sick," Gaunt said. "He has the earache."

"Poor man," Harmony said, wincing at the thunderous presses. "He probably got it listening to this noise."

"Go to the coach," Daniel said to her. "I'll handle the rest."

Gratefully, she turned and hurried out. "Now," Daniel said to the foreman, "how long will this take?" Gaunt riffled through the papers, stopping to read the notes Harmony had attached to each item. "Can't even get to them for over two weeks. Then, three days, maybe four."

Daniel pulled a soft chamois bag from his pocket, hefting it so Gaunt could hear the clinking of heavy coins. Daniel set it down on the table and unfastened the top. Gaunt hesitated, then stuck his nose over the opening. He stepped back as if he'd been stung. "You want someone killed, m'lord?"

"I want this job pushed ahead of everyone else's. I want you working night and day—hire more men if you need. You have two days to get it finished. Do you understand?"

Gaunt's eyes widened. "I get it all? I don't have to share?"

"I don't care what you do with it. Just keep silent about our arrangement." Daniel turned and wove his way out of the building. Behind him, the presses stopped.

* * *

He took her to Talbourg House for tea, a particular request of the duchess. Upon arrival, the women forgot him entirely. Clothes were discussed. Before he could protest, they decided to *run to the shops*.

"Just a few shops," his grandmother promised.

"Just for an hour," Harmony pled sweetly.

Daniel stayed home and ate strawberry puffs, scheming devious ways to break Harmony loose from her habit of secrecy. It was an understandable trait, he decided, for keeping things from her father must have branded the habit into her heart.

Poor darling, she needed him, but could not admit it.

Finally, he took a nap and woke four hours later.

"Daniel," the duchess whispered urgently, jarring his shoulder to awaken him, "it's Harmony. She's fallen asleep in the coach and she's burning up with fever."

Twenty-two

Harmony lost two days, at least that's what they told her when she finally came back to life. She fevered and dreamed that Daniel had been there, holding her hand, kissing her forehead. During the day, and secretly at night when Laura, an angel, bade him enter.

The duchess came too—for it was her house, after all—and she, too, let Daniel in to see her. Sorrel nursed her and tipped liquids down her while others—Bessie and Tessie and even Moffet and Bernard—came to pat her hand and made a garden in her chamber.

On the third day, she was well. Daniel let her go down to the parlor as she asked, walked beside her while the duchess stood waiting in a pool of sunshine just inside the parlor door. Daniel bustled her to the settee and settled himself beside her as if, Harmony thought, she might fall over at any moment.

"Have you been busy?" Harmony asked politely.

"Aye."

"Pacing the halls outside your door," said the duchess with a laugh.

"I've been to Jackson's—"

"Where he beat everyone who would fight him," the duchess said proudly. "He's all the rage, you know."

"Oh, no," Harmony said, "you didn't see poor Tony Lewis there, did you? He said you'd dropped him like a rock before."

"Aye, he was there."

"Did you . . . ?"

"Drop him?" he said with a smile. "He kept talking about how your lips were like roses and your eyes were like sapphires—I couldn't shut the damned puppy up."

"So . . . ?"

"So, I dropped him."

Lord Robert Beckman paced the floor of Sir Roan's library. "Why did you let her stay there, Sir Roan? Why didn't you bring her home?"

"By the time I knew about it, the duchess had her snug in a bedchamber with the doctor there. What was the point?"

"Rockburne is the point. Do you want him to seduce your daughter?"

"Beckman! The duchess wouldn't let such a thing happen as that."

"The duchess, the duchess—that's all I hear these days. You're being seduced yourself—by money."

"Not at all, Lord Beckman. She's a grand lady."

"And her grandson?"

"Well," Roan said scowling, "he's in charge of the money, and he's half scared of me. He won't give me any trouble."

"If you cannot manage this situation, I will."

"For heaven's sake, Daniel, light somewhere. It's Harmony's first day downstairs and you've barely talked to the girl."

"Sorry, Harmony." He dropped onto the settee beside her. "Are you sure you feel all right—do you want to go back to bed?"

"We're expected somewhere this afternoon, Daniel."

He looked at her pale face and remembered the terror of the last two days, seeing her lie lifelessly in a bed with her skin afire. "Don't even think about it."

"It will be your first test."

"Test?" He leaned back with a suspicious scowl. "What test?"

"A test one might expect from a tutor. Choose something you've read. I'll send a note to Lady Beckman—it's her salon we are attending—and they will discuss that reading with you."

He leapt to his feet. "Why would I want to do something like that?"

"Daniel," she said with a laugh, "how else will you know if you're ready to take your place in society?"

He ran a large hand through his hair, ruining the style his new valet had so carefully arranged. "That was an *excuse,* something my grandmother concocted to get me into your life." He looked across the room where the duchess sat serenely sewing.

"I've promised." Harmony gave him a hopeful look he could never resist.

"Aye." *But not without a bargain more to his liking.* "We'll make a pact."

Eager now that he had agreed, she leaned forward, smiling at his acquiescence. "Of course."

"The game I suggested . . ."

"Game? The one where we pretend *not* to be sweethearts . . . ?" At his devilish nod, she leaned back against the corner of the settee.

"Want to know the rules?" She shook her head, her hand gripping the wood.

As if she were as delighted as he, Daniel outlined the routine. "In secret, we play out the game of love—"

"Secret?"

"Well, not secret, exactly. Lovers steal kisses in gardens and hallways and empty rooms." As her face turned crimson, he suppressed his laughter. "They send secret messages across crowded rooms and touch when no one is looking."

"Goodness!"

"D'you want me to die of boredom, Harmony? I'll never manage all this strain without some relief."

"Relief?"

"Truth, Harmony, didn't you find our masquerade in Shingle Spit just a little thrilling?" He leaned forward and lifted her chin. "D'you think you could handle a kiss or two, just to keep me from going crazy? A bit of therapeutic treatment, you might say?"

When she stared at him as if he'd gone mad, he brought in the big guns. "Didn't I drag myself out of a sick bed and come to your rescue?"

"Oh, Daniel," she said, gulping back a mixture of laughter and tears. "Of course, I'll play your game. I'm a selfish beast to even be thinking of saying no."

Daniel stopped at the entrance to Lady Beckman's parlor. He was early, just as he planned, for as the lady tripped forward to greet him, he could see no others in the room, save an overfed cat in a bentwood rocking chair.

Officially, Lady Beckman was his mother's cousin, but somehow along the way she had become Aunt Rose. He could barely remember her.

"How charming of you to be prompt," she whispered, her frightened gaze flitting out to the hall behind him to discern if she was to be left alone with this *smuggler* relative of hers. Upon seeing it empty—except the footman who did not count— she backed up. As if seeking a lifeline in a stormy sea, she turned her glazed eyes toward the servant. "Tell my son that we have guests."

To give her some measure of security, Daniel deliberately looked away to examine the room. "Interesting parlor."

The room was every man's nightmare.

A bird of a woman, she clearly had no concept of *weight* upon furniture or *width* between the sides of the same. Fragile chairs and settees littered the room like a flock of tiny sanderlings wintering on the beach.

He reconnoitered quickly. The gold chair might do, if he

could just trust in those spindly legs and the common sense of its builder. What manner of groans, he wondered with a faint smile, might Bernard allot to this collection of furniture?

"Thank you," she said, politely, in answer to his compliment. She fumbled inside her sleeve and brought forth a lace-trimmed handkerchief to pat the moisture from her upper lip.

"My grandmother had a previous appointment, Aunt Rose, but if she can make it, she will drop in later."

Lady Beckman turned crimson. "How kind . . . I wasn't sure when my secretary sent the cards if Her Grace could fit it into her schedule."

She's not dense, thank goodness. The truth was that Lady Beckman had never sent an invitation—not because Lady Talbourg's presence would not elevate any hostess, but because she never came.

Daniel positioned himself near the coveted gold chair and waited for his hostess to sit. She did not—could not, evidently—instead, she *fluttered*. She adjusted painted replicas of Robbie on the mantel, moved a silver phosphorous candle case precariously close to the edge, then back again. Next, a round table drew her, where a half-dozen bells—cloisonné, Russian gilt and enamel, porcelain—jangled off key as they slid along the cherry wood.

He ran out of patience.

"Sit down, Aunt Rose. You're making me nervous."

Luckily she was near an armless chair, for she obeyed immediately. "Now," he said, in a no-nonsense voice, "tell me what goes on at these parties."

She gripped the mangled handkerchief between two clenched fists and stared at his new emerald stickpin. "Well, we talk about things . . . books and paintings and cultural events. We have music . . . singing, instruments, the pianoforte . . ." As she enumerated the familiar amusements, her voice steadied.

"How long does everyone stay?"

"Well, as long as they wish . . ."

"No, I mean what's the soonest time a person can leave."

She smiled then, as a mother might smile at a boy in his first formal clothes. He smiled back. "I don't mind admitting this is not my usual fare, Aunt Rose. I've managed to evade these things before, but my grandmother's decided it's time to smooth off the rough edges, and she's bullied Miss Roan into the job, poor girl."

Her smile dimmed. "Miss Roan?"

Daniel frowned. "You don't like the girl?"

"Oh, no," she said, "I mean, yes . . ."

"Because your son's after her?"

She blinked, then blinked again. She couldn't seem to believe they were having such a conversation, but Daniel hadn't been charming widows all these years without learning how to cajole them. "She's not right for your boy, then?"

"Well," she said, glancing at the door where her son might appear at any moment, "I was prepared to like her, but when she moved to town, she became an absolute *byword* in Grosvenor Square . . . stealing all the good servants and spending money in such an *uncouth manner.*"

Daniel gasped—then roared with laughter. "She poached the neighbors' servants?" Tears ran down his cheeks, and Lady Beckman began to giggle. "Did she steal any of yours, Aunt Rose?"

"Well, no. She seemed to keep to the square . . ."

He wiped his eyes and leaned forward. "She's a country scholar, green as grass, Aunt Rose, but if she's interested, she could figure out the system in the blink of an eye." She shrugged her shoulders and tried to believe him. He was happy to see that there must be more to her worry. He hoped to gain an ally in Lady Beckman, who despite her fragility, might have something to say about who would be her daughter-in-law.

A guilty expression accompanied her hesitant explanation. "She's poor, untitled and doesn't know how to live in Robbie's world."

"I don't blame you for worrying," he said, his agreement erasing the lines between her eyes. "For all that she *could* fit in, I doubt that she can keep her nose out of a book long enough to *want* to. And then," he added truthfully, "any husband of Harmony Roan will have to take on the burden of the father, and he's not an easy man."

"My son thinks so highly of her, though . . ." Her voice trailed off helplessly.

"My grandmother likes her too," he ventured. "I think she's decided the girl will do for me."

Lady Beckman's eyes opened wide, then narrowed in speculation. Daniel shrugged. "Don't tell Robbie or Sir Roan, though, I wouldn't like to stir anyone up until we see where the lady's interest lies."

Then he leaned forward, an imploring look softening her. "D'you think we would suit? We come from the same village and except for an occasional visit to town, we both like the country."

She sighed and gave him a lovely smile. "I think she'd be perfect for you. I wish you well."

The words had barely gladdened two hopeful hearts, before a steady stream of guests filled the room. Daniel rose so many times to bow that he soon lost his chosen roost and spent the rest of the time standing near the mantel, which was just as well since boredom made him long to pace, and at least he could rock back and forth on his cane to keep from bolting from the room.

And Harmony *would* be the last to arrive.

Pink, Harmony thought . . . no, *raspberry.* Pale, it was true, but the color was unmistakable. She smoothed her hand over the fine silk and kicked her new *raspberry* slippers to make the double row of flounces dance out where she could see them. She shook her head slightly just to feel the curls around her face move against her cheeks and forehead. Bless the duchess for taking her shopping. Bless Sorrel for her brilliance and her clever scissors. And even bless Lady Beckman for giving her somewhere to go—a place where Daniel might see her in company with her first real gown.

She'd gone to Roan House to dress, and left in a state of excitement, for there was not a servant who had not sneaked into the foyer to see the spectacle of their benefactress out of the dreary brown and grey and into the confection that had arrived while she was abed across the square.

Her father and his crowd had gone somewhere, and although she knew it was a hopeless cause, she wished they could just stay away for a few hours. Days . . . months?

Beside her, Laura squirmed in her new finery. In truth, probably not so much over her modest apparel, but the thought of mingling with new people, of whom she seemed inordinately shy. It was interesting, she thought, that only Bernard's rough encouragement had allayed Laura's fears.

Biggins opened the door, and Harmony sailed blithely out of the carriage with Laura behind her. A cold wind gusted, lifting the edge of her dress. Two gentlemen strolling past stopped to tip their hats and then walked backwards for a few feet before continuing on. A little thrill lifted Harmony's spirits. She'd been *noticed*.

As the footman announced Harmony to the company, she ran a swift glance round the room, looking first for her father, for should he be there, her behavior was thereafter prescribed. *He was,* she discovered with a sinking feeling, as were Beckman and all the young men whom she met underfoot every day. Others attended, many of whom she had not met. Finally, although she had sensed his presence, there was Daniel Rockburne leaning against the mantel, making the rest fade into the background.

Daniel was a sorcerer. With the simplest of glances—his eyes darkened, the pupils dilating. Her lips parted at the sight of him and her body began to hum. A languid sweetness lifted the corners of her lips as she turned away to receive heady accolades from the young puppies who could scarcely believe she was the drab they'd left home this morning.

She made her way around the room on the arm of her hostess, meeting strangers whom she discovered were not so forbidding to a girl in a raspberry dress. Beckman pressed toward her with a lecherous look she'd never seen from him. As his hand slipped round her wrist, she swallowed as a surprising feeling of panic took over.

Help came from a surprising direction. Lady Beckman snapped her fan on her son's marauding arm. "Behave yourself," she hissed and then, sending Harmony a genuine smile, she pulled her away from the clustered men. "Come meet our guest of honor, Joseph Turner, the artist. We have mutual friends, and he has agreed to honor us today."

Daniel watched the vision that was Harmony Roan cross the room, held closely in affection by their hostess. Pride filled him. He didn't need a pink gown to love her but, damn if it hadn't been a shock to see her transformed.

He made his way slowly toward her, unobtrusive to all save Lady Beckman who shared a smile with him. "Joseph Turner?" he heard Harmony say, then watched her face light with joy. "I heard about your work," she exclaimed, "Such incredible light and shadow, they say, and wonderful detail in the foreground."

Turner seemed a rather unpolished, humble man, and his face—rosy cheeks with a great beak of a nose—glowed with pleasure at her praise. "Do you paint?"

"Alas, no. But will you be bringing back *Hannibal* this year? I wanted so to see it . . ."

As their conversation continued, Daniel began adjusting his plans for Harmony. He could not immure her in the country, that was clear. London then, part of the time; perhaps they would follow his parents' footsteps and travel. One could do no better.

Lady Beckman's voice intruded. "Turner?" She pushed her cat off the rocking chair. "Take this chair. Everyone else, find chairs and we shall begin." It was a ridiculous command, for the few chairs were already occupied by ladies. The young men

made themselves comfortable on the thick carpet while Lord
Beckman propped an elbow on the other end of the mantel.

Harmony perched on a square velvet pianoforte stool. Daniel
watched as her silken shawl fell from her shoulders to rest at
her elbows, drawing another round of attention from the
younger set. The girl needed to be locked up for her own good.
She hadn't a clue what she was doing to raise the temperature
of the room.

Their hostess was still giving directions. "First, Lord Beckman will read our literary selection, from *Marmion* by Sir Wal-
ter Scott." It was the selection Daniel had chosen. He sent an
inquiring glance at Robbie—surely he would balk at that ig-
nominous task of reading aloud?—only to find his cousin's narrow chest expanding with pride.

Satan's teeth, he was never going to understand London.

Robbie, leafed through his book. "Shall we skip the introduction and go straight to the first canto?" Several ladies sighed in
disappointment, no doubt preferring to hear the mood-inducing
description before being plunged directly into Marmion's battle-
gloried story. Robbie glanced toward Harmony for his answer,
but upon finding her watching the flames dancing in the fireplace, nodded smugly and began:

> *"Day set on Norham's castled steep,*
> *And Tweed's fair river, broad and deep,*
> *And Cheviot's mountains lone:*
> *The battled towers, the donjon keep,*
> *The loophole grates, where captives weep . . ."*

Daniel found his own gaze directed toward Harmony's bent
head as Robbie read Scott's poetry in a droning, singsong voice.
On and on it went, without a break to marvel at the skill of
verse or the actual story as it unfolded.

While Robbie was so occupied, Daniel caught Harmony's
gaze and sent her a wicked look. Satan's teeth, he thought, at
her immediate catch of breath, it wasn't going to be easy to
play this game of seduction with Harmony—she was transpar-
ent as air.

He renewed his efforts to stay with Robbie, listening for the clever exchange of insults and elaborate intrigue, but finally lost the thread. Too bad that Robbie was so entranced with his own voice. He managed about half the canto, then stopped to dampen his throat with a few delicate sips of sherry. He seemed to take the silence as an accolade to his performance, and for a moment Daniel worried that he intended to plunge back into it.

Robbie, however, had other plans. "Rockburne, I understand that *Marmion* was your assignment this week."

"Yes it was." Daniel waited, calm and rather amused.

His eyebrow elevated, Robbie waited for Daniel to elaborate— and obviously, give him an excuse to sneer. His eagerness waned as Daniel remained silent. "Well . . . ? Did you understand it?"

"The reading, or the story?"

Robbie frowned. "They are the same, are they not?"

"Depends on who is reading, I suppose. I've always liked the story, but today I did learn something new."

"Indeed?" Robbie drawled, fairly drooling over the chance to humiliate Daniel. Especially, he suspected, now that Daniel was curtailing his courting time with Harmony.

"Oh, yes." Daniel rubbed the back of his neck where his stance had induced an uncomfortable stiffness. "I never realized how soporific the rhythm was . . ."

Harmony sent him a warning glare as Robbie sputtered, but damn it, she couldn't expect him to ignore an attack. "Reminds me of a drummer's slow cadence when the soldiers need steadying. Very effective, actually."

Lady Beckman rang one of her little bells. "Lovely," she announced, as if the contretemps had never occurred. "Now we shall have some harp music and—" A rustling of skirts at the doorway drew Lady Beckman's attention.

She gasped. "Your Grace—"

The butler made it official. *"The Duchess of Talbourg."*

Twenty-three

Daniel watched as the arrival of the duchess changed the mood entirely. Even Beckman's condescension toward Daniel faded in the reality of Lady Talbourg's presence and her graciousness to his mother. She took the time to greet her hostess and then charmed Roan's young puppies, one and all—which courtesy seemed to enliven Roan's mood to a noticeable degree.

When the duchess saw Harmony—that was another matter. Lady Talbourg's attentiveness to her far transcended the cordial manners shown to the others. Her face glowed on spotting the girl rising from her stool and walking swiftly to meet her. As Harmony kissed her cheek, her face softened, lending a youthful mien to her usually stern face. It was not the first time he'd noticed her delight with Harmony.

Then the duchess turned to find Daniel—and the truth finally hit him, a finer truth than he deserved. With her arm around Harmony, the duchess seemed to be offering him the lovely lady. *Wouldn't you like her?* she seemed to say. *She loves you,* she offered, *she'd make you happy.*

And underneath that eagerness to confer this precious gift, was the same purpose that had always been the focus of his grandmother—his happiness—and always before, he had tossed it away.

How selfish he had been. How ignorant. How like a child he had measured her every irritating trait against his own comfort, forgetting that she had never been as small-minded as he. Year after year she had welcomed him back and offered what she thought would make him happy. Never chided or whined when he rejected her overtures. Just kept trying . . . which, he suspected she would do to the very end.

In recognizing this, he wondered—had he finally gained some true measure of maturity? After thinking for years that he'd become a man at his first fight, his first woman, his first rescue of his father? Or had the strike of the Rockburne Curse sliced the edges off his male pride, created a true prism through which the colors of love might shine?

Full of newfound affection, he strode to her side—just in time to hear her ring a peal over his head. Fairly hissing her displeasure, she pinched his hand. "I heard you baiting Robbie, you ungrateful cub. What do you think you're doing, enraging him and stirring things up for Harmony?" He couldn't help it. He laughed.

When Her Grace's footmen marched into the parlor with armloads of boxes, she gave a sigh of relief. "Ah, Sir Roan's books," the duchess said. "I thought I'd bring these along to the gathering, Rose, since most of us here can understand the exhilaration that accompanies a man's first published work. The carrier said the product went with the reckoning, and I could send them where they belonged on my own time. . . . Dreadful man."

Daniel watched in horror as the leading footmen headed for a delicate table near the middle of the room, intending to drop his heavy load onto its bell-littered surface. He moved swiftly, barely able to intercept the footmen and convince him to deposit the boxes on the floor, all to the grateful squeals of his hostess.

"I only brought one box of each," Lady Talbourg said. "I've sent the rest to Roan House."

Roan stood frozen and red-faced as the young men scrambled to break open the parcels. Harmony gently urged him back into his chair, kneeling beside him as the youths piled the various items onto his lap. It was her glorious moment as well as her father's, and her beaming face showed it.

As they read off the titles, Roan began to enjoy himself and his ruddy color receded. "Take one, each of you," Roan said to the company. "A gift for all your help."

Lord Beckman chimed in. "Wonderful, Sir Roan. I'll choose something for our next discussion."

Daniel watched Harmony, enjoying seeing her so content. Then her smile faded—and the color drained out of her face. Clutching a thin, olive-green book to her bosom, she sank from her kneeling position to sit upon the floor.

Daniel reached over the shoulder of one of the men near the boxes. He extracted the puzzling culprit and retreated to the fireplace for a quick examination. Gilded into the dyed leather was a simple title: *A Frenchman's Walking Tour, The Pleasure of the English Seaside.*

He frowned. Was the title wrong, misspelled? Harmony had not opened the book, so her frightening reaction came from the cover itself. He turned it over, examined the spine. Except for a scrolled medieval design below the words, the cover held no mystery.

He looked in her direction. She had lifted her attention from the book and looked across the room—imploring his aid. He nodded briefly and began moving toward her. No one seemed to have observed the small drama, nor did they take note of his dropping down beside her.

"What is it?"

She leaned toward him, an imperceptible motion, until their shoulders touched. *"Pierre's book."*

"Pierre . . ." Then he remembered. "The bizarre directions, right?" At her nod, he fanned through the pages, not really reading the text. "Published by mistake, and if your father sees what you have done," he mused, imagining the reverberations, "you will bear the burden of his anger."

"I don't care about that, Daniel—this is a tragedy. When people discover how ridiculous these directions are, my father will become a laughingstock, a fool. All the respect he's gained, the acclaim and admiration, will be gone in a moment. Our entire life's work will be for nothing."

"Well, then," he said briskly, "let's fix it."

She patted his hand. "Too late."

He caught her fingers and gave an angry squeeze. "Why are you so blasted stubborn, Harmony?—I'll do it for you. I'll go round and buy all of them from the bookstores, and you can snatch the rest from your house. We can do it in a day."

At the thought, her fingers clenched his tightly. "It's too complex, you cannot imagine."

"*Harmony,*" he murmured intently, "look at me."

She turned her head. The hope in her eyes was awash with despair. "Do what I tell you," he told her. "I'll make it work."

After Daniel left, Lord Beckman came to stand beside her. "May I speak to you? We can retire to the library next door." He offered his hand to assist her rising. Good, she thought, it was the very thing she wanted as well.

He paused while she surveyed the room. "It was my father's study before. I have added the bookshelves. He wasn't much of a reader."

"Your mother is the scholar, I understand." He nodded and seated them in a pair of chairs.

"Sir Roan told me that he had spoken to you," he began. "I'm sorry your father blurted out our plans—he said it made you angry."

She was surprised by his candor, and pleased that he understood. "It sounded more like slavery than a marriage," she said, smiling in relief.

"I planned to court you when we came to London, to see how you felt before I offered for you. Can we just forget your conversation with your father and begin over?"

She almost said yes, almost allowed the courting to keep everyone *calm.* It would have been so easy, so *nonconfrontational.* But then . . . her father would be far more adamant, far more violent when she declined Beckman's inevitable offer.

She shook her head and told the truth. "I don't wish to marry now, Lord Beckman. I have always longed to travel like my father, and my aunt. When the season is over, I will begin with a small trip—perhaps Scotland or Ireland, maybe the Netherlands if I'm feeling brave. I don't plan to marry for years."

"Has your father agreed to do this? Just as his books are released?"

"Did I not explain? I am going alone. With servants, of course, and my chaperon."

He shouldn't have laughed.

If he had even blinked his disbelief and swallowed it silently, she would have understood. If he had argued or even become angry, she was used to that. But not outright laughter.

She stood abruptly.

Surprise wiped the laughter from his face and he scrambled to his feet. "My dear, you must understand—"

She turned to leave. "I do understand, Lord Beckman. You are no different than my father—you have no *respect* for me—and I do not want to spend the rest of my life with either of you."

"But, Miss Roan, a woman does not travel alone."

She stopped and turned. "Not many travel, it's true, but that does not make idiots or freaks or fallen women of those who do."

He reached her side. "Miss Roan, you have mistaken my feelings entirely. I admire you, *have admired you* for years."

"Have you? What have you admired, Lord Beckman?"

"Well," he began, turning red in the process, "your intellect, of course and your kind care of your father."

"You want a *smart* housekeeper?"

"No . . . that is, your loveliness—"

"I'm a plain dab, Lord Beckman."

She should not have said that, evidently, for the strangest expression came over his face. A inner stillness steadied him, imbued his normally pleasant mien with something more resolved, *rapt*. "No, Miss Roan, you are not. It's just that no one has discovered your beauty yet. You are enchantingly lovely, untouched, ready to be brought to life." He motioned to her dress. "Today has proved my point."

Uneasy, she tried for humor. "You've looking for the perfect rose?"

"I have found her," he said, and for the first time she understood that distant look she had misinterpreted all these years.

She was torn. If his feelings were so involved, he had not deserved her brusk dismissal. "I'm sorry, Lord Beckman . . ."

His expression changed instantly. "Do not say no, Harmony," he said, using her name for the first time.

"I have no other answer."

"Then you leave me no choice."

Daniel went directly from the salon to the most respected bookstore in town—Hatchard's on Piccadilly. He plowed his way through young girls making eyes at flirting gentlemen behind the back of the chaperons, crawled over clerks stocking shelves, and barged into John Hatchard's office. The proprietor stood at his entrance and gave him a bow. "Lord Rockburne, I am honored."

Daniel stopped. "Have we met?"

"Oh, no, but your fame—or infamy—has gone before you."

"My fame?"

"Gentleman Jackson's. I hear you didn't leave a man upright in the place."

"Had a lot on my mind," Daniel said, somewhat chagrined, for he hadn't quite realized what damage he'd done. He'd only gone there distraught over Harmony's illness—with the urge to kill something. He'd thought he'd been rather civilized.

"How can I help you?" Hatchard asked. "A special order?"

"No, we've run into a bad turn with the Roan books. One of them was a book composed for a private party—the French walking tour book—and we shouldn't leave it on the shelves."

Hatchard's friendliness dimmed a bit. "What do you propose?"

"I'll buy them back."

"At cost?" He was still worried, Daniel could see that. What did the man think he was—a tightfisted cheat?

"Hell no, Hatchard. Just let me buy them as if I were a customer. Pack them up and send them to Talbourg House. Give me the bill, I'll pay you now."

"Well . . . well!" Hatchard's face beamed with renewed enthusiasm. "You are what they say, Lord Rockburne, a gentleman to your toes."

Daniel went to Hookam's next and met with an almost identical conversation. *Satan's teeth,* if he'd known last time he was in London that the way to the damned aristocrats' hearts was to beat the hell out of them, he wouldn't have left so soon.

Colburn wasn't in when he visited his bookstore, but his team of salesmen almost smothered him with idolization of his boxing skills, and couldn't care less what he paid for the books. He made his way to the damned foreign stores, grateful for the bit of gutter French and German he'd picked up in his travels.

By the time he got home, he felt like he'd been keelhauled twice over. And he had a lot more respect for the ladies who could do this all day, five days a week.

Twenty-four

Was it raining? Harmony could hear the windows rattling with the sound of a storm.

A sliver of light from the hall swept over the rug and Laura slipped into the room. "Hsst, Harmony."

"I'm awake—is that a storm?" Laura ignored her, crossed to the window and opened it. "Stop throwing gravel, she's awake."

"What on earth?" Harmony flew to the window and looked down. Zeus, there were Daniel and Bernard, happy as drunken sailors standing in the garden.

"Come down," Daniel whispered. "Hurry."

Laura closed the window, while Harmony lit a candle. "What time is it?"

"Sun will be up in an hour. Dress quickly."

Harmony was breathless with excitement when she reached the garden. As she got closer to the men, she could tell that they had, indeed, warmed themselves up with a grog or two. "It's Bernard's turn at the watch," Laura whispered, "and His Lordship came over to share the last half."

Daniel took her arm and Bernard was even cozier with Laura as they hurried toward the gazebo. Once inside, they could talk easier, thank goodness, for Daniel was ecstatic. "I got them all, Harmony."

"All?"

"The blasted books—they are all on their way to my house. Did it before the sun set."

"Where did you go?" As Daniel rattled off the names of the twelve booksellers, she listened intently. "Aren't you happy?" he asked. "You seem a little glum, considering . . ."

She was deliriously happy, and the painful ache of worry began to ease. "That's wonderful . . . how many lending libraries were there?"

"The *what?*" Daniel asked, wishing before she got through her wretched explanation, that he had another drink.

He wasn't any happier about her own news for him. "Break away today at three," she said, "We are going to a musicale at Lady Haughton's house—Lord Haughton's mother. She's a bit of a fusspot, I understand, but music is her love. She's generous with her table," she said to encourage him, but she had already rendered him blue-deviled with her news of lending libraries.

Finally, she gave up trying. "I'm sorry, Daniel."

"It's worse," he said glumly. "Roan sent round a note. He wants to see me at ten."

For once, Daniel liked the fact that he bore the Rockburne title, liked that being a duke took precedence over Roan, the baronet, and Beckman, the earl—both of whom seemed zealous as vultures too impatient to wait for natural death.

Bows and greetings exploded in the room, all in a haphazard manner, for Roan still seemed oblivious to proper procedure. Harmony, bedecked in the colors of sunlight, stood beside her father looking apologetic and apprehensive. Evidently, they had imported her to witness his demise—from what, Daniel had yet to discover.

"You sent a note, Sir Roan?" Daniel asked the question in the manner he'd seen his father use to speed a meeting along. He *leaned* toward the exit, as if waiting for the wind to come by and carry him off to the next errand. It only made Robbie nervous—a reaction Daniel was beginning to wonder about— but it put Roan in his place.

"Won't keep you long, Rockburne. Expect the duchess will

be quizzing me before long about your progress." Rockburne nodded solemnly, taking a mental note to have her to do just that.

"You have some questions, Sir Roan? Just ask away, although when you learn how ignorant I am, you'll be scouting the nursery for primers."

"Not at all," Roan returned, a row of beaded sweat breaking out on his upper lip, for the last thing Roan wanted was to report a failure to his sponsor. He gave Beckman an accusing look, telling Rockburne exactly who had engineered this meeting. *And what the devil were Roan and Robbie so cozy about now? He had hoped Robbie might go off in a snit at the snub of Roan accepting another sponsor, but no, they were still close as thieves. No doubt that was the problem . . .*

"So, Rockburne," Roan began. "Where do we start with this tutoring? Can you read?"

Robbie choked with laughter, and even Harmony smiled, but with a different expression—remembering, Daniel knew, the tea shop and his book-reading travails.

When Daniel nodded, Roan sighed happily. He poised his pen over a piece of paper. "What have you read?—*Who* have you read?"

"Who? . . . Wordsworth, Scott, Coleridge, Gibbon—"

Roan's eyebrows rose to high mast. "You've read the *Decline and Fall . . . ?*

Daniel shrugged. "The first volume. When you're on the water, you read what you can find."

Still wide-eyed, Roan scratched away on the paper. "Go on."

Daniel was having trouble remembering author's names. "I read whatever I could find, Sir Roan. One time it was *Tom Jones,* and once it was *The Castle Rackrent.* Something Miss Roan might have liked," he said with a sideways glance to see if she caught on. Her blush was worth admitting that he'd read the blasted book.

"What was your favorite book?" This from Harmony.

That was easy. "The *Nautical Almanac.* My father liked

Johnson's dictionary. Used to challenge me to word matches—
he always won."

Roan cleared his throat and pulled off his spectacles, rubbed
them hard on his sleeve and put them back on. Clearly, he didn't
know what to do with Daniel. "Work with my daughter," he
said, waving generally in her direction. "Report to me
every . . ." Here he paused and shook his head as if to clear
away the confusion of so unwanted task. ". . . every few days."

Robbie, the oily snake, turned to Harmony with a cozy smile
that made Daniel's fists clench. "What are you teaching today,
Miss Roan?"

"I'm showing Lord Rockburne the lending library."

Daniel swallowed a surge of laughter. How like this witty
Harmony to torment him with that unpleasant reminder.
"Then," she continued with an upward peek to see how Daniel
fared, "we have Lady Haughton's salon at three, and . . ."

". . . the Egyptian Hall," Daniel added. "Or was that tomorrow?"

Beckman watched their interchange with hooded eyes. Suspicious eyes, Daniel thought, and Harmony was definitely *flirting* with him. Robbie would not like his prey attracted to Daniel
Rockburne.

Tonight, he was going to do a little sleuthing around town.
A snake like Robbie didn't get this old without making a few
talkative enemies.

When the two men left, Harmony leaned over the table. "You
really read Maria Edgeworth's book?" When he nodded, she
prodded for more. "Did you like it?"

"It was all right. I traded it for a play named *Polly.*"

"Daniel! That was *banned.*"

"What should have been banned was the damned castle
book," he grumbled. She fell back into her chair and laughed.

In repayment for her sins, Daniel bullied Harmony into going
with him to the lending libraries—or thought he had. Once in

the coach, she pulled out a map marked with lines and dots. *Many* dots, all of them denoting lending libraries. He realized then that she must have spent the interim preparing a route, and intended to go from the first.

It was amazing, he thought, that such a benevolent trick could make his blood run hot and his body heavy with desire. He wasn't sure, but he thought he heard James's laughter floating in the air.

She poked her finger at the first dot in the string. "We'll begin here, and then the fastest route follows this line."

He leaned toward her, resting his chin atop her shoulder. "I think I shall be *very* bored today."

She turned her head and nudged him off her shoulder. "Daniel, behave! We cannot play your silly game in libraries. There are people in every aisle, there's no place to . . ."

"That's what makes it a game."

Once inside, Daniel found an empty aisle, and kissed her on the ear.

"Daniel," she hissed, "someone might see us."

"But," he argued, "are you bored?"

They made their leisurely way to the office in the back and waited to see the manager, whereupon he trailed his fingers across her palm. She started nervously, gave him scolding looks, but her lips were curving upward.

Lending libraries, he found when they were finally ushered into the office, were a far different matter than bookstores. "I wish to buy all your books called—"

"We do not *sell* books, m'lord." The clerk, a thin bespeckled man whose hands were always moving, looked down his nose at Daniel—a clever trick considering he sat behind a desk. He rolled his pen sideways on the desk, impatient for Daniel to leave.

"Why not? You are in the business of making money."

The pen went upright and tapped furiously on the flat surface. "And what should one charge for a *lending* book when we have yet to ascertain how many times it might be *lent?*"

"Make a guess."

"I just told you," he said, tossing the pen on the desk, "It's impossible—"

"Make a guess and double it."

His hand flew, barely halting the pen at the edge of the desk. "Double it?"

They stopped at Gunther's for refreshment. Harmony leaned back into the corner of the coach, map on her lap, while Daniel gave the waiter their order. The day had turned gray, and a low fog crawled upon the ground.

His business over, Daniel joined her in the coach. He gave the map a killing look, picked it up and threw it on the opposite seat. "Damned octopus." He looked grim. "That's it, I'm hiring runners to do this job."

He gave her an assessing look, and ran his fingers leisurely through her hair, down her neck . . .

"Daniel, the waiter is coming back!"

They were late to the musicale. Not too late to see the program begin, but good manners had been breached. Another flutterer, Daniel thought as the hostess, Lady Haughton, greeted them at the door. A plump little woman who resembled her son, Mark, fluttered them in, chattering without end, as did her other son, Tony, when they were passed on to greet him. The brothers snatched Harmony away and managed to settle her between them on the back row, there to rudely vie for her attention throughout the first event, a violin and piano composition of Beethoven's.

Unable to stop the little party on the back row, Daniel moved to the front, soon getting lost in the music. "I love it too," came a sultry voice beside him. He opened his eyes and found the woman who owned the seductive voice, sitting on his left. "I am Lady Cowper," she whispered. "And you . . . ?"

"Rockburne."

She was a beauty, he had to admit, with those dark eyes and lovely features. And, he realized, she was not flirting, she simply liked music and people. "Rockburne," she said with laughter in her voice, "the gentleman with the handy fives."

"I should charge fees," he murmured, enjoying himself.

She laughed softly. "You are very much like your grandmother. I admire her immensely."

"As do I."

"You came with Sir Roan's daughter—is she someone special?"

"Aye."

"I'll send vouchers to Almack's for you both. Come tomorrow night, on King Street off St. James. The food is paltry, but we hostesses get to terrorize the *ton* with the power of our approval."

"Am I coming to be entertained—or be the entertainment?"

"Both, I hope."

The music began again, a piece by Haydn, and they lapsed into contented silence. When it was finished, their hostess, Lady Haughton, broke the spell. "And, now my dear Tony will clear our musical palate with a little poetry, after which we will enjoy the second course of music."

Chairs screeched in the back as Tony rose to come forward. Laughter followed him, and Daniel soon realized why—he was pulling Harmony behind him, blushing and protesting. He began to rise, but Lady Cowper's fingers on his sleeve halted him. "Let them go. Tony's the kindest of boys, and she'll come to no harm."

Daniel sank back onto his chair and waited. Laughing, Tony assumed a pose—hands on hips and his head raised to the ceiling—like a howling wolf, Daniel thought without humor. Then, Tony collapsed the pose and arranged Harmony in the same manner, lifting her chin when she began to giggle.

"This is a poetry duet," he announced to the amused crowd. "I shall do a stanza in English and Miss Roan shall echo me in another language. When she runs out of languages, I shall have mercy and stop."

He cocked his head at Harmony who stood relaxed beside him. "Ready?" When she nodded, he assumed his pose and began. She listened quietly and when he was finished, she assumed her pose and returned it in French. She followed with Portuguese.

Harmony's lips were twitching when she translated into Russian—and a lady near Daniel began to laugh.

Daniel recognized her immediately, for her thin, exotic beauty was legend. *Countess Lieven,* whose husband had served as Russian ambassador for over twenty years.

Harmony winked at the countess, and finished with a flourish. "Oh, my dear Miss Roan," the countess said. "How very clever."

Tony scowled at being left out. "Are you cheating, Miss Roan?" When Harmony shrugged silently, he turned to her admirer. "Countess Lieven?"

"She said . . . let me translate . . . *This demented fool beside me is dangerous when ignored. Please give him applause, lest he run amok among you.* That's close enough," she said, still grinning. She turned to Lady Cowper. "I shall send her a voucher."

Harmony slid onto the seat of the coach, laughing at his expression. "You're not having fun?"

"Fun?" he growled, intending to grumble about her flirting with Tony and Mark—then realized he would only sound like a jealous swain. His purpose was to give her space and time to find she loved him, not to smother her as her father did. Instead, he decided with a chuckle, to claim the prize he missed at the musicale.

"I've missed the game, and I had a perfect score."

"We were competing? You mean someone wins?"

"Oh, yes."